SUR

"Kev! Up!" Wade h ..... up as the second helo made a pass at the stern. Bullets smacked into steel and fiberglass around them, and both Blackhearts ducked, Curtis throwing himself flat just below the lip of the helipad.

He rolled over onto his back as the bird went by, wrenching the EVOLYS around and sending a burst at the receding aircraft's tail. He couldn't tell whether he'd hit it or not.

Levering himself to his feet, he hauled the EVOLYS up and searched for the helo. It was nose down, making tracks fast, banking off to the west, far astern of the yacht.

I still might be able to hit it. He shifted to the aft rail, bracing the machinegun and tracking in on the fleeing helicopter. He squeezed off a burst, but his range was off. Red tracers arced just beneath the bird, which jinked hard to avoid the fire and dove even closer to the water, turning away from the *Dream Empire* and banking violently from side to side to avoid the gunfire.

He fired one more burst, but between the helicopter's motion, the widening range, and the yacht's own rolling ride, he missed off to one side. Finally, with a blistering curse, he came off the gun.

Wade clapped him on the shoulder. "You'll get another chance." He nodded toward the north, where the remaining speedboats had now come about and were heading away from the yacht as fast as they could. "They got a nasty surprise, but if they really want this boat, I think they'll be back."

BRANNIGAN'S BLACKHEARTS

MARQUE AND REPRISAL

PETER NEALEN

CHAPTER 1

The attack was swift, brutal, and completely unexpected.

Carl Hild hardly noticed the roll of the deck beneath his feet as he headed below, toward his cabin. For the most part, he was just used to it, but he was also so thoroughly miserable that he probably wouldn't have anyway. *I never should have taken this gig.*

The money wasn't bad. The job itself, though…

Hild had been to just about every port in the world over the last twenty years. He'd sailed with all kinds of crews, from the good, to the bad, to the incompetent and depraved. None of them quite matched this nightmare.

Not that the crew itself was bad. Even the captain, drunk though he was, knew his business and generally treated his subordinates fairly. Even the route wasn't bad.

No, it was the client.

The MV *Tonka Canyon* wasn't the biggest oceangoing cargo ship out there, and her cargoes often only just about broke even. This time, though, the container at the forefront of the hold was supposed to pay for the whole voyage by itself, and that was leaving aside the other stuff they'd taken on to fill the rest of the hold.

It just didn't feel worth it. The container had come with its own security detail and supervisor. And that was where the pain started.

1

The supervisor, who had introduced herself as simply Ms. Schrute, had never been to sea before, and it showed. Her intermittent seasickness, though, hadn't humbled her, or even kept her out of the way. Instead, it had apparently strengthened her determination to be underfoot every minute of every day, obnoxiously reminding them of the importance of the cargo, questioning every single decision made by the captain or the officer of the watch, and generally making every second of the voyage a study in misery. She knew nothing about how to sail a cargo ship, and yet she had to be a part of every single action and decision.

They couldn't get to Lisbon fast enough.

He got to his cabin, still morosely brooding over how many days they still had at sea, when something made him stop dead.

Hild might be miserable, but that hadn't changed the fact that he was a professional. He'd been on too many ships, too many times across the ocean, not to quickly become attuned to every noise aboard the vessel. Sometimes realizing that something didn't sound right might mean the difference between getting to port intact and becoming another statistic of ships lost at sea. Ocean voyages might not be as dangerous as they had been back in the early days, but the sea was still a dangerous bitch, and mechanical failures could happen to anyone.

This sound was different. It resonated through the hull, like someone had just taken a jackhammer to the bulkhead.

Tired as he was from his shift, it took Hild a moment to identify the sound. When he realized what he'd just heard, his blood ran cold.

Gunfire.

He froze in the hatchway leading into the cabin he shared with Ignacio Ybarra. Another burst of gunfire rang through the hull.

He was a merchant sailor. He'd been in his share of bar fights, but that was hardly the same thing as gunfights. He didn't know what to do. Even the piracy drills they'd run just after

2

leaving port didn't seem to fit the situation at the moment. The drills were all about keeping pirates off the ship. Whoever was shooting was already on board.

Another hammering report, that sounded like it came from only one deck up, decided him. He ducked into the cabin, swung the hatch shut, and dogged it. Then he scrambled into his bunk and crammed himself into the corner, watching the hatchway and hoping that the pirates took out Schrute and her goons and left the rest of the ship alone.

***

The short, wiry man's dark eyes had looked on carnage and torture, had seen atrocities that would have made a serial killer blanch. The dead bodies lying on the deck, leaking blood out onto the steel, didn't even merit a passing glance.

He walked calmly down the ladderwell into the hold, passing two of the men in storm gray fatigues, maritime plate carriers, and helmets, their faces covered, black Vector R4 rifles in their gloved hands, as he approached the lone cargo container tied down to the deck, separated from the rest of the ship's cargo by a space of about ten feet. Six more of the men in gray stood there, weapons in hand, covering the two still-living maritime security men and the woman, all three of them down on their knees on the deck. One of the security contractors was bleeding, dripping red fluid into a growing puddle of crimson in front of him, his head bent. The other was battered, bruised, and drooling a little. He was probably concussed.

The man whom even his gray-clad subordinates only knew as El Salvaje stepped in front of the woman and stood there for a moment, silently, until she finally looked up. He pointed to the container. "Open it."

Her eyes were wide, but she was apparently still in some denial about the realities of the situation. "I don't know who you are, but you've picked the absolute *wrong* ship to try to hijack. Do you have *any* idea who *owns* that container? You're going to be hunted down, no matter where you try to hide."

If El Salvaje had been a little more inclined to humor, he might have smiled. She hadn't even tried the "if you go away now, no one will follow you" gambit. She'd just blustered.

He let his rifle hang on its sling, drew his Star M-43, and shot the bleeding contractor through the head.

The report rang through the hold, and the woman flinched violently as the man's blood and brains spattered on the container behind them and he fell on his face. El Salvaje shifted the weapon toward the woman's face. "Open it. Or we will kill you and open it anyway."

The woman was shaking, now. She nodded, the movement spasmodic, and two of the gray-clad pirates hauled her to her feet. With trembling fingers, she began to put in the code on the container's cipher lock. She was shaking so badly that it took three tries, especially since El Salvaje still had his pistol pointed, unmoving, at her head.

Finally, the cipher lock opened, and she stepped back. El Salvaje shot her in the head, a fine mist of blood spattering the container side as she crumpled to the deck. The other pirates had stepped back as soon as the lock had disengaged, knowing what was coming.

The last contractor started at the pistol's report. "Hey, what the—" He was cut off by another gunshot, and fell on his face, motionless.

El Salvaje stayed where he was and motioned with the pistol toward the container doors. The pirate who had pushed the woman toward the doors hesitated, just for a moment, but when El Salvaje turned those cold, black eyes on him, he quickly stepped forward to pull the doors open.

The short, dark murderer joined the pirate and peered into the container, holstering his pistol and drawing a flashlight to shine it around the inside of the container. He scanned the contents for a moment before nodding in satisfaction. "Close it up." He turned on his heel. "Get the rest of the crew up on the deck."

***

Hild tried not to move or make a sound as someone rattled the hatch, then banged on it loudly. He did his utmost to stay absolutely still, a hole in the very atmosphere of the ship.

Whoever was out there hammered on the hatch again. He forced himself to hold his breath. It was ridiculous to think that anyone could hear his breathing through the steel hatch, but he tried it, anyway.

A muffled voice sounded outside. Then he heard a *pop*, then a hiss. A moment later, that hiss got louder, and then a point of brilliant light burst through the hatch, just below the first of the dogs.

He scrambled back, or he tried to. He was already up against the bulkhead. All he could do was watch as the torch burned through the hatch, until finally it was wrenched aside and tossed on the deck with a *clang*.

Two men in gray, their faces covered beneath their helmets, pointed rifles at him. "Get out. Now."

For a fraction of a second, Hild considered trying to fight. That lasted about as long as it took for the thought to form. After hearing the gunfire echoing through the ship, he had no doubt that they'd shoot him dead in a heartbeat. Putting his hands up, he wormed his way out of his hidey hole and went with them, trying not to burn himself on the still-smoking bits of metal where the hatch had been attached as one of them let his weapon hang and reached out to grab him roughly and haul him through.

Neither of the men in gray said a word as they shoved him roughly up onto the fantail, where he blinked in the sun as a gloved hand pushed him from behind and made him stumble. It took a few seconds for his eyes to adjust to the brightness, at which point he saw that the rest of the crew, minus the security contractors and Ms. Schrute, were lined up at the rail, their hands on their heads, facing out to sea. Half a dozen men in gray fatigues, combat gear, and helmets, with wicked-looking military rifles in their hands, stood behind and to one side of the crew.

His captors shoved him hard again, and he staggered toward the rail. "Put your hands on your head." He stumbled again as he tried to comply, and he was grabbed roughly by the back of the neck and propelled the rest of the way by main force, shoved between Rafe Munoz and Kit Harris. "Don't move."

He wanted to look to either side, to see if the others were okay, and if they might have some consolation, some reassurance that they were going to get through this. They'd be hostages, he was sure, but the crews usually made it through, right?

The sight of a speedboat coming from the Ro-Ro cargo ship just off the stern, loaded with men in coveralls, didn't lift his spirits. That looked like a skeleton crew for a freighter, not more pirates. Why were they coming here?

He tried to look over his shoulder, but he was suddenly prodded by the hard jab of a rifle muzzle. "Eyes front!"

Hild strained his ears for anything that might tell him what was going to happen next. He suddenly found himself thinking about home. Even his ex-wife didn't seem like such a bitch, right then. And to think, he'd been bitching and moaning about Schrute and her goons less than half an hour ago.

The first shot startled him. He snapped his head around, just in time to see the captain go over the fantail and fall limply toward the ocean.

Then the row of pirates behind them opened fire. He heard a thunderous chorus of hammering reports for just a split second before a fiery pain stabbed through his torso, and then he was falling.

He was dead before he hit the water.

***

"You think this is worth adding to the fleet?" The short, stumpy man spoke with a slight Afrikaner accent. He hadn't bothered to cover his face; there was no need, with the crew having been disposed of.

El Salvaje didn't know for sure why most of these men saw fit to do that, since the crews were all expendable, regardless. No one was going to be left to report on any of them, no matter the target.

"Do you have the men or equipment to offload that container?" El Salvaje studied the Afrikaner with hooded, dead eyes. The blond man looked away quickly.

Any other man might have turned away from the other pirate in disgust, but El Salvaje had not survived jobs with cartels, the Venezuelan-backed FARC, or any number of other such groups around the world by relying on his own formidable reputation for his safety. He watched the Afrikaner until the pirate turned away to find some other task that needed doing.

El Salvaje stood where he could keep his back to a bulkhead, and still see what needed to be watched, and thought. Taking this cargo would be a warning shot. He didn't necessarily agree, but he wasn't there to strategize for the fleet. That was Cain's job. It was his fleet. El Salvaje's job was to kill whoever Cain wanted killed, and collect his share of the loot, at least until it was time to disappear and move on again.

Of course, the warning implicit in making this particular package disappear was probably superfluous, given what had gone down over the last month. But again, that wasn't his problem.

Behind the freighter, as the pirate crew brought it around toward the north, the sharks began to gather, ready to feast on the corpses still floating in the ship's wake.

CHAPTER 2

"Dad? Looks like Uncle Hector's here."

John Brannigan looked up from the table. Hank, leaner and shorter than his father by several inches, was peering out the door at the driveway, noticeably staying out of the light, off to one side, where a newcomer shouldn't be able to see him. The boy had been an officer, but he'd learned. He should have, given the fact that his old man had been something of an infantry legend. Still. He'd learned even more since he'd left the Marine Corps and become a member of the secretive mercenary team that called itself Brannigan's Blackhearts.

Brannigan shut the ledger in front of him with a faint frown and got up to step around the table and move to the other window. Sure enough, that was Hector Chavez's car pulling up the driveway. "That's weird. Usually he calls ahead."

"Maybe the cell signal's not working up here again."

"Wouldn't that be a shame," Brannigan growled. The only reason he had the infernal device in the first place was because of the Blackhearts. Otherwise, he would have been perfectly happy to go completely off grid up here.

Thrusting his .45 into the back of his waistband, just in case, he opened the door and stepped out as the dark blue sedan came to a halt and the driver—it was Chavez, he could see clearly enough through the windshield to be sure of that—shut off the engine. Then the only sound was the wind whispering through the tops of the pines all around.

Chavez opened the door and levered himself out, holding up his hands. "I know, I know. I didn't call ahead." He looked around at the shadows under the trees. "I think you'll agree that it was probably better to leave this off the airwaves."

Brannigan raised an eyebrow at that, but he just waved the smaller man toward the house and turned to go back inside. It was a nice day, but if Chavez was that worried about surveillance, then they probably should head inside, just in case.

Chavez was about a head shorter than Brannigan, but at the former Marine Colonel's six-foot-five, that wasn't that difficult. He had slimmed down since his retirement, just shy of getting stars, which had come shortly after Brannigan's own somewhat unwilling departure from the Marine Corps, but that had also been necessitated by Chavez's heart problems.

Hank greeted his father's old friend, then stepped back toward the rear of the cabin, unsure as to whether he should stay or not. "Stay put, Hank. This concerns you, too." Chavez was slow to sit down, stretching as he looked around the small log house that Brannigan had built for his wife, now in her grave for several years. It was neat, but it was a military neatness, the result of long habit on the part of both father and son, without the homey touch that a woman would have brought. He glanced at Hank, but if he'd thought of something to say about that, he kept it to himself.

Brannigan had been working outside most of the morning, and he and Chavez went *way* back, so he didn't stand on ceremony. He went to the cupboard, pulled down a bottle of bourbon, poured two glasses, and shoved one across the table to Chavez as he sat down. It was early, but this was apparently a business visit, so he figured it was appropriate. And while Chavez was a pro, and wasn't one to wear his feelings on his sleeve, something about his manner told Brannigan that this was going to be a doozy.

"What have you got, Hector?" He leaned back in his chair as Chavez took a sip of the whiskey.

10

Chavez took a deep breath before he answered. "My company just recently got solicited for a job." Chavez had been running an aboveboard maritime security concern since his retirement, which often served as a useful front for his side gig of setting up jobs for Brannigan's Blackhearts. He had contacts throughout the military and security worlds, and he heard a lot, not to mention having logistical connections that often came in handy for transportation and support. "On the surface, it looks like any other maritime security gig."

Hank stifled a groan. Chavez chuckled slightly. Maritime security, for all its romantic air of fighting pirates, often boiled down to months of unutterable boredom aboard a ship, in cramped quarters with bad food, with bare-bones weapons and equipment. For those who knew the security contracting world, it was decent money but generally undesirable work.

It also wasn't up the Blackhearts' usual alley. They were problem solvers, not security guards. They went into dark, dangerous places, killed who needed killing, and got out.

"*On the surface*, I said." Chavez finally pulled up a chair. "The more I looked into it, the more I saw that there's more going on than it appears.

"There's been a string of pirate attacks over the last several months that have been outside the usual pattern. Ordinarily, pirates tend to congregate near choke points, like the Horn of Africa, the Straits of Malacca, places like that. High-traffic sea lanes where they can dart out, take a freighter or a tanker, hold it for ransom, or, like the West African pirates, just kill the crew and sell the cargo.

"These attacks, though, haven't gone down near any of the usual hot spots. They've all been way out in the open ocean." He took another sip of the bourbon. "In fact, the whole thing might have been put down to a series of unlikely accidents if not for one ship that managed to get a message out before they were cut off. After that, looking at the pattern of high-value, often secret, cargoes that have gone missing over the last six months, it's become apparent that there is a highly sophisticated pirate group

11

operating in the Atlantic. To make matters worse, it looks like whoever they are, they're following the Nigerian pirate model of making the crews disappear and taking the cargo. They might be sinking the ships, or they might be transporting them somewhere else after disabling their transponders. We simply don't know.

"Insurance companies are starting to quietly panic. So far, the problem isn't advanced enough that it's gotten much notice, but it's only a matter of time." He chuckled slightly. "There is another reason it hasn't necessarily been in the news lately, though. Apparently, a Navy counter-piracy task force went out looking for the pirates last month and came up empty. The Pentagon does *not* want that getting out."

"So," Brannigan mused, "the client wants some actual pirate hunters?"

"Not in so many words, but it can be read between the lines. The owner of the *Dream Empire* wants as elite a maritime security team as he can get for a passage from Charleston, South Carolina to Cyprus." Chavez took another sip, watching Brannigan closely.

For his part, Brannigan didn't react except to sample his own drink. "You say that name as if it means something, but I'm not familiar with the ship."

"It's a super yacht, sister ship to the *Octopus*. Four hundred feet, with two helipads and even its own submersible. It's one of only two such yachts in the world. And Joshua Fontaine is the owner."

Brannigan did raise an eyebrow at that. Even as far up in the hills as he lived, and as generally disinterested in the world of celebrities and the rich and famous as he might be, he'd still heard of the billionaire playboy and philanthropist. He trusted such people about as far as he could throw his truck.

"So, Fontaine is worried about his toy?" Hank was leaning against the wall near the back door, his arms folded. Shorter than his father by an inch and lighter by about fifty pounds, he took more after his mother, and Chavez could see it.

"So it would seem. Once again, that's the surface level. Turns out that a cargo that went missing last month belonged to one of Fontaine's shell companies. From what I've been able to ascertain, it's the first time any of his interests have been targeted. He's worried." Chavez turned back to Brannigan, who was thinking things through, his eyes narrowed. "I know that security guard on a ship isn't exactly your bailiwick, but between the irregularities about this job and the size of the offered paycheck, I thought I'd bring it to you."

"How big a paycheck?" Brannigan asked.

Chavez named a figure. Hank's eyebrows shot up. Brannigan just nodded coolly. "It's a chunk of change. Almost enough to offset the fact that a maritime security gig is going to be a tough sell to these guys. Most of them could probably retire on what we've made over the last few years. Except for maybe Curtis." He leaned his elbows on the table and swirled the whiskey in his glass. "The 'irregularities,' as you put it, might be the selling point. We'd have to know more about exactly what Fontaine has in mind, though. Is he just trying to keep his investment safe, or is he really looking for a paramilitary force to cross swords with the pirates?"

"That's a little hard to say." Chavez poured the last of the bourbon down his throat. "The job description was necessarily vague. He probably can't come out and say that he's looking for private pirate hunters, not legally. Since it *is* Fontaine, though, and he's got more money than Midas, I'm sure that it'll come out sooner or later, probably once you're twelve nautical miles out to sea."

Brannigan snorted softly. "Sounds about right." He ran a hand over his mustache. "I'll put it to the boys. No guarantees at this point, but if there really *is* somebody out there disappearing ships, it might be something we should look into. Even *if* the client just wants nice, quiet security guards."

Chavez chuckled. "Wouldn't be the first time."

Brannigan poured them each a second drink. "Won't be the last."

CHAPTER 3

Joe Flanagan scanned the water carefully, considering the angles. There was a good spot just upstream, where a sizeable boulder lay just beneath the surface, visible only as a slightly more noticeable stirring of the water. He saw another spot closer to the bank, though, where a fallen tree and a partially collapsed overhang had formed a sheltered pool.

He stayed where he was, motionless, quiet, set back from the bank so that he wouldn't cast a shadow on the water, and watched for a while. After a few minutes, he circled around toward the pool formed by the fallen tree. Crouching down by a pine, he watched the water carefully for a few more minutes, before finally casting into the end of the pool.

It took a couple of casts, but finally the line tautened and the tip of the rod bent. He flicked upward, setting the hook, and then started to work the fish in toward the bank.

Even as he reeled in his catch, he heard the crunch of gravel under tires, the sound of a motor stopping, and then a door being shut. Despite the battering his hearing had taken over years of gunfire and helicopters, he could still pick out the footsteps through the woods behind him. He had his back to a tree, and wasn't easy to see, but he still shifted his position so that he could spot whoever was approaching, even as he continued working to land the fish.

The big German Brown came out of the water, lashing its tail, and he caught it under the gills before removing the hook and putting it on the stringer. Then he turned to where Brannigan stood leaning against another tree.

"Colonel."

"You're a hard man to find, Joe." Brannigan shoved off the tree trunk and came down to join him. "Nobody at the cabin, no note, and your phone's turned off."

Flanagan shrugged as he prepped his line again and went back to studying the water. "Rachel's friends came to take her into town for the day. Something about shopping for the baby. So, I had the day to fish." He cast again. "I take it we've got a job?"

"Possibly." Brannigan found a fallen tree, well back from the water so as to avoid disturbing Flanagan's fishing, and sat down. The Colonel was considerate that way. "It's not necessarily our usual thing. Maritime security. Pay's good, though. Better than usual." He repeated the number he'd gotten from Chavez, which raised Flanagan's eyebrow, even as the black-bearded man finished reeling in and looked for the right spot for his next cast. "From what we know at the moment, it's *probably* just going to be a boring security guard job for the month or two it'll take to cross the ocean, but it pays well."

Flanagan looked over at him. "John, you know as well as I do that nobody pays *that* much just for glorified rent-a-cops. There's got to be more going on."

"I'm sure there is." Brannigan filled him in on the brief he'd gotten from Chavez. "The problem is, I'm not exactly sure what the catch is, and right at the moment, it doesn't look like we're going to get any more info before we're committed."

"That could be a problem." Flanagan cast again, but he wasn't just talking aimlessly while he fished. Flanagan wasn't the kind of man who ever talked aimlessly. He was thinking it through, just like Brannigan had been for the last day or so. "Good payday or no, it might suck to find ourselves out on the ocean with only a few popguns for months, while somebody's making entire ships disappear."

16

"If Fontaine really is worried about high-end pirates, I doubt that we'll be underequipped." When Flanagan turned to him with another raised eyebrow, Brannigan just shrugged. "There are a lot of variables, and *if* enough of the boys sign on, we'll do what we can to nail as many of them down as possible before we set sail. Fontaine's probably not going to be an easy nut to crack, information-wise. Nobody gets as rich as he is by being forthcoming when he doesn't absolutely have to be."

"Hmm. How much time do we have?" Flanagan reeled in his line one more time, but this time he kept bringing it in, catching the line and securing the hook to the small loop just above the reel before tightening it down to keep the lure from swinging free.

"About two weeks." Brannigan levered himself to his feet. Flanagan was in. He hadn't needed to say much more than that. "We actually got a good amount of forewarning this time."

Flanagan nodded as he and the Colonel started back toward the vehicles, picking up his stringer as he went. "Well, I think we've been on the bench long enough since Kyrgyzstan that most everybody will be up for this one, even if it does turn out to be a snore-fest." He paused as they threaded their way through the trees. Flanagan hadn't taken a trail down to the river. That was a good way to find a spot that had already been overfished. "Split the calls again?" Originally, that had been between Brannigan and Santelli, but Flanagan had taken over that side of the operation when he'd taken Roger Hancock's place as the team's Number Two.

"Sure."

Flanagan thought for a moment. "Do we call in that Tackett dude? He seemed interested."

Brannigan mused on it. "No, he seemed pretty set on just going after the Humanity Front. This doesn't feel like them, somehow. They wouldn't keep this so quiet. When they come out of the woodwork, they're trying to sow chaos, to cover for whatever sick game they've got in the works this time, to 'improve the state of the world.'" He shook his head. "If we have a good reason to think it's the Front, we'll call him in. Until then, it's just us."

"Fair." Ahead, they could see the faint outlines of their respective trucks. Flanagan didn't live all that far from Brannigan's place, which made contact simpler. "I'll get the usual."

"One other thing." Brannigan paused before turning to his own vehicle. "We're down a medic again, after Herc went down. Have you got any ideas?"

Flanagan stowed his fishing gear in his truck. "Actually, I do. One of our old platoon corpsmen."

"Which one?" Brannigan frowned. Flanagan glanced over at him, knowing that the Old Man probably knew exactly who he was about to name.

"Puller."

Brannigan frowned. "Haven't heard that name in a long time. He was a bit of a hothead, wasn't he?"

"He could be." Flanagan chuckled. "I still don't know how you manage to remember every single dude who served under you by name, John."

"It fills up memory that might otherwise be wasted with movies and random bullshit." Brannigan pulled his door open. "Okay, give him a shot. I'll leave it up to your judgement whether or not he's good."

"Meet at your place?" Flanagan climbed up on his own running board.

"I'll let you know. It might be better to go straight to Charleston and put our ears to the ground." Brannigan slid behind the wheel of his truck. "With the limited amount of information we have, I want as much time to snoop around as we can get."

***

Carlo Santelli looked up at the *bang* and the curse that followed immediately after it. He shook his head. Prado could be a bit high-strung. He was a good mechanic, though.

Santelli returned his attention to the search for parts. Parts for the 1960 Chevelle currently in the garage were getting harder

18

to find, and more expensive as a consequence. He'd found what he was looking for, but he was still hoping to find a better deal.

His little auto restoration business was booming, and that was why he'd brought Don Prado on. The man was a great mechanic and had a passion for old cars, and he and Carlo had known each other for the better part of forty years, anyway. The partnership had been natural.

The phone buzzed. Santelli sighed. They had a full job list for the next six months. There simply wasn't room for any more projects. Still, he should at least answer it.

It wasn't a customer looking to get old car fixed up. It was Brannigan.

"What have we got, sir?" If Santelli's Boston Italian accent had softened a little during his many years in the Marine Corps, moving back to the old neighborhood had only made it thicker.

"On the surface, it's a maritime security op. Might be more to it. It'll probably be a couple of months." As always, Brannigan was pretty terse over the phone. What the Blackhearts did often skated the edge of illegal, where it didn't throw itself right over that line at a dead sprint. "Can Melissa and the business spare you that long?"

"I've got a partner now, and it might slow things down a little, but he's a good dude. He can handle it. As for Melissa..." He sighed. "I'll talk to her."

Brannigan paused. "Anything wrong?"

"No, sir. Nothing's wrong. We've had a long talk about it. Several long talks, as a matter of fact." He sighed again. "It's not as hard on her anymore. She understands that I can't just let you guys go while I stay back. She gets it. I never thought she would, but she does."

"You've got a remarkable wife, Carlo."

"I know it, sir. When and where?"

"Charleston, as soon as you can get there. There's a lot of snooping around that needs to get done before we go to sea. A lot of unknowns on this job. Drills can happen once we're underway."

19

Santelli did some reading between the lines. "Understood. Need me to handle any of the calls?"

"Not right now. Flanagan and I have it covered."

"Roger that, sir. I'll see you in Charleston." He hung up the phone and headed into the garage to let Prado know what was going on. The other man didn't know a lot of details about Santelli's other career, but he knew enough that he wouldn't be that surprised.

Another *bang* was followed by another curse. It was probably going to get a little louder in there in the next few minutes.

***

"Cease fire! *Cease fucking fire!*"

John Wade stormed across the range and shouldered between two of the students, snatching the pistol out of the young man's hands, careful to keep the muzzle pointed up and downrange. "What the *fuck* was that?"

"What?" The kid looked shocked and angry. "I was just talking to her."

"You had your fucking muzzle pointed at her leg and your finger on the *fucking* trigger!" The sheer force of Wade's rage made the young man, his curly hair not quite long enough to get Wade to call him a hippy, but far longer than he liked, take a step back. "Get off the range!"

"Hey, I paid for this!" The kid apparently didn't have a great sense of self preservation.

For a long moment, Wade just stared at him, unblinking, his icy blue eyes finally making the kid second-guess his indignation at getting yelled at.

"Yes, you paid. And I'll make sure you get fully reimbursed." That almost physically hurt to say. *Damn, I hate working with civvies.* "You aren't staying on this range one more minute, though. You're a threat to yourself and everyone around you. Get moving."

At first, it looked like the kid was going to argue. Everyone else on the line was looking at him, and anger stirred in his eyes, but as Wade took another step closer, the kid realized that a fight was not going to go his way. John Wade, formerly of the 75th Ranger Regiment, stood half a head taller and easily seventy-five pounds heavier. He hadn't gone slack at all since his retirement several years before, and he really hadn't mellowed much, either.

"Hey, I'm a paying customer!"

"Not anymore, you're not. Get off my range." He took another step, and the kid finally decided that discretion was the better part of valor. With a bitter curse, the young man spat on the ground and turned to leave, his departure becoming somewhat speedier when Wade took another fast step toward him, murder in his eyes.

As the kid retreated rapidly toward the parking lot, Wade unloaded the pistol, grimacing as he considered that he was going to have to give the weapon back. *Not with bullets in it, I'm not.* He shucked the rounds out of the magazine. "Everybody take ten, jam mags, get some water, take a bathroom break." He started after the kid, gritting his teeth at the knowledge of how this was probably going to go.

His phone buzzed in his pocket before he'd gotten halfway to the parking lot. Glad for a moment's reprieve from having to give the moron's Glock back, he stopped and looked at it.

"Joe. Tell me we've got a job."

Flanagan sounded slightly nonplused. "How's the range going, John?"

"Well, the business is actually running slightly more smoothly without Jenkins around to screw it up." The former SEAL had gone down like a hero, and that had regained him some points in all of their eyes, but Wade was not a sentimental man. "The quality of the customers, however, is wildly variable."

He wondered if Flanagan could hear him grinding his teeth over the phone.

"It can be that way sometimes." Flanagan knew Wade well enough to know what his temperament was like. "We do have a job. On the surface, it's a straight-up maritime security op."

"Gross." Wade looked up at the parking lot and grimaced. "Not looking forward to sitting on a ship for a couple of months. What's the pay?"

Flanagan told him. "That ain't nothin'." He sighed. "It can't be much more frustrating than this. When and where?" That was the matter of moments. "I'll be there. Now I've got to go give this idiot his Glock back and give him another lecture on the importance of gun safety before I finish kicking him off my range." Technically, it had been Don Hart's range, but he'd left it to the Blackhearts when he'd been killed in Chad.

"Just don't kill him. I'll see you in Charleston."

CHAPTER 4

Vincent Bianco opened up the official contact email for *The Legend of Morval* and groaned. "Two hundred twenty-three?" He leaned his elbows on the desk and put his head in his hands.

The good news was that the epic fantasy role playing game that he and his buddy Tom Glenn had painstakingly put together over the last few years was a hit. A huge hit. The bad news was that with that success came a *lot* of questions, some great, most stupid. And since the company was just him and Glenn, that meant one or the other of them had to go through *all* of them. And it was his turn.

He got up from the desk, went to the fridge, and got a beer. It was going to be one of those nights. He'd gotten to know a lot of other game designers and creators over the course of putting this game together, and most of them were energy drink fiends. Not for Vincent Bianco at seven at night, though. He might be a self-professed, unapologetic nerd, but he was also a grunt, and that meant it was time for alcohol.

Glancing at the computer, he sighed and pulled out two more. He'd probably need them.

Settling in at the keyboard, he popped the top on the first beer and took a long pull, that got longer as he read the first email. It was borderline incoherent, and it took about three read-throughs before he could piece together what the sender was trying to say.

That wasn't a great help, because the question didn't make much sense, either.

I've got to come up with some *sort of reply.* He finished the beer, knowing he was already off to a bad start, and hovered his hands over the keyboard. He was drawing a blank. *"You're an illiterate moron who probably shouldn't be allowed around technology or small children," probably isn't the best response from a customer service perspective.*

He sighed, but the cursor continued to blink unhelpfully in the empty reply box. *What do I say to this idiot?*

When his phone started playing Hammerfall's "Fury of the Wild," he snatched it up like a man grabbing a lifeline. Anything to put this odious task off for a little bit longer.

"Yeah." He hadn't even bothered to look at who was calling.

"Vinnie, you sound like a desperate man." Brannigan sounded amused. "Did I call at a bad time?"

"Colonel, you called at the best possible time." He spun his chair halfway around so he didn't have to look at the screen, snagging a second beer as he went. "What have we got?"

"Could be something. Could be two months of boredom. Chavez hunted up a maritime security gig on a billionaire's superyacht." He chuckled. "Before you get too excited, no, I don't expect that we'll get to sample most of the fleshpots on the way. We'll be security, not passengers. The pay's good, though."

Bianco glanced sideways at the computer screen next to him. "Right now, I'd take a tour as a corrections officer."

"What's going on? The game business not going so well?"

"It's going well enough, sir. A little too well. I'm sitting here with my second beer in the last fifteen minutes, staring at customer support emails."

Brannigan chuckled dryly. "Well, if I'm reading things right, I'm sure that the yacht has wifi. You can probably keep up while we're underway."

Bianco blinked slowly. "Thank you, sir. Thank you *so* much for that."

24

The laugh was a little louder this time. Brannigan might have been an officer, and a full bird colonel at that, but he'd come up from the enlisted ranks before that. Now that they were all just contractors on a small team, a lot of the formalities had gone by the wayside, and Brannigan could rib his boys a little more than he might have when he was still in uniform. "We'll meet up in Charleston, South Carolina, as soon as everybody gets out there. We're not scheduled to go to sea for about two more weeks, but I want to do some recon and intelligence gathering before we leave. Something about this has my spidey sense tingling. See you there."

Bianco acknowledged and put the phone down, feeling a little better. A Blackhearts job was better than sitting here answering interminable emails, many of which might have been written by bots designed by methed out monkeys.

Then he realized that while he could set up transportation to Charleston that night, he still wasn't going to leave yet, and that meant that he still had several hours of mind-numbing emails to respond to. With a groan, he took another pull off his second beer and got back to work.

***

Flanagan stepped around the corner and settled into the shadows in the alley between the furniture store and the H&R Block. The glow of the Strip filled the sky to the west, closer than he preferred, but this was the spot.

Another figure stirred in the shadows, and Flanagan's hand moved toward the .45 in his waistband until he heard, "It's me."

He didn't know what Mario Gomez was doing in Vegas. Given what he knew about their quiet, half-Apache teammate, he probably didn't want to know. The Blackhearts had gone to war for Gomez and his family before, when the Espino-Gallo cartel had seized the Gomez ranch in New Mexico. That hadn't worked out well for the Espino-Gallos, but others had tried the Gomez clan since then, and many of them had ended up as food for the buzzards and the coyotes in the desert. When it came to Gomez's comings and goings off-mission, most of the Blackhearts thought it prudent not to ask too many questions unless he needed help.

Flanagan relaxed slightly. Gomez was a stone-cold killer, sure, but he was *their* stone-cold killer. He was a brother, and they'd relied on each other for their lives in dangerous places all over the world.

"Should be a few minutes." He tried to keep the tired frustration out of his voice, though he knew that Gomez would probably commiserate. Curtis was a magnet for trouble. Even now that he was—last Flanagan had heard—engaged, he was still getting into it to the point that his fellow Blackhearts had to come in and back him up, even before the job started.

Flanagan's phone vibrated, and when he pulled it out, the message said, "Two minutes. Coming from the north."

He showed Gomez the message, and the other man nodded. They faded into the shadows and waited.

Almost exactly two minutes later, the short, heavily muscled form of Kevin Curtis, in his usual tight white t-shirt and jeans, came around the corner. He spotted them even in the dark and moved to join them. "These guys ain't getting the hint."

Flanagan handed over Curtis's Glock 19 with long-suffering silence. He still hoped they could get through tonight without a shot being fired.

Three young men, two of them wearing baggy shorts and wife beaters, the third in long pants and a jacket—which seemed a little odd, given how warm it was—came around the corner quickly, apparently trying to catch up with Curtis. One of the men in shorts was carrying a MAC-10. Their intent was pretty clear.

Almost as one, the three Blackhearts drew their own concealed pistols. Gomez had a light mounted on his CZ P-10, and it blazed in the three men's faces first, while Flanagan had a handheld light that he clamped in his off hand, held to one side of his own Springfield TRP 1911. Curtis was the only one without a light, but he was partially silhouetted in the glow from the streetlights at the other end of the alley, making it obvious that he was pointing a weapon.

26

"There are two ways this can go, boys." Flanagan's voice cracked out through the alley from behind his light. Flanagan was generally a quiet man, but he'd also been a Marine NCO once upon a time, and that command voice wasn't something that just went away. "You put the guns down, back away slowly, and forget that there was ever any money you were trying to take, or you get ventilated right here and now, and we disappear before Vegas PD shows up. Personally, I'd prefer the former, since you've got nothing that I want, and a killing could result in all sorts of red tape I'd rather avoid. On the other hand, my friend here hasn't killed anyone in at least a couple of hours, and he's probably getting the itch."

Gomez didn't say anything. If asked about it, he'd probably just shrug and nod.

The three would-be robbers squinted into the brilliant weapon lights. The two in the wife beaters were covered in gang tattoos, and the third probably had the same, as Flanagan could just see something tattooed on his knuckles, currently turning white around the grip of the MAC-10, which was pointed in the wrong direction. The three Blackhearts had the thugs dead to rights, and they knew it.

For a moment, it looked like they might still make a fight of it. They were all younger than the Blackhearts who currently had them covered, but they were just as clearly hardened criminals. All of them had probably killed people before.

Which still made them amateurs compared to the three gunfighters who were currently about a pound of trigger pressure away from a massacre.

The man in the jacket must have been in charge. He slowly held out his empty hand and lowered the MAC-10 to the street. He nodded to the other two, who equally slowly and carefully put their own pistols on the asphalt.

"Now turn around and get moving." Flanagan's voice was cold. "If I see a face within the next block, I'm putting a bullet in it."

The guy in the jacket was clearly pissed, but he was smart enough to know that he'd just been ambushed, and that he was outclassed. He was also smart enough not to try to save face when he was on the wrong end of a gun barrel. He just turned around and walked out of the alley, hitting one of his compatriots when the smaller man looked like he was going to try to make an issue out of it.

The Blackhearts didn't follow to make sure they'd broken contact, but just fell back toward the parking lot on the far end of the alley. "Are they going to give up, or take another crack at it for revenge?" Flanagan asked.

"They'll find an easier mark." Curtis sounded confident enough. "You're lucky you were in town to get to play, Joe. Otherwise, I would have had to deal with them myself."

Gomez snorted. Flanagan just shook his head. "I hope you're right. I wouldn't want to have to come back here to haul your ass out of the fire *again*, because we just started a new vendetta tonight."

"Nah." If Curtis was worried, he didn't show it. "I know these scumbags. They pick out winners, follow them, then mug them somewhere off the Strip. They're low-level trash. I *guaran-fucking-tee* you that they were shitting themselves just now. They don't go after the hard targets. They'll probably beat each other up tonight, blame each other for the way it went down, then go try to find some skinny soyboy to rob next week."

"Well, if you say so." Flanagan was already heading for his truck, parked next to Gomez's. "If there's nothing else, we've got a long way to go to get to Charleston."

Curtis had stopped. Flanagan and Gomez both turned slowly to face him, murder in Flanagan's eyes. Curtis looked from one man to the other, then shook his head and laughed. "Okay, fine. I guess if we're getting paid enough, I don't have to swing by the Palace again tonight." When Flanagan closed his eyes with a deep and long-suffering sigh, Curtis slapped him on the shoulder and strutted past him toward the truck. "Let's go, then, shall we?"

***

I'm really not getting any younger. Tom Burgess tried not to think too much about how much his feet and his knees hurt. There'd been a time, more years ago than he liked to remember, when this little hike wouldn't have bothered him in the slightest. Now, though, it seemed like every muscle ached as he followed Ignatius Kirk down the mountainside.

Kirk had invited him out to scout for elk, and since he really wanted to get a good hunt in that fall, he hadn't hesitated to accept the invitation. It was somewhat embarrassing that the older man was running him into the ground, despite the sucking chest wound that he'd taken a couple years before. Kirk was a machine.

I need to get out more, or the actual hunt's going to kill me.

He spotted Kirk's cabin with a sense of relief that he hadn't expected. The cabin had been built out of several shipping containers, set well back from the nearest road and heavily camouflaged, so by the time that they could see it, they were already awfully close. The hike was almost over. Still, it had been a good trip. They'd gotten eyes on a sizeable herd, up in the high country about five miles from the cabin, and then had spent several hours just watching and cataloging their movements. It had been a productive day.

They got to the cabin only about half an hour later, and Burgess lowered himself into an armchair with some relief. "That was a long day."

Kirk smirked behind his massive beard as he handed his old friend a beer. "It ain't even dusk yet."

"And we ain't junior enlisted all full of piss and vinegar anymore, either." He accepted the bottle and took a long pull.

A phone jangled. It didn't startle Burgess this time. Kirk was an extremely private person and was also extremely careful, some might say to the point of being borderline paranoid. Burgess knew that his old friend had a cell phone jammer on the property, but he'd started leaving it off since he'd joined the Blackhearts, just in case.

Burgess didn't doubt that Kirk had found some sort of technological work-around to keep his phone from being easily located, even while maintaining contact in case a job came up.

Kirk reached across the couch and pulled the phone out. "Yes, Colonel." He listened for a moment. "Yeah, Tom's here. Probably has his phone turned off." Another pause. He squinted one eye with some disgust. "Maritime security? Doesn't sound too much like our kinda thing." Then he nodded. "Ah. Gotcha, sir. Yeah." He looked over at Burgess, who nodded. "Yeah, we're in. Tom's probably going to have to go home first. How much time have we got?" Another nod. "Roger that, sir. I'll be there by the day after tomorrow."

Hanging up, he turned to Burgess. "Looks like we've got a mission. Maritime security out of South Carolina."

Burgess didn't groan, only because he'd heard just enough to know there was something else going on.

"I would have turned it down, but apparently there's a pirate hunting angle that the Colonel thinks is worth it," Kirk continued. "We've got a week and a half, two weeks in Charleston to figure out more about what's going on, then we set sail."

Burgess nodded and took another pull off his beer. "Sounds like a plan. I'll swing by the house and get things settled for the next couple of months." He leaned back in the chair. "*After* I get a little rest."

***

Flanagan stepped into the bar and looked around with a sinking feeling. The place was a dive. Dark, lit only by neon beer signs above the bar and dim ceiling lights with green shades, wreathed in cigarette smoke, it was the sort of place where you expected the floor to be sticky and the clientele more than a little sketchy.

It already took too long to find him. Now he's in a place like this. He knew that Marines and Corpsmen weren't always known for frequenting the highest-class places, but if Doc Puller was hanging out here, it didn't necessarily bode well for his life choices. *Maybe I need to look for somebody else.*

30

He was already there, though, so he may as well at least see if Puller was up to the task.

It took a minute to thread his way through the tables, trying not to cringe at the too-loud music that would simultaneously make conversation extremely difficult and make it nearly impossible for anyone to listen in.

If there was anything to talk about that they might be worried about somebody overhearing.

Doc Puller was there, all right, just like his former girlfriend had said that he probably would be. Flanagan's eyes narrowed as he took in his former platoon corpsman, still fit but now leaning heavily on the bar, his back to the door, with several empty beer bottles in front of him. Apparently, this was the kind of bar that only cleaned up after the clientele had left.

Fortunately, the stool next to Puller was unoccupied. For that matter, most of the bar was empty. It was still three in the afternoon.

He slid onto the stool and leaned his elbows on the bar, glancing up at the TV above. It took Puller a second to realize he had company, and then, beer bottle still held to his lips, he turned his head to look. It took another second for him to recognize the lean, black-bearded man sitting next to him.

"Joe!" He slammed the bottle back down on the bar. "Holy shit! Joe Flanagan!" They shook hands, and if Puller's handshake was slightly weaker than it had been, he tried to make up for it with drunken enthusiasm. "Damn, I haven't seen you in forever." He grabbed the beer again and slammed the last of it down. From the looks of it, he was already north of a six pack. "What brings you out here?"

"Looking for you." Flanagan kept his voice down just far enough that Puller had to lean in to hear him. "Had a job come up and thought about you." He looked around the bar. "Didn't expect to find you in a place like this, though." The question was implicit.

"Oh." Puller looked around almost as if just noticing the sort of place he was drinking in. "I'm not a regular, or anything. Not really." He waved at the bartender for another beer, holding

31

up two fingers. The portly man with a ponytail slid two bottles across the bar, and Puller caught one, missed the other, but Flanagan got it before it went careening onto the floor. "I just come in here every so often."

Flanagan had known Puller long enough to know something was wrong. He'd been a good doc and a good fighter. He'd put down his share of alcohol while they'd been in the same platoon together, but he'd never been a raging drunk, or the kind to be drinking heavily at three in the afternoon on a weekday. What had changed since they'd both gotten out?

Puller, though, was going to tell the story in his own good time, and Flanagan wasn't the type to push. He needed to know that Puller would be honest, too, or else this wasn't going to work.

"Truth is, your timing's great. I'm kinda between jobs right now." Puller took another gulp. "Seems that some ambulance people don't like getting called out on their bullshit."

"What happened?" He had his opening. Now to find out if Puller was up to the task.

The former corpsman slammed the bottle down on the bar, but he didn't look at Flanagan. "Bad accident. I got there late. Turned out that I'd dated the gal in the front seat. Just last month, as a matter of fact." He took another drink. "I waded right in. Seems I violated some safety protocol or something. They wanted to suspend me, have me take all these blood tests. I told 'em to get bent." He drained the last of the bottle. "So, here I am."

Flanagan thought it over. It fit. Puller had been slightly bombastic but always willing to give the shirt off his back when they'd served together. He'd been a skilled corpsman, and he'd never put too much stock in procedure if he thought that a life hung in the balance. He'd seen enough combat that he *wouldn't* have a lot of patience with civilian SOPs that had been designed to minimize liability, especially if he really cared about whoever the injured person was.

"Well, the job's maritime security. The catch is that it's for an *extremely* wealthy client, and they might be a target for...other parties." He didn't want to go into too much detail, especially not in a dive bar and while Puller was drunk. He studied his old friend. "Think you can dry out for a couple of months?"

Puller laughed. "No problem, brother. Especially if it's an *extremely* wealthy client." He grinned. "When and where?"

"Charleston, South Carolina. No more than two days from now." Flanagan clapped Puller on the shoulder, turning it into a vise grip as he leaned in close. "Don't make me regret this."

Puller seemed to sober a little bit, and he put the beer down more gently. "Bro. Trust me. You won't." He gripped Flanagan's hand. "I'll be there, and I'll be sober as a bird. I promise."

Flanagan nodded. "I'll see you there, then." As he turned toward the doors, he sincerely hoped he had nothing to worry about.

CHAPTER 5

"Hey, Joe. Check this out." Gomez didn't point, but nodded slightly to indicate the end of the pier. "See that blue boat with the white canopy, second from the end?"

Flanagan didn't look right away. The two of them were strolling down the wooden pier at Patriot Point, trying to look like tourists and, he was sure, failing miserably. Sure, the USS *Yorktown* and the USS *Laffey* were both behind them, making the place a genuine tourist trap, never mind the massive hotel and spa on shore, but two athletic men in their late thirties to early forties were either meat eaters on business or…something else. They didn't fit the profile of something else, so they stood out a bit.

The sky was a deep blue, with only a few scattered, white clouds scudding by overhead. The water underfoot was a little green, though not as vibrant a shade as the trees that lined the shore. The boat club and the marina were reasonably crowded, which helped them get lost in the noise a bit.

As he casually scanned the marina, he spotted what Gomez had seen. Sure enough, there was a small yacht docked at the pier, close to the end. Unlike most of the boats in the marina, however, this one was occupied.

By itself, that wasn't all that strange. There were people aboard a few other boats tied up in the marina. Two of them were obviously living aboard their boats, while a few more appeared to just be doing maintenance or cleaning. These guys were different, though.

He glanced past the end of the pier, where the *Dream Empire*, all four hundred feet of her, massive enough to rival the *Laffey*, was anchored just off Schute's Folly Island. The two men sitting in the cabin of the docked boat were obviously watching the superyacht. One even had binoculars to his eyes.

"Might just be curious." He kept his voice low, pausing as they passed a family with two young kids, getting stares from the children while the parents did what they could to avoid looking too closely. "It's not every day that a four-hundred-foot superyacht drops anchor in the middle of the river mouth." He kept moving, not missing a step. "Or it might be more of Fontaine's security." They were pretty sure they'd spotted two teams already, and that was without checking the hotel, where if Flanagan had been in charge, he would have put an OP as soon as the yacht sailed into the harbor.

"Maybe." Gomez was as deadpan as ever, but he was also clearly skeptical. "They don't fit the same profile, though. None of the rest of Fontaine's people have been scoping the yacht out. They've been watching the crowds and the traffic."

"You've got a point." He tried to study their targets as best he could without staring. That was doable in some circumstances, but with the sheer number of people out and about, not to mention the distance and the obstruction of multiple boats tied up at the pier, it was next to impossible here. They'd have to circle back around and hope they didn't get spotted doing it. "The other question is, if those are the ones we can see, where are the others?"

"And who are they?" Gomez crunched a sunflower seed in his teeth and spat the hull over the rail and into the water. "If they're not Fontaine's people, then that means that we've already got another player on the board."

"The pirates, you think?" Flanagan wasn't entirely willing to put money on the guess, but if Fontaine had hired the Blackhearts because he was worried about said pirates, and an unidentified bunch of surveillance spooks was watching the yacht… They had to have a serious intelligence gathering apparatus if they were hitting secret cargos on the open ocean.

"Maybe." Gomez leaned on the rail and spat another sunflower seed hull into the water. "The other thing is, if Fontaine's as filthy rich as he's supposed to be, how much do you really want to bet the Feds *aren't* watching him day in and day out? Even if he's clean as the wind-driven snow…" Gomez laughed a little at Flanagan's derisive snort. They'd both heard a few things about Joshua Fontaine. Nothing that would necessarily hold up in court, but enough to make them suspicious. A lot of people with the kind of fortune he had weren't shy about bending the rules when and where they could. "Even if, you know that the Feds are going to be *looking* for something to try to nail him with. Especially since he doesn't have as many cozy relationships as some people in his position."

"I wonder about that." Flanagan lifted his eyes to the superyacht lying at anchor out in the estuary. Blue and white, it currently had an MD-500 helicopter sitting on its aft helipad. "With the kind of money he's got, I find it hard to believe that he hasn't bought a few of those sorts of relationships."

Gomez shrugged. "If he has, everybody's being *real* quiet about it."

Flanagan decided they'd been in one place long enough and turned to keep going down the pier. He didn't ask why their ordinarily taciturn teammate knew so much about Fontaine. Gomez might not talk much most of the time, but he wasn't dumb. Killer he might be, but like most of the Blackhearts, and the Recon Marine he had been before that, Gomez was a thinker, and when there was so little intel to go on as they had this time, he'd done some research.

After all, they were stuck on shore for the next week and a half, so they might as well do as much open-source intelligence gathering as they could.

It said something, too, about the relationship that the two quietest members of the team had forged that Gomez felt comfortable talking this much around Flanagan. When the

Blackhearts were all together, Gomez usually wouldn't say more than half a dozen words in a day.

"They're moving." Flanagan glanced over just in time to see the boat with the two observers chug away from the pier and turn upriver, heading away from them and the yacht.

"You think they know they got spotted?"

Gomez paused, leaning back against the rail as he appeared to look up toward the fancy hotel behind them, but in the process, he was able to surreptitiously scan their surroundings. "Maybe. I don't see anyone who looks like they might be a relief, and nobody's heading out to the yacht yet."

Flanagan sighed and turned back toward the parking lot. "We'd better make ourselves scarce then. Somebody else is going to have to keep an eye on the wharf for a while."

***

The Holiday Inn wasn't nearly as swank as the resort at Patriot Point, but it was lower profile, and they hadn't gotten accommodations from the client, since they weren't even supposed to be in Charleston yet. Brannigan had considered having the team spread out, taking rooms in various different hotels around the city, but the communications and logistics issues with that plan had led him to scrap it. So now it was easier to gather the whole team in his room, up on the fourth floor.

A knock came at the door, and Burgess checked it, his hand on the P365 at his waist. Some of the Blackhearts were probably carrying illegally, here in South Carolina, but Brannigan knew that Burgess, at least, along with him, Flanagan, Kirk, Hank, and Gomez, all had concealed carry permits that were recognized in South Carolina.

He pulled the door open, and Santelli ducked inside. "Well, I'm sure of it, now. We've got surveillance."

"You were followed?" Brannigan looked up from the laptop where he was looking for any information on recent ship disappearances.

"I wasn't, but Bianco and Curtis sure were." He shook his head. "I'm no spook, but these guys weren't much better than me at hiding in plain sight. They were obviously following the car."

Brannigan looked up at Gomez and Flanagan. "And we're *sure* these aren't just Fontaine's people being paranoid?"

Both men shook their heads. "It's *possible*, but like Mario said, it doesn't fit. They were definitely watching the yacht, not the surrounding area."

Brannigan nodded, turning back to the laptop and bringing up some overhead imagery of Charleston. "So, we're still a week and a half out from mission start, and we've already got complications." He ran a hand over his mustache. "Okay, they want to play stupid games, let's oblige them. I'm tired of groping around in the dark."

He pivoted the laptop around so that the rest could see the screen. "Let's see if we can't draw our new friends in and find out what it is they want."

CHAPTER 6

"This is stupid. Why the hell am *I* the one who has to play the rabbit?"

Kevin Curtis didn't like all this skullduggery bullshit. Give him a belt-fed and a whole lot of terrorists, or pirates, or whatever, and he'd be fine. It wasn't even that he was opposed to sneaking. He was good at it in the bush. It was this playing tag with parties unknown in the city, where he had to worry about whether or not it was a good idea to engage, that bugged him.

So, how is this different from what you, Joe, and Mario pulled in Vegas a couple nights ago?

Shut up.

It didn't help his mood much that he was currently dressed like a peacock, in an eye-searing white, blue, and purple windbreaker and garish sunglasses. Nobody was going to miss him, unless they had their face so buried in their phone that they couldn't see anything.

He still wondered if he was just being that dense, or if he actually *had* been missed. By the time he got to Patriot Point, he still hadn't picked out a shadow. Whoever had followed Santelli the day before hadn't showed themselves yet. Maybe it had been a fluke.

Still bullshit. Why should I *be the one to stick my neck out for them to take a swipe at?*

He knew he was just being grumpy, but the windbreaker was hardly his usual style. While he might be engaged now, Curtis had always been a ladies' man, and with that had come a finely tuned fashion sense. The windbreaker offended every bit of that sense.

"Should have made Joe wear this stupid thing." He knew that the other man would have hated it just as much, if for different reasons, which was why the thought gave him a grin. Unfortunately, Flanagan was the number two man on the team, and just happened to be much better at prepositioning himself to take action, along with Gomez, so he was shadowing Curtis, watching for their opposition.

Curtis pulled his phone out as he strolled out onto the pier. *Anything?*

It took a moment for the answering text to pop up. *No. This is going to take some patience. Unless we've got a leak, they can't have identified us all, and nobody's going to put surveillance on every tourist in the city. They're going to have to see you watching them first.*

"Dammit." Curtis shook his head. Of course, Flanagan's explanation made sense, which only made Curtis hate it all the more. *Why can't we just board the damn yacht and wait for the pirates with some booze and bikini babes?* He might be engaged, but old habits die hard.

For a moment, he paused in the parking lot, scanning the marina and the museum. The old USS *Yorktown* dominated the naval museum, and after a moment, he made his decision. There weren't a lot of places on the marina piers to hang out, and while he was *trying* to be noticed, at the same time, he didn't want the Charleston cops to show up because a yacht owner thought he was casing their boat. He *was* a black man in South Carolina, after all.

So, he walked up to the ticket booth and shelled out twenty-seven bucks for a ticket to the museum, grumbling a little to himself at spending his own money as operational funds, and strolled down the concrete wharf to the stairs that led up to the *Yorktown*'s flight deck.

He spent just long enough admiring the aircraft on deck, even though he always had been a ground pounder and didn't really like flying, never mind how many times he'd jumped, even after getting out and joining the Blackhearts, to make it look like he was actually there as a tourist. He had to strike a balance between being just obvious enough to draw the opposition's attention and so obvious that he brought museum security or the local cops down on his head.

Despite his grumbling, Curtis was actually far better at this than he'd admit to anyone, even himself. Nobody joined the Blackhearts without being able to adapt and act tactically in all sorts of different environments.

Casually, he sauntered to the chain link fence that lined the edge of the deck, installed to make sure no museumgoers toppled over into the water. He'd brought binoculars, which weren't out of the ordinary for a lot of the other tourists, but now it was time to play his role all the way.

First, he pulled his phone out of his pocket again. *In position on the* Yorktown. *Going to try to drill a hole in their heads with my eyes now.*

Roger. Typically, Flanagan didn't include anything more than that.

Not even a "good luck," Joe? Curtis briefly considered sending that message just to piss his brother from another mother off, but there was work to do. Instead, he shoved the phone back in his pocket and lifted his binoculars.

He scanned the superyacht where it still sat at anchor first. It hadn't moved since Flanagan and Gomez had observed it the day before. *Damn, that thing looks swank.* He was almost looking forward to a boring two months or so aboard. Even the security quarters should be pretty comfortable.

Unfortunately, there were no girls on deck, but he supposed that that stood to reason, since it looked like the superyacht was in a maintenance and resupply cycle at the moment. Finally, he started scanning the marina piers, looking for the boat that Flanagan and Gomez had spotted.

43

There. It wasn't hard. They'd gone right back to the same spot, and he could even see one of them inside the boathouse with a pair of binoculars, watching the superyacht.

Leaning against the fence, Curtis put his binoculars to his eyes and settled in to stare at the surveillance boat until he got a reaction.

***

Flanagan looked down at his phone as it vibrated in his hand. *They've made me. One of them is on the phone right now.*

Copy. He looked up at Gomez and nodded. Game on.

They were sitting in one of the two rental cars the Blackhearts had picked up in Charleston, currently parked facing the trees at the edge of the Patriots Point parking lot. Their lines of sight were limited, but they were out of the way and effectively out of sight. Flanagan had positioned the rear-view mirrors so that they had a decent view of the parking lot behind them. It wasn't perfect, but both men had seen enough on the way in that they figured it was better to conceal the fact that they were both sitting in the car, watching the parking lot, than to be able to see every nook and cranny. They should be able to see enough of their surroundings not to miss anything of consequence. Flanagan could see where Curtis would come out of the marina, and hopefully that meant they could see anyone who took up a follow position behind him.

"There he is." Gomez sounded dryly amused as Flanagan ducked his head to get a better look in the side mirror, just in time to see that glaring white, blue, and purple windbreaker.

Flanagan chuckled, just a little. He and Curtis went back a long, long way, and the constant shit-talking was part of the territory.

They watched as Curtis threaded his way through the parking lot and headed for the exit. They weren't watching Curtis so much as they were watching the rest of the crowd.

"Bingo." Flanagan nodded toward the mirror without taking his eyes off it. "Blue t-shirt, green shorts, just got out of a red Camaro, directly behind us."

44

Gomez shifted his gaze to the main rear-view mirror and nodded. "Got him. You want to follow on foot, or in the car?"

Flanagan was already putting the car in reverse, though. "We can get ahead of him in the car. We already know where Kev is going."

"Unless they catch up with him before he gets to our ambush site." Gomez settled back in his seat, though.

"That's a chance we'll have to take, but we're not exactly the only ones out here, either." He nodded toward the phone in the center console as he backed out of the parking space and headed for the exit, driving past Curtis without even looking at him. "Give Carlo a yell, just in case."

Gomez scooped up the phone and called Santelli rather than texting. "Hey, it's Mario. Curtis is on the move. Got at least one tail, blue shirt, green shorts." He paused. "Roger." Putting the phone back in the console, he adjusted the P-10 in his waistband and glanced behind them, though Curtis and his tail were currently out of sight. "He's ready."

Flanagan nodded and turned down Coleman Boulevard, heading for the residential neighborhood they'd picked out as their ambush site. It wasn't the best place to do this, but there were a lot of trees to obscure their presence, and less chance that they'd be spotted during the day than if they'd tried to intercept their opposition in the parking lot of the strip mall just on the other side of the road. Hopefully, there weren't any nosy housewives peering out their windows with cell phones in hand.

Or househusbands, these days.

Pulling up to the curb underneath a spreading tree that all but obscured the car entirely, Flanagan killed the engine and cracked his door, though he didn't open it so far that he couldn't use the side mirror to watch the street behind them.

They waited in silence. If Curtis was in trouble, he'd let them know. As it was, they couldn't expect him to send a running commentary all the way. It would both distract him and look suspicious.

The minutes went by, the tension getting higher. Flanagan let his eyes move, scanning their surroundings rather than staying fixed on the mirror. If they were made, this was the time that things might get hairy.

The street remained as quiet and still as a graveyard. If anyone was looking out a nearby window, they didn't think that the green sedan sitting under a willow tree was all that strange.

"Here he comes." Gomez spotted Curtis first. He was still wearing the windbreaker, even though it was pushing eighty degrees. If the opposition, whoever they were, were on the ball, they might find that suspicious. Hopefully, they didn't look the gift horse in the mouth.

Flanagan cracked the door a little farther as he shifted behind the wheel, getting ready to launch himself out and engage in some extreme violence.

Curtis hadn't slowed down or sped up but maintained his relatively casual pace as he moved down the street toward the car, his hands in his pockets. He got about halfway to the vehicle before two men came around the corner behind him, one of them the guy they'd spotted earlier, in the blue t-shirt and green shorts. The other was dressed a little more conservatively, in cargo pants and a slightly too-small t-shirt.

Flanagan and Gomez both stayed where they were. The intent was to intercept these guys and find out who they were. If they played their hand too soon, Curtis's shadowers would be gone before they could corner them.

The man in the cargo pants slowed, though, putting out a hand to forestall his companion. He'd spotted something, or else just sensed that something was off. The man in the blue t-shirt looked around, his eyes narrowed, and stopped.

"Damn it." Gomez started to open the door, but it was too late. A second later, both men had retreated back around the corner and disappeared.

Curtis reached the car and only then looked back. "Well, shit. What gave it away?"

"Don't know." Flanagan had stepped out of the car, watching their back trail carefully. He wasn't sure if the others had simply broken contact, or if they were circling around through the surrounding residential yards to hit them from another angle. After a moment, though, he shrugged and slid back behind the wheel. "It was worth a shot, but it looks like they're a little too alert. They're gone." He sighed. "No leads today, boys, unless somebody else manages to pick them up and tail them."

Gomez was already on the phone, passing the word to the rest, as Flanagan started the car back up and headed out of the neighborhood.

***

Flanagan and Gomez hadn't been the only ones in the parking lot, though. Tom Burgess had the Blackhearts' other rental car, and had been sitting in the parking lot outside the Beach Club, under the trees where he could see out to the piers. He saw some of the text traffic but paid it no mind. His objective wasn't theirs.

He'd already spotted what he was pretty sure was the yacht's outer security. They'd moved since Flanagan and Gomez had pinpointed them the day before, but they still fit the description, and their attitudes and watchfulness fit the bill as well. Burgess was sure that there were probably other parties in the vicinity that needed the extra security, but given the proximity of the *Dream Empire*, it made sense that these were Fontaine's people.

Keeping an eye on them without *looking* like he was keeping an eye on them was made somewhat easier by the fact that he was sitting in a car. He'd pushed the seat far enough back that someone would have to walk right up and peer in through the window to see that he was there, and he'd spaced the sedan far enough from the nearest vehicles that it was unlikely—not impossible, but unlikely—that anyone would get that close.

Only a few minutes had passed since Curtis and his followers had left the parking lot when things started moving.

The men in the car he was watching started stirring, and one of them lifted a phone to his ear. A moment later, another "tourist" up on the deck of the *Yorktown* also answered a phone, or maybe a radio. Something was happening.

Burgess didn't move a muscle. He'd done this before. This wasn't the time to get excited. This was the time to wait, watch, and document what he saw.

After the initial short flurry of movement, which would have been downright imperceptible if he hadn't been watching for it, everything went still again. At least, until the three-vehicle motorcade pulled up a few minutes later.

Burgess watched the SUVs with interest. They were all Lexus LX570s, luxury SUVs, and obviously up-armored. There was a lot of money in that three-vehicle motorcade, and he thought he knew who had sent it. He settled back a little more in the seat, getting almost all the way down below the dash, holding his phone at such an angle that he could just get the camera over the dash to take some pictures of the motorcade as they pulled through the parking lot and stopped in the entrance of the Charleston Harbor Resort and Marina, a massive, red-roofed hotel sitting next to the Beach Club.

There was some foliage between him and his targets, but he could still get usable shots, and he could zoom in just enough that when one of the security men, dressed in khakis and a dark blue polo shirt, stepped out and opened the back door of the middle Lexus, he got a good shot at the man who got out.

Maybe a couple inches under six feet, the man was dressed in a white polo shirt and khaki slacks that probably cost almost as much as the car Burgess was sitting in. The sunlight glinted off the gold watch on his wrist, and his sunglasses were probably almost as expensive as the watch. His auburn hair was longish and swept back, gelled until it glistened in the sun.

Burgess let out a low whistle, glad he had the windows up and the AC running, so nobody was going to hear him. He snapped several pictures as the man looked around the parking lot, then, flanked by two of the men in blue polo shirts, walked around the corner of the building and down the lane toward the piers. He wasn't going inside. He was heading for the boats, and presumably the *Dream Empire*.

Only after the man had disappeared around the corner and the Lexus SUVs had driven back out of the parking lot did Burgess lower the phone and send the photos and a short message to Brannigan.

Joshua Fontaine was just dropped off and headed toward the piers. Appears that our client might be making the voyage with us.

Tom Burgess settled back into his surveillance position with a sigh and a reflective scan of the area. He'd been on contracts where that kind of close contact with the client had been the norm, and with few exceptions, they had often been nightmares. Given what they knew about Fontaine's reputation, this could go either way.

If the pirates they'd been warned about were after Fontaine, this could get *very* interesting. Especially if they already had the yacht under surveillance.

He was starting to suspect that this wasn't going to be nearly the boring voyage it had initially shaped up to be.

CHAPTER 7

Brannigan looked over as the phone rang, expecting another report from either Gomez or Burgess. This was getting *very* interesting, indeed. Active surveillance that didn't appear to be Fontaine's people, active surveillance that was good enough to spot an ambush and back out of it, and now Fontaine himself was apparently coming along on the voyage. *Just what is the game, here?*

When he looked at the phone, however, he didn't recognize the number. His eyes narrowed. Not many people had that number, but Chavez was one of them, and he must have passed it along. He knew that the Blackhearts wouldn't have let it out.

Scooping it up, he hit the "answer" button and put it to his ear. "Yes."

"Mr. Brannigan?" The voice on the other end sounded clipped and impatient. Brannigan already found himself taking a dislike to its owner.

"That's me." His own tone wasn't especially patient.

"My name is Sorley. I'm the security coordinator aboard the *Dream Empire*. When are you going to get here? I'm waiting at the pier right now."

Brannigan didn't answer immediately, though his jaw tightened, and his knuckles whitened around the phone for just a moment. They'd been on the ground for a couple of days already, and they'd even gone to the yacht to see about getting aboard and beginning to familiarize themselves with the vessel's layout, and had been denied. Now this jackass was acting as if they were late.

"We've been ready." He kept his voice level, though he might have bitten off a syllable or two. "We already got told we had to wait."

"Well, the wait's over. How soon can you get to the pier?"

"Give us twenty minutes." The hotel wasn't far, and they could *walk* that distance in that time.

"Fine. Twenty minutes. Don't keep me waiting." Sorley hung up.

Brannigan looked down at the phone in his fist, his eyes hard. When he looked up, Santelli was watching him skeptically.

"This is going to be one of *those* contracts, isn't it?" The former Sergeant Major might not have as much of a history in the contracting world as some of the other Blackhearts, but he'd been around. He'd stayed in the Marine Corps as long as he had so that he could do what he could for his junior Marines, not because he'd been one of those who simply couldn't cope with life outside the Corps. He knew more about the contracting world than many with his history and experience might. Furthermore, both men had seen commands that functioned much like some of the worst contracting companies in the market.

"Looks like it." Brannigan shoved the phone in his pocket. "I sure hope those pirates actually take a crack at us. This is going to be the worst job we've taken yet if they don't." He looked around the room. Most of the Blackhearts were gathered there, except for Gomez, Flanagan, Curtis, and Burgess, who were still out on surveillance duties. "Grab your stuff and head for the marina. Space it out, too. If we've got snoopers on the ground, it probably isn't a very good idea to go hiking down the street all together like an aging Boy Scout troop."

That got a few chuckles as he got on the phone to give Flanagan and the others their instructions. He and Santelli would grab their stuff. They needed to get moving.

He wondered, though. Even if this really was a pirate-hunting job, and not just a billionaire looking for the shiniest toys, even to include his security, then it was already off to a bad start.

***

Flanagan and his companions beat the rest to the parking lot by several minutes. He pulled into a parking space just off the Beach Club, and when he looked around, he saw the other rental car not far away. There was no sign of Burgess at first glance; the other man had leaned back far enough that he wasn't immediately observable.

Burgess had apparently seen them, however. He climbed out of the sedan and locked the doors as he walked over to Flanagan's side of the car. The client had paid for the rentals, and paid for the duration of the voyage, so they weren't worried about returning them just yet.

Flanagan didn't get out immediately. He rolled down his window as Burgess approached. He wasn't sure if the opposition—whoever they were—was still around, but it didn't feel like a good idea to expose themselves too much just yet.

"There's still an OP set up somewhere on the marina." Burgess kept his voice down and kept watching his surroundings as he spoke. "I went for a walk just now, and there are definitely a couple guys in the boat you spotted yesterday. Different spot on the pier, but the description matches."

Flanagan nodded. "Heard you saw Fontaine himself head out there."

"Sure looked like him." Burgess ran a thumb through his beard, under his chin. "He hasn't come back out, either, so he's either in the Beach Club, or he's aboard the yacht." He shrugged. "Or I was mistaken, and it was somebody else who just looks like Fontaine, and he's out fishing or joyriding on the river."

"I guess we'll see." Flanagan looked down at his phone.

"I gotta wonder. Why would Fontaine hire us to protect him, and then not tell us that he's the one needing protection?" Curtis sounded uncharacteristically thoughtful from where he sat

53

in the back seat. "I've done some close protection stuff off and on, and you *always* meet the principal. Get to know their patterns, their schedule, stuff like that. Why the secrecy?"

"*Especially* with the amount of money he's paying," Flanagan agreed. "I don't know, Kev. Something's weird about this whole setup, but maybe he's the kind of billionaire who just figures the security stuff is beneath him, and since we're going to be on a yacht, out at sea, there's no reason to dirty himself dealing with us knuckle draggers."

Curtis sniffed. "Maybe you're a knuckle dragger, Joseph, but I can just as easily be a man of high culture. I *do* live in Vegas, after all."

Even Gomez snorted at that.

Gomez looked up. "Carlo just got here." When Flanagan followed his gaze, he saw the short, stout former Sergeant Major walking toward the gap between the two resorts, a pack over his shoulder. Some distance behind him, Kirk appeared, looking a little like ZZ Top with his long beard and sunglasses on.

"Time to go." While Kirk had an extra pack with him, probably Curtis's, Flanagan and Gomez had brought their luggage with them in the car, just in case. All of the Blackhearts had packed light, not knowing exactly what they were getting into and assured, via Chavez, that gear would be provided. Mostly, they had a few changes of clothes, toiletries, and one or two diversions to keep them from going stir crazy on a two-month transit aboard the yacht.

More of the Blackhearts were filtering into the parking lot as the three of them got out and locked the car. None of them got too close, so that they would appear to the casual observer to be separate beachgoers until they closed in on the pier.

Brannigan was about midmost of the group, on the phone as they passed between the two massive hotels and out into the marina. Flanagan fell in next to him, spotting Sorley almost immediately. Something about the man drew his attention, aside from the phone he held to his ear. Short, stocky, with a shaved head and almost no neck, the man didn't look like most of the rest

54

of the tourists and boatmen out on the piers that day. There was an edge to him that Flanagan could pick out even from a hundred yards away. His blue polo shirt and light khakis couldn't disguise it.

Sorley looked over as the Blackhearts converged on the pier. He managed to look impatient and angry even as they closed in.

"About time." He looked at his watch. "We have a strict schedule to keep."

Flanagan felt his own anger rise, but Brannigan beat him to the punch. The Blackhearts' commander loomed well over a head taller than Sorley, and there wasn't much fat on his massive frame, either. He stepped into Sorley's personal space, glowering down at him while stroking his mustache with one big, calloused hand. Brannigan might have been an officer for a long time, but he'd always been a very hands-on sort of commander, and his lifestyle since his forced retirement hadn't exactly been soft or sedentary.

"I'm only going to say this once, Mr. Sorley." Brannigan's rumble was amiable and threatening at the same time. "Your employer hired us for a reason. We're not some dimwitted rent-a-cops you can push around. You didn't specify any timetable, so if you're going to get pissy about us not knowing information *you* failed to disclose, then we walk. Right now." He stared the smaller man down, his icy blue eyes almost as steely and intimidating as Wade's. It probably helped that Wade was standing off to one side, his arms folded, watching Sorley without blinking.

Flanagan was watching him, too, but with a further objective than intimidation. He was observing the man's mannerisms, and he saw the calculation behind Sorley's eyes. The wheels were turning in that shaved skull, and the man was reassessing the situation as it happened.

This dude's more than just a facilitator. He's dangerous.

Granted, dangerous might well be a plus when selecting a security coordinator. Someone without experience of violence is rarely well-qualified to prepare for it. Something about Sorley struck Flanagan as off, though.

Just like the rest of this job, if we're being honest.

But Sorley wasn't just recalculating. Even as Flanagan saw the realization dawn in the bald man's eyes that he was dealing with extremely dangerous professionals, instead of the usual low-level grunts puffed up as SEALs or some other JSOC black magicians on maritime security contracts, he could also see another change in the man's attitude. This wasn't the kind of man who took loss of face well. He was going to assert his place as top dog, regardless of the fact that he'd just been called out. In fact, now he *had* to assert that place. He might not do it immediately, but it was coming.

"Well, we have a timetable, whether you got it or not. So, if this is everybody, let's go."

Flanagan watched Sorley carefully. He'd brushed off the implicit threat in Brannigan's words, but Flanagan was pretty sure he'd picked up on them, anyway, and that he was taking them seriously. It was a thoughtful bullet-headed security coordinator who turned, deliberately not looking back at the band of killers behind him, and headed for the end of the pier.

The Blackhearts followed, not without a few dire looks aimed at his back, but Brannigan was composed as he held his pack over one shoulder and paced along only about a yard behind Sorley.

Flanagan wondered if the "security coordinator" knew that every man behind him had a gun somewhere on his person. Probably not.

Sorley, his face taut and a quiet anger now burning behind his eyes, led the way to a launch with another man, about Sorley's height but a lot skinnier, his hair sun-bleached blond and long, at the tiller. Sorley got in at the bow, looking back at the Blackhearts, but if he was thinking about giving brusque instructions to get in, he reconsidered at Wade's glare. Instead, he just waited, looking angry, until everyone was aboard, and then he nodded to the blond coxswain. The younger man looked like a stereotypical surfer, not an employee of one of the biggest billionaires on the planet.

He knew his way around a boat, though. The ride out to the *Dream Empire* was as smooth and quick as it was deadly silent.

The massive vessel's stern doubled as a dock, and the coxswain steered the launch carefully in to one side of what looked like a miniature submarine. Apparently, the *Dream Empire* had mirrored her sister ship in just about every way, including the submersible.

Once docked, Sorley clambered up onto the catwalk and waited. The yacht was so big that while the faint swell was noticeable, it was considerably less violent than it might have been on any other, smaller vessel.

"This way. I'll show you your quarters, gear locker, and where you'll be expected to post watches." He glanced over his shoulder as he passed through the hatchway. "Yes, before you start to get butt-hurt about it, your movements aboard this tub are going to be very strictly circumscribed. The top two decks are off limits. Don't even think about trying to find out the nature of the cargo, either. That's none of your business. Do your jobs and you'll be paid handsomely. Get out of line and you get nothing."

He led the way through the extensive galley and into a forward compartment that appeared to have been hastily refitted into an arms room. Green-painted weapon racks had been bolted against the far bulkhead, with several pistol-sized safes mounted above them. Lockers stood against the other bulkhead, and Flanagan caught a glimpse of some storm gray through the openings in the locker doors. What he could see looked brand new, which was probably to be expected for Joshua Fontaine's security.

One corner of the room had been set up as a sort of command center, with at least two radios, camera monitors—none of which displayed any of the forbidden top decks—and a charging station with a dozen portable walkie-talkies all set in their ports with the lights showing green. Sorley looked around the compartment, which was rather crowded once the entire team was inside. "There are four lookout positions, so you should be able to switch off fairly regularly." He folded his arms. "There's a lot going on aboard this ship that is need-to-know, and you don't need to know. You're here to do a job. That's protect this yacht and its cargo. Any other details are no never mind to you. You're getting paid enough. There is a considerable chance that the pirates who have been hitting transatlantic shipments lately will attempt to attack this yacht. You need to be prepared for it. I have set up a schedule for three alert and lockdown drills on the first few days out of port." He pointed to a white three-ring binder lying next to the radios. "I'll leave the specifics of the duty roster up to you, but I do expect the plan to be followed to the letter."

He started toward the hatch and the ladderwell just outside of it. Before he got there, though, he turned to Brannigan. "You might be the company CEO or whatever, *Colonel*, but I'm in charge of overall security aboard this tub. Which means you answer to me. Maybe you didn't get the timeline earlier." He pointed to the binder. "You've got it now. I suggest you follow it, if you want to get paid." Without another word, he turned back to the hatch.

Except Wade was standing in his way. Wade might be slightly shorter than Brannigan, but he made up for it with an aura of barely restrained violence that was *always* there. He hadn't gotten the callsign "Angry Ragnar" for nothing.

Sorley looked up at him. "We got a problem, big man?"

Wade met his gaze with a smile that was as warm and friendly as a shark's, and a good deal more dangerous. "That depends on you, little man."

Once again, Sorley seemed to pause and recalculate his position. He wasn't backing down, but he was adding to what he'd already put together about the Blackhearts. His wasn't an expressive face, but for those who could read people, it was obvious that the plan was changing, the more he saw of the Blackhearts.

Finally, Sorley stepped back and looked over at Brannigan. He smiled disarmingly, but there was still the same cold calculation in his eyes. "My apologies, Colonel. It seems that Mr. Chavez found us a more tight-knit crew than I was expecting." He glanced at Wade, who hadn't stepped back an inch or relented at all, but still had him fixed with that serial killer stare. "My compliments on your boys' dedication. But there *is* a timetable, and if we *don't* follow it, we might get caught with our pants down, and I don't think any of us want to see that happen. Particularly not out on the water, with no support in sight."

Brannigan didn't answer, but just nodded, his arms crossed over his chest. Distinctly uncomfortable now, Sorley eased around Wade, who pivoted to follow him with those laser turret eyes, and headed out the hatch.

"What an asshole." Curtis wasn't even looking after Sorley as the hatch closed behind the "security coordinator." He was looking at the weapon racks. "Nothing but SBRs for a damn maritime security gig. How the hell are we supposed to engage pirates out at range without belt-feds?" He kicked the weapon rack. "What an unprofessional setup."

"Hate to tell you this, Kev, but there aren't that many maritime security operations that get actual machineguns." Kirk looked over the compartment. "This is actually pretty nice for one of these gigs."

As Brannigan walked over to the table and picked up the binder, the deck vibrated beneath them, and the engines began to throb. Bianco looked up and around. "I thought we weren't leaving for another week."

Brannigan was unperturbed as he flipped open the binder. "Seems that we didn't get told a lot of the timetable. If they're really that worried about pirates, that might make some sense. Still pisses me off, though." He sighed, looking down at the crisp, professionally printed plans and diagrams in the notebook. "We're committed now, regardless. So, I suggest everybody gear up, arm up, and start familiarizing themselves with every bit of this bucket we can reach."

CHAPTER 8

"Five hours until the next drill." Bianco glanced over the camera feeds again. Nothing. Just like the last four days. "I can't wait."

Kirk had his feet up on the desk, reading a magazine. His MCX Virtus SBR was leaning against the bulkhead along with his storm gray plate carrier, and his Glock 19 was on his hip, along with spare mags for both it and the carbine. Most of their personal weapons were secreted in their quarters. No reason to expend their personal ammo. "At least we're getting paid, and we're not getting hunted by the Front over the Tian Shan mountains this time."

Bianco glanced at the cameras, then the overhead. "Not sure we should be talking about that."

"What, the Front?" Kirk dropped the magazine for a moment. "Who *doesn't* know that the Front's dirty, at this point? They've been doing damage control for the last few years, and if they didn't have billions stashed away from all the people they duped before that, they'd be as dead as the dodo by now." He chuckled and picked up the magazine, something about cars and mechanics. "No, I'm not worried about these clowns learning that we've killed a bunch of Front goons."

"What if…" Bianco trailed off for a moment, glancing up again. He really wasn't confident that the compartment wasn't bugged. Just because *he* couldn't see it on the cameras didn't mean there wasn't another monitor somewhere, with Sorley watching and listening. He dropped his voice to a whisper. "What if *they're* Front? I mean, there's a *lot* of money here. And all this secrecy…"

Kirk frowned, dropping his boots to the deck and putting the magazine down on the desk. He scanned the monitors for a moment, chewing on the question.

"It's possible." He chuckled a moment. "Trust me, Vinnie, nobody ever accused me of being anything less than paranoid. Still, nobody ever linked Fontaine with the Front. I looked into him a little once we found out he was behind this op. He's clean as a whistle…at least on the surface."

Bianco frowned. "You think he's dirty?"

Kirk laughed out loud at that one. "Kid, show me somebody with the kind of money Joshua Fontaine has who *doesn't* have a baker's dozen skeletons in their closet, and I'll show you a unicorn. Trust me, *nobody*'s that rich without bending a lot of rules when they don't flat-out break 'em. That might make me sound like a pinko, but I've been around too long. When they don't cheat outright, they buy politicians to make cheating legal— for *them*. And probably give them some taxpayer money along the way." He shook his head. "No, I don't think he's squeaky clean. If he's Front, though, he's done a *damned* good job of hiding it."

"Wouldn't that be just what somebody in the Front would do, though, these days?" Bianco knew he wasn't the only one who was uncomfortable with this entire setup, though he had to admit that on some level, it was probably just the fact that they were doing glorified security guard work while shut up in a command post, when they were usually high-speed mercenaries who did the dangerous, secret jobs where nobody else could or would.

"Maybe, except that Fontaine made most of his money *before* the Front got exposed." Kirk reached over and gripped Bianco's shoulder, giving him a bit of a shake. "Relax, kid. Whatever's going on, I *seriously* doubt that it's the Front. This time."

Bianco let his head bob ruefully as Kirk shook his shoulder. "You're probably right. Still…"

Kirk sobered. "I know. Still." He looked over the bank of monitors again. "Well, either we get hit and get to kill some pirates, or else we have a nice, quiet working vacation with a fat paycheck at the end of it."

"Is it bad that I'm kinda hoping for the former?" Bianco had to admit that he'd been bored. The fact that the yacht had amazing wifi wasn't a comfort, because it meant he couldn't in good conscience leave all the customer support emails to Glenn.

"Nah." Kirk laughed and picked up his magazine again. "That's just how we're wired, brother. We want to get some action to earn our pay."

The two of them settled back down to watching and waiting. Aside from the drills—which had been simplistic to the point that Bianco suspected they'd either been designed to make them easier for the civilian passengers to follow the instructions, or else Sorley really didn't know what he was doing—all they had to do was keep two men in the command post and two on exterior watch, one in the bow and one at the fantail. It was a pretty bare-bones security setup, despite all the voiced concerns about super pirates.

They knew nothing about Sorley's background, and after his little performance when they'd first come aboard, they hadn't exactly been friendly enough to find out anything more. The questions kept coming up, though.

A knock came at the hatch, and Flanagan stuck his head in, a faint frown on his face. "Is Doc in here?"

Both men looked at each other, then shook their heads. "Haven't seen him since shift change," Bianco said.

Flanagan's frown deepened. "He's not in our quarters, either." He took a deep breath and started to pull away from the hatch. "I'd better go find him."

"Something wrong?" Kirk asked.

Flanagan hesitated. "I don't know. He's not quite the same guy I used to know. Something's happened to him since we served together." He stayed in the hatchway for a moment, thinking. "The Doc Puller I knew wouldn't have been getting

63

drunk in a dive like the one where I found him. Not over something like that. The dude used to be *obnoxiously* cheerful."

"Like, Curtis obnoxious?" Bianco asked. "Or just normal obnoxious?"

Flanagan laughed softly. "Dom Puller could make Kevin Curtis looked positively *dour* by comparison."

Kirk managed to look horrified. "That's…that's kind of nightmarish to think about."

"He could be a handful," Flanagan admitted. "He was a hell of a doc, though. He'd low crawl through broken glass to get to a wounded Marine. Then stick you with an IV on libo so you could keep drinking." He quieted and shook his head again. "Like I said, something happened. I don't know what. But I think I'd better go find him, just in case he's getting into trouble."

***

Puller knew that while it hadn't been spelled out as such, the spirit of the rules Sorley had given them had effectively restricted the Blackhearts to quarters when they weren't on watch. There were even prescribed routes to and from the bow and stern watch posts in the SOP binder. He needed to clear his head, though, and he couldn't do that in the relatively small compartment that was their berthing. Sure, it was far bigger than any bunkroom he'd seen in the Navy, and posh as hell, but he needed the open air.

There wasn't any booze available for the Blackhearts aboard, and to his dismay, he was finding that that was a problem. While he might have done his share of drinking both before and after his time in the Fleet, he'd been sure that he wasn't really an *alcoholic.* Yet here he was, wanting a drink so bad that it hurt.

It wasn't just the lack of alcohol that was getting to him, though. There was something off about this whole thing. Not the Blackhearts. He remembered Colonel Brannigan and Sergeant Major Santelli from back in the day, with respect if not quite reverence. Just from what he'd seen, the Blackhearts were a close-knit group of utter professionals, Curtis's antics aside.

No, it was something about this job. He just couldn't put his finger on what it was. So, here he was, out by the rail, taking in the sea and the open air, trying to think.

"Hey." He turned to see one of the girls that he'd gotten a glimpse of from time to time out on the upper deck. She'd wrapped a towel around her waist, but she was still wearing a bikini top, and she was stunning. The wind whipped her blond hair around her face, and her skin was a flawless honey color. And he could see enough of it that he was pretty sure she didn't wear that bikini when she tanned.

"Hey." He knew he should be on his guard. She was too hot, and if the Blackhearts were supposed to be separate from the guests—presuming that was what she was, rather than a working girl—then there wasn't a good reason for her to be down here, mixing with the proles.

She sidled closer, leaning on the rail and looking out to sea, letting the wind blow her hair back. "I haven't gotten to see much of you guys."

"Well, we're just the help." If anything, Puller's headache was getting worse. "We're not supposed to mix with the bigwigs."

She laughed and rolled her eyes, then glanced at him sideways, the look on her face changing. There was something strange in her expression, as if she was slightly confused. "Is that what they told you?"

He frowned, his thoughts suddenly dragged back to the here and now. He hardly noticed her amazing body anymore. "What do you mean?"

Before she could answer, though, her eyes moved to look at something behind him, and her face was suddenly shuttered, wary. He turned to look and saw Flanagan coming up along the side. "It's okay. He's good." He turned to meet his old friend. "What's up, Joe?"

Flanagan eyed the girl, then turned back to Puller. "Wondering where you got to, that's all."

Puller took a deep breath. The girl was shying away, now, though she reached out and touched his arm before she headed

65

forward with what might have been a regretful smile. "Just needed some air."

Flanagan's voice was suddenly hard. "Get back to the arms room."

Puller frowned. "Look, Joe, I wasn't doing any harm…"

Flanagan gripped his arm. "I don't mean that, Doc." He pointed. "We've got incoming."

Puller followed Flanagan's pointing finger. It took a second to see what his old platoon mate had seen.

The dark specks of two helicopters raced through the air toward the yacht, above the white wakes of at least four speedboats.

CHAPTER 9

Flanagan hadn't been the only one to spot the oncoming pirates. Gomez had called in the alert from his position up in the bow, just before Bianco had seen the enemy on the monitors in the command center. In less than two minutes, all the Blackhearts who hadn't already been on watch were in the arms room, already geared up and armed, watching the incoming forces on the monitors.

"Those helos are going to be a problem." Brannigan was leaning over the desk, watching the approaching pirates. They had minutes, at most.

"Well, then you'll be happy to hear that we do have some more firepower than just what's in this compartment." Sorley came through the hatch, wearing his own vest and carrying what looked very much like an MP7, which raised a couple of eyebrows. Those little 4.6mm PDWs were *not* easy to get outside of military or police forces. It said something about Fontaine's resources and connections. "Come with me." He disappeared through the hatch, heading across the hull and past the dock in the fantail.

Brannigan nodded as all eyes turned to him, and Curtis and Bianco were the first ones out the hatch, following Sorley. Most of the rest followed, while Brannigan and Santelli stayed in the command center for the moment.

Bianco caught up with Sorley in a few strides, as the man opened a hatch to reveal yet another hatch just inside it, with a cipher lock on it. He quickly punched in a code, and while he tried to shield the pad with his body, Bianco could see what numbers he'd entered, and made a point of memorizing the code as best he could. *Never know when that might come in handy.*

The lock beeped and flashed a green light, and Sorley pushed the hatch open, flipping on an overhead light as he went through. The compartment was less than half the size of the command center on the starboard side, and it was packed with plastic equipment cases.

Sorley started to open the nearest ones, and Bianco heard Curtis swear behind him. The first case held two FN EVOLYS machineguns with red dot sights.

Curtis shoved past Sorley and snatched up one of the lightweight, 5.56 belt feds and tossed it to Bianco, but not without shooting the security coordinator a venomous look. "Couldn't *possibly* have let us know about these *before* the bad guys were on our back porch, could ya? Fucking asshole." He looked around, ignoring any reaction he might get from their prickly supervisor. "Where's the ammo?"

Sorley might have reacted, except that Bianco, who was even bigger than Wade, was glowering at him with a heat that was enough to make anyone no longer notice the big man's apparent boyishness. Instead, he just pointed to the far corner, accessible by a narrow lane between the stacks of gear, where ammunition crates were stacked against the bulkhead. Curtis threaded his way through and started attacking the crates with gusto. They didn't have a lot of time.

While Kirk and Hank stood in the hatchway, since there wasn't really enough room to enter, Sorley opened another case, and pulled out a Carl Gustaf 84mm recoilless rifle.

Kirk held out a hand. "I'll take that, along with however much ammo you've got for it." Sorley handed the weapon system over without a word, pointing to more cases against the port bulkhead. Kirk nodded to Hank, who ducked in past Bianco—who

68

was gathering drums of 5.56 ammo from Curtis, who was simply wrecking the crates where he could, because of time, and started pulling out HE rounds.

"Any more of those?" Hank asked.

Sorley shook his head, his expression flat and tight. "It was enough of a chore to get that one."

There was something off about the man's expression and manner. Almost as if he was still reluctant to hand over the weapons and ordnance. Almost as if this hadn't been the plan.

There was no time to deal with him, though. The pirates were almost on top of them.

Laden with armfuls of weapons, ammo, and ordnance, the four Blackhearts clambered out of the compartment and sprinted for the ladderwell.

**

Kirk was glad for every mile he'd hiked through the woods and the mountains as he stormed up the ladder, hauling not only his body armor and rifle—and the client hadn't sprung for the nice, lightweight, modern plates, either—but also the Carl G and two 84mm High Explosive warheads. It was heavy and awkward, and a man of his age in lesser shape probably wouldn't have managed it.

He reached the open deck and turned to race toward the bow as Hank Brannigan came out of the hatch behind him, ready to move to join Wade at the stern. Breaking into a trot, he headed for the forward helipad.

Before he could get to the helipad and join Gomez, the first of the helicopters roared by overhead.

To his relief, it wasn't one of the combined designs that the Front had used in Kyrgyzstan. It appeared to be a fairly standard MD-500, not unlike the two birds carried aboard the superyacht itself. It didn't look like it was that heavily armed, but there was a man with a weapon in the side door. Kirk couldn't tell if it was a machinegun or just a rifle, and he didn't slow down to try to see more clearly. He'd seen all that he needed to.

He ducked behind the gunwale and cranked open the flange at the rear of the Carl G, sliding an HE round into the chamber as the helo started to bank and come back around.

***

Bianco was swearing a blue streak as he climbed awkwardly up the ladder, trying to lever the half-plastic, half-nylon canvas 100-round drum into its clip on the underside of the EVOLYS while still holding two more drums under his arms. He tripped as he got to the top and fell on his face on the deck, just barely managing to keep from falling on top of the machinegun as he hit. The drums went skidding across the deck.

"So much for that." He scrambled to his feet, slapped the rounds onto the feed tray, and smacked the cover shut. The EVOLYS had a sideways feed tray, instead of the top-mounted one he was used to from the SAW, the M240, and most every other light and medium machinegun he'd ever fired. "Just hope the optic didn't get knocked off zero." Keeping the muzzle high, he scooped up the fallen drums and ran across the helipad to the port rail.

There was zero cover, but he threw himself prone, flipped out the EVOLYS's bipods, and got behind the gun, searching over the sights for the speedboats. He wasn't sure he could hit one of the helicopters, but he could put some holes in those boats.

As the second MD-500 snarled over the stern, though, he realized that he might just *have* to engage the birds. They were sitting ducks out on the deck if the helos had guns. Or even passengers with guns.

He rolled onto his back to bring the deceptively lightweight belt-fed to bear, but the MD-500 was already past and coming around. Wade was in his lookout in the stern, tracking the helicopter with his MCX. Bianco hesitated for a moment, then cursed and flipped back over onto his stomach, his plates and mag pouches keeping him propped up off the helipad, as he extended the bipods further, wishing he had something more concrete to brace them on. The rubberized feet weren't slipping too much on the helipad's surface, but he still couldn't load them as much as he wanted, especially with a weapon that only weighed about thirteen pounds loaded.

The speedboats were coming on fast as the helicopters circled. A loudspeaker blared from above, the voice flat and distorted, as if using an electronic voice changer. *"Put down your weapons and power down your engines. You will be boarded. Any attempt to resist will be met with deadly force."*

Bianco didn't need to look over to where Flanagan was barricaded on the gunwale, just forward of his position. Unless the client came out there and demanded they disarm—which wouldn't make much sense, given the amount of money they were being paid and the firepower Sorley had revealed—they weren't going to be surrendering.

He found a speedboat, about a fourteen-footer, skipping across the waves toward them, and leaned into the gun, flipping the selector to "Auto" and letting his breath out as his finger came to rest on the trigger.

***

Kirk locked the chamber shut, cocked the Carl G, and glanced over his shoulder. He didn't have an assistant gunner to check his backblast area, so it was all on him. If he did some property damage to the yacht, he didn't especially care, but he did need to make sure that none of his teammates were about to get smoked. "Backblast area clear!"

It was amazing, how easily those words came back.

Turning back to the business at hand, he lifted the recoilless rifle above the gunwale and searched for the MD-500. This was going to be tricky. The Carl G wasn't a MANPAD. There was no seeker head—though he knew there were warheads for it these days that had them—and so he couldn't just get a lock and fire. He was going to have to make this shot count, and that meant remembering just how fast the round traveled and correctly gauging the helicopter's flight path.

He found the dark-colored MD-500 as it leveled out and approached the yacht again. There were definitely men hanging

71

out of the doors, their weapons in their hands, as the bird came in low and fast.

"Firing, firing, firing!" That was old habit, too, that he slipped back into like a nice jacket. Kirk let his breath out, relaxed so that he didn't flinch against recoil that wasn't really there, and fired.

The Carl Gustaf cracked off with a deafening *bang*, redoubled by the backblast bouncing off the bulkhead behind him. Kirk's head immediately started to ache abominably, but he kept his eye to the sights, practicing good follow through as he kept the target helo in his crosshairs.

For a second, he wondered if he shouldn't have just ducked right back down and started reloading, since if he missed, he was going to be Target Number One for any guys on that bird with weapons.

His timing and his calculations had been right on, though. The pilot barely had time to notice the puff of smoke from the shot before the 84mm HE round punched right through the windshield and detonated.

The entire front of the helicopter briefly disappeared in a short-lived fireball, before the rest of the bird came apart in a much bigger blaze, fragments of fuselage, engine, rotor, and bodies flying through the air to tumble into the ocean just off the *Dream Empire*'s bow.

***

Curtis hadn't followed Kirk forward. He'd decided that the nearest threat was probably better serviced first. So, instead of going forward, he ran toward the stern, where Wade had just turned back toward the speedboats after the second MD-500 had gone over.

"Oh, *now* they bring out the heavy stuff," Wade bit out, even as he braced his MCX Virtus on the rail and started to sight in on one of the oncoming speedboats.

"I know, right?" Curtis found a firing position and leaned into the EVOLYS's SCAR-style stock before coming off the gun with another curse to adjust the "Ugg Boot."

Wade was already shooting, though the accuracy of even the really nice SIG rifles was sketchy, at that range and with an eleven-and-a-half-inch barrel. But it was the tremendous *bang* of a Carl G from the starboard side, and the subsequent catastrophic *boom* of the first helicopter going up that really kicked things off.

Just as the fragments of the helicopter rained down into the water, Curtis got the machinegun as steady against the rail as he could, let out a breath, and squeezed the trigger.

Given the machinegun's weight, he'd expected to get rocked. To his surprise, though, the recoil was shockingly smooth and gentle. He didn't have any trouble keeping control of the machinegun as he walked his red tracers up from where he was spitting up little white geysers of water and into the speedboat.

Bullets chopped into the boat's bow, the windscreen, the coxswain, and at least one of the men behind him. The *Dream Empire* was moving on the waves, but not nearly as much as the speedboat was, making for a much more stable shooting platform.

The boat slewed to one side and slowed as the coxswain went down. Curtis came off the trigger, shifted his position behind the gun slightly, and raked it again. More of the pirates went down.

Then he was shifting fire to the next boat, even as Bianco hammered it with a long burst of his own.

"Kev! Up!" Wade had pivoted, bringing his MCX up as the second helo made a pass at the stern. Bullets smacked into steel and fiberglass around them, and both Blackhearts ducked, Curtis throwing himself flat just below the lip of the helipad.

He rolled over onto his back as the bird went by, wrenching the EVOLYS around and sending a burst at the receding aircraft's tail. He couldn't tell whether he'd hit it or not.

Levering himself to his feet, he hauled the EVOLYS up and searched for the helo. It was nose down, making tracks fast, banking off to the west, far astern of the yacht.

I still might be able to hit it. He shifted to the aft rail, bracing the machinegun and tracking in on the fleeing helicopter. He squeezed off a burst, but his range was off. Red tracers arced just beneath the bird, which jinked hard to avoid the fire and dove even closer to the water, turning away from the *Dream Empire* and banking violently from side to side to avoid the gunfire.

He fired one more burst, but between the helicopter's motion, the widening range, and the yacht's own rolling ride, he missed off to one side. Finally, with a blistering curse, he came off the gun.

Wade clapped him on the shoulder. "You'll get another chance." He nodded toward the north, where the remaining speedboats had now come about and were heading away from the yacht as fast as they could. "They got a nasty surprise, but if they really want this boat, I think they'll be back."

CHAPTER 10

El Salvaje scrambled up off the speedboat and onto the steps leading up to the MV *Lyubov Orlova*'s main deck, even before the crane had attached to the boat to bring it up on deck. He clattered up the steps, unconsciously shifting his weight to maintain a straight line as the massive old cruise ship rolled on the swell.

He'd never been particularly nautically inclined. This job had forced him to learn. It was good. He'd had to stretch himself, more than he'd needed to in many a year. The cold of the ocean this far north didn't tend to agree with him, though. He preferred the heat of the tropics, the deserts and the jungles where he'd cut his teeth with narcos and guerrillas.

The *Lyubov Orlova* wasn't the first pirate ship he'd been aboard, of course. There were pirates working in many of the places where he'd furthered his trade, and he'd had to deal with them. Just never on the kind of long-term basis that this job had required.

After some of the pirate motherships he'd been aboard in the Caribbean, the Straits of Malacca, and off the coasts of Africa, the *Lyubov Orlova* was in startlingly good shape. Especially considering her history.

Having been built in Yugoslavia for the Soviets as an ice-strengthened cruise ship for Antarctic cruises, she had been taken out of service after running aground in Antarctica. After sitting in St. John's, Newfoundland, for several years, she'd slipped her moorings and drifted out into the North Atlantic. From there, she'd been believed lost.

She hadn't been, though. She'd been found, and carefully secured, kept out at sea far from where anyone was likely to look for her. And now she was Cain's ship.

He didn't know much about Cain. He didn't care to, either. The man had resources, and he ran a tight ship. And he was a predator. That was all that El Salvaje needed to know.

What he didn't have, apparently, was good enough intel on this particular target. At least, not that he'd shared with his subordinates.

The lithe, pantherish man headed inside, leaving the recovery of the surviving boats and helicopter to the rest of the pirates. He hadn't been hired for that kind of drudgery. He'd been hired for his tactical acumen and his experience at revolutionary and criminal war.

Weaving his way through the passageways, he climbed up the ladder to the bridge and walked inside.

Cain must have been warned, because he'd turned to face the hatch just before El Salvaje walked in. If he'd been expecting some kind of roaring tirade, he wasn't going to get it. That wasn't El Salvaje's way. He had long ago left such displays of emotion behind him.

He'd have to feel to get that angry, and he couldn't remember the last time he'd felt much of anything.

"The intel said that they'd have SBRs and pistols." His voice was as low and flat as it had been when he'd threatened the woman aboard the *Tonka Canyon*. "The intel was wrong. Two boats shot to pieces. One of the helicopters blown out of the air."

Cain's eyes flashed at that. "What? They took enough fire to bring the bird down?"

"It didn't take much. They used a rocket." El Salvaje watched for the pirate's reaction, but he only saw the man shut down any emotion, going cold and calculating. "I was too far

76

away, and it was on the other side of the yacht from my boat, but I would say an RPG or an AT4. It flew straight, and there was no smoke trail like there might be from a MANPAD." He might look like a narco thug, he might have *been* a narco thug, but El Salvaje knew weapons as well as he knew operations and tactics.

Cain's scowl deepened. He turned back to the chart table, rubbing his chin.

"Is this target worth the losses?" That wasn't sentimentality speaking. El Salvaje had none. He was simply calculating the unforgiving mathematics of war. It was something that his enemies in the Western world had never been good at. They'd drop a $24,000 bomb on a man in a shalwar kameez and carrying an AK-47 as old as he was, just to make a statement. El Salvaje wasn't that interested in making statements. He was interested in winning.

Cain looked at him sharply. "This target? Yes. It might not look like it, but this is the biggest target we've ever gone after." He didn't seem to be all that inclined to elaborate.

Another man might have become angry at that reticence, but El Salvaje was used to it. Few of the warlords, terrorist masterminds, and criminal emperors he'd worked for over the years had been particularly forthcoming about their deepest thoughts and plans. That was a necessity when waging revolutionary war.

"We will need to take a different approach, then, if they are as well-armed and prepared as they appear to be." El Salvaje stepped up next to Cain at the chart table. "This will not be quick or easy. Especially since they are now forewarned."

Cain glowered down at the chart and the various intelligence reports scattered over it. "They had to know something was coming. They wouldn't have hired extra security otherwise." He thought for a moment, chewing on the problem, then sighed. "Call in all the other platforms. We're going to have to do this the hard way."

***

Aft, one of the *Dream Empire*'s two MD-500s was spooling up, the rotors already turning. Brannigan came out of the command post and looked around for Sorley.

The security coordinator was jogging forward from the bird, and Brannigan intercepted him before he could head up the ladderwell to the top decks. "Where's the helo going?"

"Recon." Sorley didn't seem to be willing to go into any more detail than that. "We need to find them and monitor them, so we know when they're coming back." He made to keep pushing past Brannigan toward the topside decks.

Brannigan stopped him with an inexorable grip on his upper arm. "When? Or if?" There was an edge in his words that should have been a warning. If that failed, the iron grip should have gotten the message across.

Sorley was sharp enough that he caught the warning. He clearly still didn't like it, but he must be adjusting to the realization that he'd brought thoroughly competent killers with no tolerance for bullshit aboard.

"When." The bald man almost seemed to deflate a little, though Brannigan was enough of a student of human behavior and body language that he could tell that he hadn't given up on that vicious ego trip he'd been on since they'd arrived at the marina. "They're definitely going to be back."

"Then you know more about this bunch than you've let on." Brannigan started to propel Sorley toward the arms room, the pressure such that while the shorter man tried to pull away, he simply couldn't.

With a faint shove, Brannigan ushered the security coordinator into their command post ahead of him, pulling the hatch shut behind him. Santelli was at the monitors, and glanced over but then, with the kind of professional detachment he'd perfected many, many years before, he turned back to the screens, apparently ignoring everything else happening in the room.

Brannigan folded his arms across his chest, fixing Sorley with a basilisk glare that would have done Roger Hancock proud. "You hired us to keep this tub safe. Yet you've consistently kept us in the dark, so that we can't be as effective as we could be. That ends now. Start talking." When a flash of anger crossed Sorley's face, Brannigan held up a hand. "Spare me the bluster. This is open combat now. If your ego's so bruised that you withhold pay, well. We'll deal with that later." The threat there was pretty implicit, and he saw that Sorley picked up on it. "Right now, survival is the foremost concern. So either you start talking, or I start breaking fingers."

Santelli might have made a strangled noise, but if Brannigan had looked over at him, he would have seen the short, balding man watching the monitors impassively and with intense concentration.

Sorley must have decided that he wasn't bluffing, though, which was a good thing, because he really wasn't. Ordinarily, hurting their employer until he talked would have been Wade's idea, and Brannigan would have felt morally obligated to keep their teammate in check. He was angry on a level that he hadn't been in a long time, though. Sorley's attitude had pissed him off from the moment he'd picked up the phone, and the constant game of "need-to-know" had built the pressure of that growing rage with every day they'd been aboard. He'd fought against the "shut up, don't worry about what's going on, and just do what I say" model of leadership when he'd been a Marine officer, and now here it was again.

"These pirates have been targeting high-value cargoes and passengers for several months now. We've had indications that they have begun to specifically target Mr. Fontaine. This yacht is one of his biggest assets, and it stood to reason that it was a major target. That's why you were hired. Furthermore, we had indications that the pirates might have had people watching the yacht before we sailed." None of that was particularly new information, and Brannigan's expression was growing more thunderous as Sorley talked.

"This yacht is now the pirates' primary target. We believe that is in no small part because Mr. Fontaine is aboard."

79

Santelli did look over at that, while Brannigan's scowl deepened even more, if that was possible. "That was information we could have used before we ever set foot on the pier."

"Maybe." Sorley wasn't willing to back down on that. "We didn't know your company from Adam. Security demanded…"

"Security demanded that you give the men you hired to protect you enough information to do the job effectively without scrambling at the last minute when the threat showed up." Brannigan wasn't having Sorley's excuses. "You also clearly know more about these pirates than you're letting on." He left it at that, but the demand and the threat behind it were pretty clear.

Sorley wasn't willing to give that much up, though. "They came out of nowhere a few months back. Whoever they are, they had a lot of resources to start with, and they have a *very* good intelligence organization. They have to have at least one oceangoing mothership, possibly as many as four. They're well-trained and well-equipped, with at least four helicopters, possibly up to ten."

"So, you don't actually know what we're up against." Brannigan didn't quite believe it, but he was starting to think that he was going to have to act on the presumption. Either that, or he was going to have to actually start breaking Sorley's fingers. Or have Wade do it.

"No, we don't. But we do have enough information that I'm absolutely sure that they will be back. They want Mr. Fontaine. There have been threats. If they can get to him, and use him to get access to his assets, they'll be rich enough that every one of them could retire to some island somewhere and live like kings for the rest of their lives. They have to know by now that he's aboard."

"Which you tried to hide from us, while they easily found out."

"Maybe not as easily as you think, but yeah, they found out." Something about the way he said that drew Santelli's eyes. The former Sergeant Major peered keenly at the back of Sorley's head for a moment before flicked his gaze to Brannigan. Brannigan, for his part, didn't react. He knew Sorley still wasn't telling them everything, but he was telling more than he had before. Although, he'd also noticed that there had been no mention of the cargo Chavez had told him about, either. "Anyway, that's why we need to get the bird up. They're coming, and we need to know how far out they are so we can prepare for the next strike."

"I'm not saying we don't send recon." Brannigan turned away. "You still should have filled us in."

"I had my instructions." Sorley was getting sullen. It was probably time to get back to work. Brannigan had enough experience with people to know when to push and when to back off. He'd pushed, and he had gotten some of what he'd been looking for. Now it was time to back off a little. Until it was time to push again.

"If you've got any more nasty little surprises aboard this tub, you'd better let us at them now."

CHAPTER 11

Wade had stayed in place in the stern, despite the fact that Hank had come out to relieve him. He wasn't convinced that the pirates wouldn't be coming back anytime soon, and while he had only gotten a few, relatively ineffective shots off at them the last time, he was determined that the next time was going to be different. Curtis and Bianco might have the long-range firepower all to themselves with those EVOLYS belt-feds, but there were still a few things John Wade could do with even a short barrel.

He was ignoring Hank for the moment. The kid had proved himself a couple times over, and Wade didn't have a problem with him, except for the times when he seemed to think that he still had to prove himself, that he wasn't just his father's kid. He seemed to be having one of those attacks of doubt this trip, as he hadn't talked much, and had seemed to be a little hesitant, uncertain where to step in and where to hang back. Wade really didn't want to deal with Hank Brannigan's insecurities at the moment. There were pirates out there who needed killing.

Squinting against the sunlight on the water, despite his sunglasses, he scanned the horizon. The pirates had retreated to the north, but that didn't mean they wouldn't come back from a different direction. As long as they stayed below the horizon, they had the entire North Atlantic to maneuver in. The *Dream Empire* wasn't all that far past Bermuda, and there was a long way to go.

He blinked and squinted a little harder. Of *course* the MCXs had red dots instead of magnified optics. Why would they possibly need ACOGs or LPVOs when they were out on the water? He cursed Sorley soundly under his breath as he tried to make out if he was actually seeing a dark dot just above the horizon or not.

Yes. It was definitely a helicopter. But was it theirs, or one of the pirates'? Or someone else's? They weren't the only vessel out there at the moment; they'd passed several smaller but almost as well-appointed yachts on the way past the Bahamas. He cursed the lack of optics even more soundly.

It was banking toward them, but that might just be their own MD-500 coming in to land. Why they hadn't sent a Blackheart along he didn't know.

It fit the rest of this retarded job. *Should have stayed on the range.* He knew he was just bitching, though. As badly handled as this gig was, it was still paying far more than he'd ever make as an instructor.

A new roar drew his attention to the north, off the left side of the yacht. He really didn't give two shits what the nautical types called it, even though he knew that Flanagan and the other Marines would say it was the port side.

Another MD-500, painted blue and white with the name of the *Dream Empire* on the tail, came in quickly, flaring and descending toward the stern helipad. So, that was the recon bird. Which meant the other one...

He turned his attention back to the helicopter astern. It was circling, now. He lifted his rifle, bracing it on the rail, and put his red dot on it, but it was far too long a shot for the short-barreled rifle.

"What do you see?" Hank was squinting against the glare too.

"There's a helo circling due west of us, just off the surface." He pointed, though it was hard to indicate where the target was with no real reference points. He also had to yell, as the rotor wash from the yacht's own MD-500 plucked at them.

Hank searched the water, and after a moment, brought his own rifle up, only to come off it in frustration. The red dots were great for CQB if the pirates boarded, but if the goal was to *keep* them from boarding, it got a little dicier.

Wade turned away from his younger teammate and continued to watch the helicopter. It was still circling, and it looked very much like it was pacing the yacht as it did so. He frowned and keyed his radio. "Kodiak, Angry Ragnar. We've got a helo pacing us, about two or three klicks back. It's just circling there. Can we get Gamer or Gambler up here?"

"This is Gamer." Bianco, to Wade's complete lack of surprise, was quicker to step up than Curtis. "On my way."

Wade acknowledged briefly, then settled in to watch their unwelcome shadow.

***

By the time Bianco arrived on the fantail, however, the helicopter had disappeared. That didn't mean they were clear, though.

"It's hard to see because of the waves, but there's a boat back there, now." Wade pointed, and Bianco, who had thought to bring a pair of binoculars, set his EVOLYS on the deck and braced the binos against the rail, searching the water behind them.

"Got him." The big, boyish-looking man grimaced without taking his eyes away from the optics. "He's a long way out there. A good three klicks, if not more." He straightened and lowered the binoculars. "Even with this baby, I'm not going to be able to hit them. Not with 5.56."

Wade snarled. "Watch this sector. I'm gonna go find Joe and Mario." He got up and started around the helipad. "We've got small craft aboard this bucket. We can go pay *them* a visit."

***

Flanagan hadn't needed Wade to explain the idea. As soon as the big former Ranger had described what he'd seen, he'd immediately grabbed his weapon and headed aft, toward the boats. If they couldn't get Sorley to put them on a bird—which would have been a much better mobile pirate-hunting platform—then they'd take a boat.

"I'm going to grab Gomez!" Wade had yelled over his shoulder as he headed forward and Flanagan went aft. Flanagan just waved over his shoulder that he'd heard.

Running down the ladderwell and into the boat bay at the stern, he paused for a moment and looked around. The launch that had brought them aboard was probably the best bet. He sprinted for it, adjusting easily to the roll of the yacht on the waves, and had just jumped aboard, checking the release system before he checked the engine and the fuel tank, when something changed.

The yacht's own engine coughed, a noise that the machinery on such an expensive boat shouldn't ever make. Then, just as suddenly, the engines died. A strange quiet fell over the yacht, and the rocking of the vessel on the swell got slightly more pronounced. They were dead in the water.

That's not good.

He glanced back the way he'd come, considering for a moment whether he should head back topside and help figure out what was going on. He wasn't a mechanic, though, and right then, the only contact they had with the bad guys was that boat out there behind them. Better to stay on the attack.

He might have seen movement somewhere forward, but when he looked again, there was nothing. He shrugged and got back to work.

A moment later, as he prepped the release to let the launch down the ramp behind and into the water, Wade and Gomez came down the ladderwell, weapons in hand. "What's going on with the engines?"

"Don't know." Wade clambered into the launch. "The Colonel said to go anyway."

"All I needed to hear." Flanagan had figured the mechanism out, and as Gomez got in and got low, Flanagan pushed the button, letting the boat down the ramp and into the ocean. They hit with a gout of spray, and then he yanked the starter and got the launch's outboard running in two pulls. Reversing gears, he backed water and brought the launch out from under the shadow of the fantail.

The yacht was definitely drifting now, the bow starting to turn toward the south. There was no smoke, no sign that anything was seriously wrong, but she wasn't making any headway.

There were questions there. They might have taken a couple of rounds from those helos in the first attack, but he really didn't think that any of those hits could have done enough damage to leave the yacht adrift.

As he brought the launch around, he saw Wade glance back at the yacht, his icy eyes narrowed. When the big former Ranger looked back at Flanagan, their eyes met, and each man saw the same questions mirrored in the other's.

That was for Brannigan and Santelli to worry about at the moment, though. Flanagan brought the boat around to point back toward their unidentified shadower and opened the throttle. A moment later, they were bouncing over the waves, leaving the yacht behind.

***

Santelli looked up as the engines died. "Hey, the lights are still on."

"Batteries, probably." Brannigan was already moving toward the hatch. "Something's wrong."

"*Everything*'s wrong," Santelli muttered, turning back to the monitors. "Has been since we took this job."

Brannigan didn't comment. The fact that even Santelli was bitching was a warning sign. The man was smarter than he usually let on, but long, long experience in the Marine Corps had taught him to keep his thoughts to himself. "If Marines ain't bitching, there's something wrong" might be a truism, but it applied to the junior Marines. Staff and Senior NCOs were supposed to be quiet professionals. So, when even Carlo Santelli started to mutter, it meant things had well and truly gone south.

And the situation hadn't even gotten that hot yet.

As he passed through the hatch and headed for the engineering spaces, Brannigan quietly promised that the bad guys-

-whoever they were—were going to have a far worse time than the Blackhearts.

Sorley intercepted him halfway there, already swearing bitterly under his breath. "Don't bother. You'll just get in the crew's way."

"What's happening?"

"We have a mechanical problem, that's what's happening," Sorley bit out. "Fuckin' incompetents apparently didn't check the oil or something before we left port." He glanced down toward the engineering compartment. "Of all the times to have something go wrong."

Brannigan still didn't trust Sorley, and he could feel his hackles go up at this situation, but he couldn't be sure that the man wasn't sincere in his frustration. Either things really were that bad, or Sorley was a very accomplished liar.

"How long to fix it?"

Sorley shrugged and pushed past him. "No idea. I don't even know what broke, or if we even have the parts to fix it. Like I said, I'm no engineer. But until it does get fixed, we're sitting ducks out here." He started up the ladderwell.

Brannigan watched him go for a second, considering the possibilities. There wasn't time, though. They already knew that the pirates had them pinpointed, and now they were dead in the water. Priorities. He keyed his radio. "This is Kodiak. Stand to. We are disabled and the bad guys have our location. Prepare to get hit again soon."

CHAPTER 12

Santelli started up the ladderwell topside, only to be intercepted by a crewman. "Hey, Sorley said that nobody could come up here…"

The movement wasn't all that overt, but Santelli lifted the muzzle of his MCX ever so slightly. "Shut up and get out of my way." His voice was still calm and almost gentle, but fortunately, the crewman got the message anyway, and flattened himself against the bulkhead as Santelli trotted up the steps past him. If he'd been dealing with anyone else, he might not have turned his back to the crewman, but a glance had told him that he didn't have much of anything more to worry about from this kid.

He hardly noticed the swank surroundings of the upper decks as he continued his climb toward the top deck, where an observation deck sat between and just forward of the two big, spherical sensor domes, just behind the mainmast. There were more important things to worry about than what they might or might not be missing out on, just because Fontaine didn't want the paid gorillas sullying his private sanctum. Not that Santelli had ever been that concerned with missing out on the fleshpots. At least, not for a long time.

Reaching the observation deck, he looked north first, snatching up the binoculars he'd grabbed out of the command center before he'd left it to get a better view topside. The cameras were too limited.

It didn't take long before he spotted what he was looking for. The Ro-Ro cargo ship off to the northwest looked old, but it was definitely coming toward them. If he'd been reading the charts right, there was no known sea lane that would put a freighter on that course. It had to be the pirates.

If he'd hoped that the Ro-Ro was the only mothership, though, he was in for a disappointment. After he'd called that one in, he kept scanning, just in case. He didn't have to look far before he spotted yet another, of a similar tonnage and class, almost due north, steaming toward them.

That wasn't the last, either. As he continued his scan toward the east, he spotted what appeared to be another large yacht, also pointed toward their position and steaming southwest.

Under other circumstances, his next choice of words might have been unprofessional and a violation of radio procedures, but with only the Blackhearts listening in, he didn't really care. "I sure hope we've got enough ammo, because we appear to have a metric shit-ton of bad guys coming our way."

***

Wade heard Santelli's warning, but right then there wasn't time to worry about it. He, Gomez, and Flanagan had their own target to worry about, and he was pretty sure that said target was bird-dogging the pirates in on the *Dream Empire*. After all, they were much too far out at sea for a speedboat that size to be out on its own.

Wade might not consider himself any sort of nautical authority, but he knew that much.

Flanagan hit the next wave hard, and the launch came most of the way out of the water. He was pushing that engine to its limits, closing in on the pirate speedboat fast. Wade felt the bottom drop out from under him for a second, just before they hit the water again with a tooth-rattling impact.

"Try not to give us all concussions before we even get in range, Joe!" He didn't look back as he barked over his shoulder, but he knew Flanagan well enough to be able to picture the man's gritted teeth. He wasn't having much more fun than Wade and Gomez were, even though as the coxswain, he wasn't taking quite as much of a beating.

Flanagan didn't reply as he steered the launch slightly to the side to make sure he hit the next wave head on. Wade thought he remembered that to keep the waves from flipping a boat over, you had to go straight into them. Something like that.

As they went over the crest of the next wave, he got another look at their target. It was a blue and white cigarette boat, and he could just see two men in the aft compartment, behind the coxswain. He only got a short glimpse as the cigarette boat went down into the trough of the next wave, and he thought he might have seen gear and weapons, but they were still a good five hundred yards away.

Flanagan was closing that distance fast, though. Wade got as low in the launch as he could, bracing his MCX against the gunwale. Gomez was in a similar attitude, on the other side, though he looked a lot more comfortable with it than Wade felt. It might seem a little strange, since Gomez was a desert guy, but he *had* been a Recon Marine, which meant he had done a lot of this kind of thing with Zodiacs.

They came up and over the crest of the wave, and then they were right on the cigarette boat.

Wade saw the R4s and pivoted to take a snap shot at one of them, but missed as the two boats raced past each other, barely fifty yards apart, one going up the back of a wave, the other going down into the trough. Then Gomez was in his way, and he didn't have a shot.

Gomez dumped a fast five rounds at the boat, even as Flanagan took them over the crest of the next wave and hauled the tiller over, bringing the launch around as sharply as he could without capsizing it on the swell.

Bullets *snap*ped overhead as one of the shooters in the cigarette boat took them under fire as they came over the crest of the wave in pursuit. Gomez shot back, even as Wade's aim was thrown off as his elbow slipped on the gunwale. The thunder of gunfire was deafeningly loud even over the buzzing roar of the engines.

Gomez's shots smacked puffs of debris off the cigarette boat's fantail, but the violent movement of both boats was making marksmanship difficult. Wade steadied himself, bracing his arm against the gunwale, and tried to force the red dot to stop bouncing all over the target boat.

It wasn't working, so he had to just try to time his shots. It wasn't a new skill. It was just a little harder when there was this much movement, rather than just trying to compensate for the natural "figure eight" movement of the dot at longer ranges.

His first shot smashed into the pillar of the short roof over the driver's station. The second hit the stern. The third went sailing off into the blue somewhere.

The fourth hit one of the pirates.

It wasn't a kill shot, but it knocked him sideways. He fell against the coxswain, getting in his way, while his last shot went wild, high overhead. Just for a moment, the cigarette boat slowed as the coxswain had to disentangle himself from the wounded man.

Flanagan took full advantage, arrowing in closer. The third pirate was still shooting at him, but the boat was swerving erratically as the coxswain struggled to keep it under control while still tangled up with the wounded man, especially as Gomez and Wade started getting closer and closer with their own shots.

Then Gomez shot the coxswain in the head.

Wade suspected that it had been luck, but he knew that while Gomez wouldn't boast about it, he wouldn't ever *admit* that it had been luck, either. Regardless, the dead man slumped at the wheel, bringing the boat around to hit the next wave sideways even as he dragged the throttle down to nothing with his dead weight.

If they'd been in the surf zone, closer to shore, the wave that hit next would have flipped the boat. As it was, while it didn't capsize it, it did throw the unwounded pirate overboard.

Flanagan brought them right next to the boat as it wallowed on the swell. The launch wasn't as stable as Wade might have liked, but he surged to his feet, the MCX tucked tight into his shoulder pocket, his eye to the red dot, searching for the last man left. There was no sign of the guy who'd gone overboard. They must have figured they didn't need flotation devices, or something.

Granted, none of the three Blackhearts had them on, either. Anyone who went over was going to have to tread water or drown.

As Flanagan brought the launch alongside, the last pirate, down in the bottom of the boat, wounded, soaked to the skin, and still partially tangled with the coxswain, tried to bring his R4 up. Wade shot him through the skull from about ten yards away. The shooter in storm gray fatigues and what looked a lot like the same plate carrier Wade was wearing took the round through the eye, just beneath the rim of his high-cut helmet, and his head jerked back, then lolled limply, spilling blood and brain matter into the already red-tinged water sloshing in the bottom of the boat.

"Well, we took them out, but we might have been a little late about it." Flanagan was looking up, toward the now-distant shape of the *Dream Empire*.

Wade didn't need to ask. He could see the vessels closing in on the yacht just as well as Flanagan could, along with the three helicopters now circling over the drifting luxury vessel.

***

The helos came ready for trouble this time.

Whether or not one of them was the survivor of the first attack, the two MD-500s that swooped in from the *Dream Empire*'s bow had mounted machineguns, and they raked the yacht with tracer fire, punching holes in metal, fiberglass, and Plexiglas before they banked off to either side. The decks had already been cleared, however, and they had no targets except the yacht itself.

The same could not be said for the Blackhearts.

Another 84mm HE round lanced up from the fantail as the helicopters raced away from the yacht. It missed, but the message was clear. The *Dream Empire* was far from helpless.

The southernmost helicopter came back in, banking hard to line up on the superyacht, but was met by a storm of machinegun fire. Clear acrylic starred and shattered, and the pilot dove and banked hard, smoke starting to waft from the engine housing. Pulling up just over the waves, the helicopter pilot raced away as best he could get his wounded bird to move.

The motherships, however, were getting closer, and while they were still at the outer edge of effective machinegun range, they started to pelt the yacht with fire, tracers slamming through the vessel's thin skin. Fortunately for the Blackhearts and the *Dream Empire*'s crew, they had only guesswork for targeting, especially since Curtis and Bianco had both relocated as soon as they'd fired on the pirate helo.

Unfortunately, while the pirates might not be able to kill the Blackhearts with their only vaguely targeted fire, they could do what they needed to do, which was keep the defenders' heads down while the speedboats hit the water and raced toward the yacht.

Brannigan was watching from the shelter of the hatchway just above the aft helipad. His eyes narrowed as he watched the impacts pucker the surface of the helipad in front of him. "Clear the decks and fall back inside the superstructure. Hold on the entrance hatches. Two men down to the well deck aft, in case they try to come aboard that way." Ducking back from the hatch, he press-checked his MCX, more out of habit and a need to do something with his hands than any uncertainty about the condition of his weapon.

The yacht's skin was too thin on the outside to stop bullets, but deeper in, the pirates would have to clear compartment by compartment.

And that was where the Blackhearts were going to make them bleed.

He had gone two steps before he met Sorley, heading for the ladderwell leading belowdecks. "Where the hell do you think you're going?"

The look that Sorley shot him was *almost* the arrogant, sour stare of the man in charge, but not quite. In fact, as he watched the man, geared up and carrying his weapons, he thought he saw a note of panic in his eyes.

"You worry about your part..." Sorley started to say, but Brannigan cut him off.

"Oh, hell no. That's not how this works. You've got a gun, you're supposed to be the security coordinator, so you're getting right on the line with the rest of us." He might have lifted his rifle fractionally. "Let's go."

He was pretty sure Sorley really was on the verge of panic, then, but all the same, the man realized that Brannigan could bring that MCX up and core his brains out in a split second. And he probably wasn't going to be able to get his own weapon around nearly fast enough. Sorley wasn't a gunfighter. That much was obvious.

With a look of bitter hatred coupled with a deep and terrible fear, Sorley turned and preceded Brannigan toward defensive positions, as the pirates closed in.

CHAPTER 13

The fire from the yacht died down, and the pirate speedboats converged on the stern. They were far too professional to set two assault forces facing each other.

They also didn't take the easy way and try to drive into the well deck. Instead, they closed in on either flank, raising telescoping boarding ladders to hook onto the gunwales, rifles pointed up at the rail while the first boarders started up the ladders, rifles slung across their backs.

For a few moments, the covering fire from the motherships ceased, as the pirates were reluctant to risk hitting their comrades. Pirates they might be, but there was a greater degree of discipline in this group than was usually seen in such criminal fraternities.

In the sudden, eerie quiet, the first four gray-clad shooters swung their legs over the rail and dropped to the helipad, quickly settling into a slightly crouched shooting stance and beginning to glide toward the hatches leading into the superstructure, rifles in their shoulders, searching for targets. They moved like special operators, men who'd trained for years to shoot, move, and communicate.

Brannigan saw all of this from within the superstructure, set back about five yards from the starboard hatch, two steps behind Sorley, who was down on a knee with his own rifle. There was no way he was going to turn his back on the man.

He was pressed against the bulkhead, concealed in the shadows—they'd turned off all the interior lights—and across the narrow passageway from where Bianco lay on the deck behind his EVOLYS, the bipods at their highest setting so that he could be sure his bullets would pass over the hatch coaming.

"Wait for it." More shooters were already coming over the rail. Better to get as many of them as they could all at once. If they hurt the pirates badly enough, it might give them pause. These guys were acting like professionals, which meant that they *might* be less likely to push a target that made them bleed. Pirates weren't true believers. Make the cost higher than the return, and they'd back off.

Hopefully.

The first wave had kept their movement slow, moving up and taking a knee on the deck since they hadn't taken fire yet. They must have been waiting for their buddies to come back them up before they made entry.

They probably should have moved faster. "Light 'em up."

Bianco leaned into the gun and sent a long burst sawing across the group on the helipad. The machinegun's report was brutally loud in the narrow corridor, and fire spat from the muzzle as brass and links cascaded down onto the deck.

Bullets smashed through shins, knees, and legs, cutting the first two men's feet out from under them. They both toppled, screaming, only to fall into the stream of lead. More rounds smashed through flesh and bone, stilling both of them in an instant, even as Bianco shifted his hips to move the stream of fire toward the latecomers still climbing over the rail.

Brannigan had his own shot on them, aimed over Sorley's head, and had already drawn a bead before Bianco started shooting. He blasted the rearmost pirate through the skull, his red dot settling on the man's head just above his gray balaclava just before the trigger broke. The pirate's head snapped back, and he bounced off the rail before collapsing on his face.

By the time Brannigan had transitioned to the next man forward, Bianco had already cut him down and come off the trigger. They had no more targets without pushing out onto the aft helipad, and Brannigan had already decided that was a bad idea.

A moment later, as the screaming and gunfire to port stopped, the reason for that decision became apparent.

Two of the MD-500s came in from astern, one after the other, and raked the rear of the superstructure with machinegun fire. Bursts of 7.62 rounds smashed through the thin metal and fiberglass of the superstructure, but Brannigan, Sorley, and Bianco had already fallen back and gone flat on the deck, hugging the bulkheads to either side. Brannigan hoped that Kirk and Curtis had done the same on the other side.

They'd hurt the bad guys. Now they had to see if the rest were going to call it a day or push the fight.

***

El Salvaje watched the carnage on the helipad impassively. He had no attachment to any of the pirates. Some of them might have formed a sort of team bond, but he was an outsider and he liked it that way. Instead of mourning the dead men lying in their own blood on the deck, as he rode the MD-500 in toward the pad, he was considering how to move forward. The opposition had been more ready for them than they'd anticipated, even after the abortive first attack.

The door gunners continued to suppress the forward hatches, tearing more bright, ragged holes in the superstructure, and El Salvaje considered for a moment whether he should tell them to cease fire. Cain had specified that he wanted Fontaine alive. El Salvaje knew enough of Cain's purposes that he was sure that dead or alive made little difference in the long run, but he would still have to deal with Cain's wrath if Fontaine ended up dead because the door gunners were being too indiscriminate in their covering fire.

All the same, he didn't think that they'd be too willing to cease fire altogether, not after what had just happened. They might be pirates, but those were still their buddies lying dead on the helipad.

The skids touched, and he waited for the first three pirate shooters to pile out and rush toward the superstructure before he got out and followed, moving fast with his head down to avoid the spinning rotors overhead, sprinting across the gently rocking deck to the bullet-pocked bulkhead, just offset from the hatchway, as the door gunners finally ceased fire and the helicopter pulled off the pad.

He pulled a nine-banger out of his gear and held it out in front of the next man in the stack's shoulder, where he could see it with his peripheral vision. Then he yanked the pin and tossed the distraction device through the hatch. The pyro immediately began to erupt just inside, smoke billowing out as the small explosions belled through the boat's structure. Then the pirate was going through the hatch behind his R4, with El Salvaje and the other two right on his heels.

To anyone unfamiliar with the state of the underworld of crime and irregular war, the smoothness of the assault would have been a surprise. The pirates had almost all had special operations training, but El Salvaje came from another world.

It was a world, however, where organizations like CJNG had access to top-tier equipment and equally top-tier training. The Americans didn't have the market cornered anymore.

They barged into the smoke-filled passageway but found no targets. The enemy had hit them, bled them, and faded.

El Salvaje pointed down the corridor with a hand, saying nothing. The lead pirates nodded and started deeper in, weapons up, checking every angle. They needed to find Fontaine, quickly, and kill anyone who got in their way.

***

Kirk was swearing as he settled into the compartment just forward of the pool, right next to the ladderwell leading up to the topside decks and the bridge. He and Curtis had moved fast, but not quite fast enough, as a bullet had sailed through the open hatch they'd used as a firing port, smacked off something hard, and embedded a chunk of its copper jacket in his calf. "Can't seem to get through an op without getting hit with *something*."

"Getting old and slow." Curtis wasn't looking at Kirk as he spoke, his eyes and weapon trained on the hatchway. He still grinned as he felt Kirk's glare.

"You just can't help it, can you?" Kirk suppressed a limp as he moved to stand behind Curtis's shoulder, his own MCX currently pointed at the deck since he didn't have a target. "Joe's not here, so you've got to shit-talk *somebody*."

Curtis did glance over his shoulder at that, as if he wasn't quite sure if he'd overstepped. Kirk wasn't one of the original Blackhearts, but he'd been around the block, and was probably the oldest next to Santelli and Brannigan. He'd never been much for banter, and he saw that Curtis wasn't sure about the reaction.

It was an interesting thing to see. Curtis was by far the biggest loudmouth of the team. Not that it rustled Kirk's jimmies any. He'd been in this profession for almost thirty years. Gunfighters were some of the most irreverent, wild shit-talkers he'd ever known, and he wouldn't have it any other way. He might not indulge in it that often, but it never bothered him.

That didn't mean he was going to let Curtis off the hook, though. Let the man squirm a little.

Then the reports of a nine-banger rattled through the superstructure, and it wasn't time for banter anymore.

Both men leveled their weapons, training them on the passageway, Curtis going down on a knee while Kirk leaned out over him.

More gunfire erupted from somewhere off on the starboard side. Somebody was pushing hard over there.

Brannigan's instructions had been clear. Engage, break contact, and head deeper in. Draw them in and bleed them. Kirk flexed his fingers around the rifle. This was going to get hairy, if the pirates flooded the passageway in enough numbers.

More gunfire sounded, including a long, ripping burst that sounded like it was probably from one of the EVOLYS machineguns. Then Curtis leaned out and opened fire in reply.

Kirk forced himself not to flinch at the brutal muzzle blast bouncing off the hatchway and the bulkheads around them and leaned out to get a better shot. One of the gray-clad pirates was trying to rush them, and Kirk put two rounds into the man's front plate by sheer force of habit, just as a bullet *snap*ped past his ear and another smacked into his own front plate, before he shifted aim, a fraction of a second ahead of the pirate, and shot the man in the face, punching his own round through the gray balaclava and blowing his teeth through the back of his head.

Then Curtis was pushing the fight, throwing himself out into the passageway behind a wall of bullets, holding down the trigger as he stayed low behind the gun. The EVOLYS looked like it was extremely controllable, despite its super light weight, and Curtis, Kirk knew, was a hell of a shooter behind a belt-fed as it was. He raked the remaining two pirates with withering fire as he threw himself toward the opposite bulkhead, cutting the first one off at the knees before muzzle rise brought the stream of bullets up into the second one's guts, just beneath his plate carrier. The man screamed in agony as he collapsed, his R4 clattering to the deck.

"Let's go." Kirk was already moving, sprinting the short distance to the ladderwell leading up to the next deck. He stopped at the hatchway, barricading on the corridor to cover Curtis as the shorter man turned and raced to join him.

Together, they headed up, ready to hold the next line.

***

Brannigan and Bianco watched the passageway while Sorley sulked. They'd gotten one, but the number two man in the pirates' stack had been quick. He'd thrown himself back out of the hatch as soon as Brannigan had gunned down the first man through and had dragged the other two back with him.

"We should move before they come up with some new, nasty little surprise for us." Something told him that the man who'd managed to avoid getting his head blown apart on entry was going to turn out to be a formidable enemy.

"Kodiak, Guido. Need some help up here." Santelli sounded almost bored, but under the circumstances, Brannigan suspected that things were a lot worse than it sounded.

"En route." He looked at Bianco. "Looks like we might need to barricade on the bridge already. Come on. I'm not leaving you down here by yourself." Leaving him with Sorley was completely out of the question. He turned and headed up the ladder as fast as he could go, forcing the security coordinator ahead of him.

They hadn't moved a moment too soon, either. They'd barely gotten halfway up to the next deck when a frag sailed in through the hatch, thrown with enough force that it bounced off the overhead and spun almost five yards down the corridor before it exploded, filling the passageway with smoke and fragmentation, the explosion resonating through the entire yacht.

Neither man was there to see it when the pirates stormed through the hatch and into the cloud of smoke and debris, their weapons up and searching for threats. Unlike most pirates, they didn't just spray down the hatches as they went, but they were definitely more on guard than they had been before.

Sweeping forward, the pirates began to clear the deck.

CHAPTER 14

Faced with the numbers they could see converging on the yacht, Flanagan immediately began to reconsider the wisdom of just taking the launch straight back to the *Dream Empire*. They'd be spotted and shot to pieces before they even got close.

Wade was already on top of it, though, slinging his rifle and cinching it down before he made a jump for the cigarette boat. "Leave the launch. We can come back for it later, if we really want to."

He almost didn't make it, slamming down on the boat's gunwale and starting to slip back into the water before he grabbed hold of the coxswain's roof column with one hand. Seizing the gunwale with the other, he started to drag himself aboard, cussing about "this Navy SquEAL bullshit."

Flanagan shook his head slightly. He could have brought the launch alongside, even touching the gunwale, in another few moments, but Wade could be a bit of a bull in a china shop sometimes.

He did bring the launch in close, even as Wade started heaving the bodies overboard. Gomez clambered over, and then Flanagan killed the launch's motor and followed suit.

There were a few bullet holes, but most of the blood had been washed out by the spray and the near-capsizing, so they hunkered down as Gomez took the controls and started them back toward the *Dream Empire*, hoping that their gray helmets and plate carriers looked enough like the pirates to get them close.

They might turn out to be the rest of the team's ace in the hole, judging by the volume of gunfire they could hear faintly over the waves.

***

Brannigan paused just long enough to make sure that Bianco was well set up on the ladderwell, while Hank was watching forward just beyond him, then hurried toward the hatch leading to the bridge, where Santelli, geared up and looking like his helmet didn't quite fit his rather large, round head, was standing there with his beefy arms folded over the buttstock of his rifle, tapping his foot impatiently.

"What is it?" He thought he probably already knew, since the hatch was closed and the Blackhearts were out in the passageway.

"They locked the bridge and told us we need to hold the passageway." Santelli's tone alone said what exactly he thought about that idea, as did his look at Sorley. "Apparently, on our 'security coordinator's' orders."

"That's idiotic," Brannigan snapped. "Passageways are deathtraps. I'm not sticking my boys out here." He turned on Sorley with murder in his eyes. "Get that hatch open."

Sorley shook his head, apparently getting some of his equilibrium back, though there was still an echo of that crawling fear in his eyes. He wasn't where he wanted to be, and it was eating at him, getting worse the longer the fight went on. "Mr. Fontaine sets the rules. I just enforce them. If you can't keep them off this deck in the first place, then maybe we shouldn't have hired you."

Brannigan saw red. He was on Sorley in two strides, one big hand closing on the man's rifle, the other grabbing him by the throat and slamming him against the hatch.

"I don't give a rat's ass who you think you are, Sorley. You don't know shit about tactics. If you're not going to let me do

106

the job, I'm going to break your neck and do it over your dead body. Now get that fucking hatch open."

Sorley's eyes widened, and his suddenly rediscovered bluster vanished for a moment, giving way to raw terror. Brannigan had every intention of following up on his threat, and he tightened his grip on Sorley's throat to make sure he knew it.

He held Sorley's eyes for a moment, just long enough to be sure that the man was going to do what he needed him to do. Even as he released him with a shove that bounced him off the bulkhead, Brannigan realized something else.

They were going to have to keep a close eye on Sorley from there on out. He'd just made a deadly enemy. Provided they hadn't already when he'd intercepted him on his way below.

Survival comes first.

"Now, open that hatch." He stared at Sorley as the man rubbed his throat, watching Brannigan and Santelli out of the corner of his eye, even while he turned to open the way to the bridge.

"Lumberjack, Gambler, this is Guido." Santelli had taken a step back and keyed his radio. "Be advised, your starboard flank is no longer covered. Suggest you collapse on the bridge."

"Roger that," came Kirk's reply. "We're moving." He paused. "That's going to leave Tomahawk and Doc isolated."

Brannigan had never asked where Burgess had gotten the callsign "Tomahawk." Knowing that most callsigns were not granted because they were cool, but because they were somehow embarrassing, he wondered what the story was there. He'd find out someday.

"Nothing for it. They're barricaded in engineering; they should be all right." Brannigan didn't want to think too hard about the fact that they were two men in the most vital part of the ship, and that the pirates were already throwing grenades.

Bianco sent a roaring burst down the ladderwell. The pirates were on them already.

***

Flanagan kept his distance as he swept the cigarette boat toward the yacht, circling to the south, away from the other speedboats and the Ro-Ro cargo ships that the pirates now had gathered in a rough half-circle around their prey. He really wasn't sure this was going to work, since there was no way that the pirates didn't know that the launch had gone out after their recon boat.

Yet they didn't take fire as they moved in, and they weren't even challenged. Several speedboats were gathered at the yacht's stern, more men in gray swarming up over the rail, and three MD-500s were circling overhead. They seemed to be entirely focused on the yacht itself.

He could hope that the other Blackhearts had already drawn enough blood to throw the pirates off balance. He couldn't entirely rely on it, but he could hope.

Neither Wade nor Gomez commented on it as he started to turn the cigarette boat back toward the *Dream Empire*'s bow. They were probably both thinking the same thing.

One of the helicopters flew low overhead, but they didn't take fire. The gray gear that both sides were using seemed to be working as camouflage. Plus, it was one of their boats, and they probably didn't expect anyone to abandon their own boat out on the high seas like they'd left the launch.

Still, the three Blackhearts stayed alert as he brought the cigarette boat alongside the bow. They could hear the hammer of gunfire, muted as it was by the hull, from inside. Things were not going well, presumably for anyone involved. There were a *lot* of pirates out there.

Those pirates had no idea what they'd walked into, though.

For a moment, as he brought the cigarette boat to a halt, Flanagan had the sudden, stomach-churning thought that he'd screwed up. The gunwale stood three decks above them, far too high to just reach up and climb out of the cigarette boat. However, it looked like the pirates had come prepared to join the fun once contact was made. Wade was already pulling the boarding ladder from a compartment in the stern. It was pretty basic, just a telescoping pole with flip-out footholds and a hook at one end, but it should serve to get them up to the deck.

Even with that, though, it was close. Flanagan had to keep the cigarette boat as tight against the yacht's hull as he could, taking as much shelter under the overhang of the bow as possible as another MD-500 went by, probably wondering what these three idiots were doing in the bow when everyone else was in the stern. Wade, being the tallest of them, still had to stand on the cigarette boat's prow and reach up almost over his head to get the hook over the gunwale.

It took a couple of tries, even as that helicopter circled closer again. Somebody up there had noticed something off.

Gomez then apparently decided that he wasn't going to wait around for the door gunners to shoot them to doll rags.

From his spot just behind Flanagan, Gomez snapped his rifle to his shoulder, paused for a fraction of a second to let the red dot settle, and then dumped half the magazine into the MD-500's windscreen.

Even AH-6 Little Birds, the military equivalent of the MD-500, weren't especially heavily armored. These were regular civilian helicopters, albeit with mounts welded to the sides for the machineguns that the pirates used for fire support. From less than three hundred yards away, the 5.56 rounds zipped right through the acrylic and smashed into the controls, the fuselage, and the pilot.

As the pilot doubled over the three bullets in his guts and lung, sending the bird into a spin, the copilot tried to compensate, hauling on the collective to try to stabilize the helicopter. Gomez wasn't through, though, and emptied the rest of the magazine into the door gunner and the copilot. The door gunner slumped, held inside by his harness, and the copilot jerked as a bullet went through his jaw and up into his brain.

The MD-500, under the conflicting inputs of a dead man and a dying man, flipped over and crashed into the water. It didn't stay on the surface for long.

"Now we've definitely got their attention!" Wade was already hauling himself up the ladder. "Let's *go!*"

Flanagan was still fighting to keep the cigarette boat pressed against the hull. "Go, Mario! I've got to keep this thing steady."

Gomez clambered up on the gunwale, holding onto the small roof over the coxswain's station as he moved out onto the prow. He almost slipped on the fiberglass, but caught himself at the last second, reaching up to grab the low end of the boarding ladder. He held on while Wade finished his climb and disappeared over the gunwale, then he started his own climb.

Flanagan held the cigarette boat in place just long enough for Gomez to get about halfway up the ladder, then he released the controls, clambered up onto the prow, and headed for the ladder.

Unfortunately, with the cigarette boat uncontrolled, it started moving out from under his feet. He had to lunge the last few feet to grab the ladder just before the boat slipped away from the still-drifting yacht.

Clamping both gloved hands onto the bottom of the ladder with a death grip, he brought his feet up to stop himself from slamming into the hull. Above, he heard more gunfire, as Wade engaged someone near the bow. *Got to get up there.* Doing what amounted to a close-grip pullup, he hauled himself up until he could let go with his right hand and grab one of the rungs. Already, he could feel the grip of his saltwater-soaked gloves starting to slip.

He caught the rung and started to climb. It took three rungs of pullups before he could get his boots on the ladder and start to climb normally. His arms, shoulders, and hands ached by the time he got to the top.

Wade and Gomez had already moved up to the entrance to the superstructure and were stacked on either side of it. Flanagan moved quickly to stack up behind Wade, checking the narrow expanse of deck between the superstructure and the side, then up across the windows in the superstructure itself, his muzzle following his eyes wherever he looked. The windows were dark, the tint added to the lack of lights inside to render them effectively opaque. Still, if there was anyone in there, they hadn't opened fire yet.

Lifting his rifle with his firing hand, he gripped Wade's shoulder. "On you."

Wade, his weapon pointed down into the opening, glanced at Gomez. The other Blackheart gave a short nod. Wade returned it.

Then they were going in.

The forward compartment was the master bedroom. Massive, lavishly furnished and appointed. Rich wood covered the deck and ran halfway up the bulkheads. The bed, big enough to dominate the center of the floor, was in a sunken partition that looked like it could rotate to give new views of the ocean off the bow.

There was no one in the compartment. Fontaine should probably be barricaded on the bridge.

The three of them had spread out around the edges of the compartment as they'd made entry. Now they converged quickly on the hatch that led deeper into the superstructure. There was only one, aside from the way they'd come, and Flanagan was cursing the fact that the upper decks had been off limits the whole voyage so far. They didn't have a great idea of the layout, which was going to make the rest of this that much more difficult.

The hatch opened onto a galley, one of at least three aboard. Just as richly appointed as the bedroom had been, the light came in off the horizon to cast a golden sheen over the table, the chairs, the linen, and the crystal, all set out for the next meal already.

Movement brought three rifle barrels to bear, but fingers paused just short of triggers. Several of the staff, in white chef's jackets, cowered in the corner.

They kept moving, though not without keeping tabs on the kitchen staff. Turning their backs on anyone in that situation could prove disastrous.

Flanagan and Gomez stacked on the hatch to the starboard passageway, which *should* lead around the kitchen toward the theater—at least, Flanagan thought so—while Wade watched the staff.

Gomez yanked the hatch open, and Flanagan went through, fast.

Right into two pirates who were moving toward the galley, their own guns up.

The gray of his gear must have thrown them off a little. They hesitated. Flanagan didn't.

He'd already had his rifle in his shoulder, and it was the matter of an inch's upward twitch to bring it to bear. He almost didn't even have to aim at that distance, except that against two of them, he had to make this count.

With a report that was painfully loud in the enclosed space, he shot the first man through the eye before snapping his rifle over toward the other, even as he sidestepped and pressed forward, moving to make himself a harder target. The second man shot him in the plate, then, the impact like a sledgehammer to his sternum, making him stagger and knocking some of the wind out of him. It threw his next shot off, and it smashed through his target's earpro, yanking the man's head around and tearing his ear in half.

Then Gomez, who'd come through the hatch right on Flanagan's heels, shot the pirate through the temple, just under the rim of his helmet, and ended any concerns about his ear.

Wade was right on top of them, then, quickly checking Flanagan for bleeds while Gomez stepped up to cover the passageway ahead of them. "I'm fine," Flanagan wheezed. Damn, it hurt to breathe.

"Shut up and let me make sure." Wade ran his hand over Flanagan's legs, arms, and torso, digging under his plate carrier, his own MCX pointed at the overhead. Finally, he clapped Flanagan roughly on the shoulder. "No bleeds. You're good."

"Let's go, then." Gomez was already moving. "They know we're here now."

112

CHAPTER 15

If Burgess had been a younger man, he might have gotten antsy, sitting there barricaded on the main hatch to the engineering spaces, listening to gunfire echoing through the yacht. As it was, though, he'd been around enough that he had made some peace with that urge to run toward the fight, at least when he had a responsibility much closer.

Not only that, but he'd already seen a few things since entering the engineering compartment that made him suspicious.

For one thing, the engineering crew seemed to be hunkered down in the corner and doing nothing to try to fix the engines.

Unfortunately, with the pirates aboard and attempting to clear the yacht, he couldn't quite follow up on that little detail. If they pushed the pirates off, then it would bear looking into.

Doc Puller, however, wasn't quite so focused. He kept glancing over his shoulder at the crew, which wasn't a particularly good idea. "Hey. Doc. Eyes where your muzzle's pointing."

Puller forced his gaze back toward the hatchway. "Something ain't right here."

"You know it and I know it, but right now we've got bigger fish to fry." Burgess shared a lot of the doc's suspicions. If the engines had been damaged somehow by the pirates' fire, or even gone down from an accident, then the crew *should* be trying

113

their damnedest to get them running again and get the *Dream Empire* away from their adversaries.

The fact that they weren't, coupled with Sorley's obstinate refusal to read the Blackhearts in on important details, had his paranoia running gangbusters.

He'd left the hatch open, giving him a pretty straight shot at the ladderwell leading out of the compartment and up onto the second deck. A firewall bulkhead separated the engineering spaces from the crew quarters forward, so there was really only one way in. If the pirates intended to take full control of the yacht, they'd need to take engineering and the bridge, as well as capture Fontaine.

He and Puller were also set well back from that hatch, purely because Burgess had done this sort of thing before—as a SEAL, many times—and he knew roughly what to expect if the pirates were on the ball, which they appeared to be.

Sure enough, a small, black cylinder came bouncing down the ladderwell after a moment, and he shut his eyes, tucking his head back into cover just before the flashbang went off.

The concussion was brutal, but he'd had just enough time to avoid the bulk of it, and he quickly leaned back out from behind the block of machinery he was barricaded on, just as the first pirate in the stack loomed in the hatchway.

Puller hadn't moved quite as fast, and he had eaten some of the bang. He was still trying to blink past the green blotch in his vision, even as Burgess shot the man in gray three times center mass. The guy staggered under the impacts, but his plate held, though the shock hurt him enough to slow him down just long enough for Burgess to transition to his head and splash his brains across the man's plate carrier behind him.

That one ducked out of the fatal funnel, throwing himself against the bulkhead and taking shelter behind the hatch coaming. There wasn't much cover there, but it was better than nothing. The pirate dumped a string of five shots through the hatch, blind, just trying to suppress the defenders. Puller ducked back as bullets

114

smacked shiny holes through his own cover, and swung around the other side, angling for a shot on the barricaded pirate.

For his part, Burgess just put three rounds through the bulkhead, eliciting a scream as the man crumpled.

He couldn't see any more pirates on the ladder above, but there was at least one left, because that one tossed a frag down into the hatch a moment later.

Burgess threw himself behind the engine, a split second before the little green ball of death detonated with an even nastier concussion than the flashbang. Fragmentation tore into the engines' housings and scoured paint off the deck, the bulkheads, and the overhead.

The smoke was still roiling in the doorway when Burgess threw himself onto his side, sticking his head and his rifle out from behind the engine. There was a good chance that the bullets and the explosives were going to do even more damage than had already been done, but right then, survival came first.

The anticipated pirate didn't appear, though. Through the ringing in his ears, he thought he heard a voice up the ladderwell, and then nothing.

He didn't relax, but just stayed in place and kept covering the hatch. Whatever new surprise the pirates had up their sleeves, he wanted to be ready for it.

Nothing happened. He couldn't even hear any gunfire anymore.

Something had changed, and he didn't know what.

"Hey, Tom?" Puller had recovered from the flashbang's concussion somewhat, but he wasn't watching the hatchway. He was looking at something down on the deck, next to the bulkhead, and frowning. "Check me if I'm wrong, but this doesn't look like it belongs here."

***

Bianco fired down the ladderwell again, but Brannigan knew that he couldn't hold it all by himself for long. Sooner or later, he was going to have to reload, and as advanced as the EVOLYS was, there just wasn't any good way to speed reload a belt-fed. The only ones left in the passageway at that point were Kirk and Bianco. Everyone else was on the bridge, there to protect about half the crew and Fontaine.

And Sorley, unfortunately.

"Vinnie! Turn and go!" Brannigan was barricaded on the hatchway, covering down the passageway toward the ladderwell where Bianco was crouched.

The big man didn't even hesitate but hauled the EVOLYS up to point at the overhead, turning toward the bridge with just enough of a pause to see where Brannigan was and where his rifle was pointed. Hugging the aft bulkhead to stay out of Brannigan's line of fire, he sprinted toward the bridge.

Santelli let him in, then leaned out to cover the other direction. "Kirk! Turn and go!"

Nobody, to Brannigan's knowledge, called Kirk by his first name.

Brannigan didn't turn his head to watch Kirk collapse toward the bridge. He kept his muzzle and his eyes trained on the ladderwell that Bianco had recently abandoned. If the pirates wanted Fontaine, then they had to come up one of those ladderwells.

Kirk brushed past between him and Santelli, then they settled in to wait for the inevitable firefight in the passageway.

Instead, time ticked by, and the hammer of gunfire below and forward began to die down. Only sporadic gunshots sounded throughout the yacht. The passageway stayed empty.

He frowned. Something had just shifted. He could feel it. He just didn't know what it was. He thought through the forces he had at his disposal, still considering the apparent numbers the pirates had brought to bear. This was a big crew, at least a company sized element, possibly bigger. Whoever they were, they had a *lot* of resources, too. But if something had just stalled them out, this might be the time to attack.

None of the Blackhearts liked to sit still and wait for the bad guys to come to them. They'd accomplished most of their missions so far, with such limited numbers, by moving fast,

116

staying stealthy, and getting inside the enemy's loop. Barricading and playing pure defense didn't agree with any of them, least of all him.

"Hank, Kirk, on me."

***

Wade had moved up to take point as the three Blackhearts rotated smoothly through the compartments, each man taking up whatever gap was left open by the other two. Close quarters battle was an art, and it was one that all three of them, Ranger and Recondos, were very good at.

They'd cleared the theater, which had been empty, and were working their way through the mid-level crew quarters. The yacht was the size of a destroyer, and there were a *lot* of compartments to clear. That also meant that the pirates had a lot of ground to cover, too, and so far, except for the team that had moved forward to try to intercept them after Gomez had shot the MD-500's crew to ribbons, they hadn't seen any of them. Some of the yacht's crew had taken shelter in their quarters, which had to be cleared one at a time, but the pirates seemed to be focused elsewhere.

They had almost reached the ladderwell when three gray-clad, armored men with their faces covered spilled out into the passageway.

Wade didn't hesitate. The first man had turned aft instead of forward when he'd come out, and while the second was already pushing out toward the bow to cover him, Wade was already on sights with his finger on the trigger.

He was a good enough shot that he probably could have killed both men with single headshots at that distance, but he didn't want to take chances by getting fancy. He just opened fire, leaning into the MCX and keeping the grouping tight as he hammered half the magazine into the first two men.

Several of his bullets were stopped by body armor, but enough tore through the gaps above, below, and around the plates that the first man went down hard, the last bullet tearing through the side of his head just before he fell, exposing the lead pirate,

117

who was already starting to turn around as he realized they were under attack. Two rounds went right through that guy's armpit, blasting through his heart and lungs, and he crumpled.

The third man took four rounds to the head and neck, two from Wade and two from Flanagan, who had just come up on his flank.

The three Blackhearts closed in on their prey, where the first man that Wade had shot was quivering and jerking, his life ebbing as his blood soaked his fatigues and the deck beneath him. Wade shot him through the skull, just to be sure.

As they got closer, he thought he heard a voice. It took a moment to realize that one of the pirates' headsets had been knocked askew, and he was hearing their radio. He reached down as Flanagan covered the ladderwell and the passageway aft, and Gomez covered forward. Unclipping the helmet's chinstrap, he levered off both helmet and headset, and listened.

He only heard the tail end of the transmission, but it sure sounded like they were getting the hell off the yacht as fast as they could. And something about the way they were talking told him that it probably wasn't because of the Blackhearts.

Wade had been in Iraq and Afghanistan. He knew an "Avalanche" call when he heard one.

***

El Salvaje didn't bother to count the pirates onto the boats or the surviving MD-500 as he went. That wasn't what he was being paid for. Either they made it before the boats pulled off, or they didn't. Some of these men had bonds, many of them from service before they'd gone all the way into the dark corners of the private sector, but he didn't share them.

He clambered into the MD-500, which already had three pirate shooters aboard, and hit the pilot on the shoulder. "Take off!" He needed to get back to the *Luybov Orlova* quickly.

The pilot, for his part, needed no urging. They'd already lost two helicopters, along with more dead pirates than this crew had ever dreamed of losing. It had not been a good day, and the pirates were shook. Only the realities of self-preservation—

which, ironically, had triggered this assault in the first place—were keeping them on mission.

With a surge of power, the pilot pulled the helicopter off the aft helipad and banked hard, dipping the nose and racing toward the *Lyubov Orlova*. El Salvaje just held on, watching the drifting yacht fall away behind them.

While he might take some personal pride—never expressed outwardly—in being as cold as death itself, and he would have insisted if asked—presuming he didn't simply kill the enquirer for asking—that he needed to get word back to his employer that Fontaine was not, in fact, aboard the yacht, the truth was, which even he had to admit in his deepest, darkest thoughts, that he didn't want to die. Even though he often took a quiet joy in the deaths of people whom he had never met and would never know, and his entire life's work had revolved around violence, on a primal level, El Salvaje still wanted to live, to enjoy the fruits of his labor. And what they'd found aboard that yacht had shaken even him.

He buried the fear behind blank, dead, dark eyes, and considered what the next phase might need to be.

CHAPTER 16

"We've finished the sweep, John." Flanagan stepped onto the bridge, his MCX slung and his helmet in one hand, and took in the tableau. "Two of the pirates didn't make it off before their buddies made tracks, and both surrendered. The rest are corpses." He glanced at Sorley. "All of the crew are accounted for. Two casualties there; it looks like they either got in the crossfire, or they startled a pirate and got shot for their trouble. Pretty sure none of our guys shot any no-shoots."

Brannigan nodded silently. That would have been grounds for some serious remediation. The Blackhearts might be very much a black-bag, off-the-books mercenary team, but Brannigan took some things seriously, and a code of honor was one of them. He might look the other way when Wade shot a dying pirate, but stray rounds killing civvies was another matter.

His message delivered, Flanagan stepped to one side and scanned the bridge. The tension was palpable.

The captain and two of the bridge crew were gathered on the port side, away from the controls, their backs to the windows and the open ocean, beyond which the pirate vessels had started to recede into the distance. Fontaine stood not far away, also facing Brannigan, quite pointedly at least a couple yards away from Sorley, who stood in the center, his back to the windscreen, still in his plate carrier but unarmed. Santelli had the security coordinator's weapons at his feet, his beefy hand on his MCX's pistol grip.

"So, Mr. Sorley." Brannigan's voice was quiet, calm, and collected, but Flanagan immediately heard the threat there. Brannigan was a leader and a thinker, and he wasn't given to fits of temper, but he was one wrong move away from lethal violence. "I think it's time that we got to hear all the 'need-to-know' information you've been keeping from us. Such as why you had the engines on this tub disabled once the pirates were confirmed to be on our tail, and why there's enough PETN wired up on the lower decks to flatten a city block. I'd add why you were in such a hurry to get to the launches, but I think the second question already sort of answers that."

Sorley, however, wasn't cowed. Not entirely. The fear was still there, but the man was a survivor, and he was still looking for some way out. He was going to play this out the best he could.

Flanagan almost pitied him.

"I don't have to tell you shit that wasn't in your contract," Sorley snarled. "You've done your job for the moment, and you're getting well paid for it. Or, you will get well paid, if you give me back my weapons and get back to work."

Brannigan stepped closer. "You don't understand your situation here, Sorley. You're not in charge anymore. *I* am. And I'm going to feed you to the fucking sharks, feet first, if you don't start talking." He glanced at Fontaine. "I know that's not Joshua Fontaine, now that I can see him up close. Which is, of course, why you did whatever you could to keep us away from him."

Sorley, for his part, appeared to understand that further antagonizing the mercenary currently towering over him would not work out well for him. Not that he was going to cooperate. He just clammed up. Flanagan watched his mouth tighten, his jaw working.

Whoever Sorley was, and whatever his game was, he was committed.

Or else he knew that to answer the questions posed would probably get him fed to the sharks, regardless.

122

Brannigan, however, wasn't going to be stymied. "Wade, go hang him over the stern. See if it loosens his tongue."

Wade stepped forward, and Sorley acted.

With a speed born of long training and experience, he ducked, low-rushed Wade, and made a grab for the Glock 19 in his waistband.

Wade, however, was not unprepared. Complacency wasn't in his character. He was more the type who would have a plan not just to kill everyone around, but also to kill the *client*, just in case.

He swept his rifle down to smash the forearm into Sorley's wrist, knocking the grasping hand away from his waist at the same moment that he twisted and kicked the man in the knee, dropping him to the deck before taking a long step back, snapping the MCX up to his shoulder. Without a moment's hesitation, he shot Sorley through the head.

Blood and brain matter spattered on the deck as the security coordinator dropped. The crew and the fake Fontaine flinched violently at the killing, and the body double looked like he was about to be sick.

"Well, so much for that idea." Wade didn't seem bothered, but he never did. Flanagan really didn't care about Sorley's death any more than Wade did. That had been about as clear cut as it got. Sorley had made a grab for a weapon, which made him a lethal threat. "Who else knows what's going on?"

Brannigan turned to the body double, but the young man—younger than Fontaine was in real life, it was now obvious—held up his hands as if fending off a blow and shook his head violently. "I don't know anything. I'm just an actor." He was almost crying. "They offered me a lot of money, and even covered the plastic surgery. It was more than I could make in a year, so I took it. They didn't tell me anything else. I thought it was just a gig. Nobody said anything about pirates, or bombs, or people getting killed!"

Brannigan studied the man for a moment, as if evaluating whether or not he believed his story. Finally, he dismissed him and turned to the bridge crew. "Captain?" His voice was mild, almost friendly, but with Sorley's corpse leaking blood and brains out onto the deck only feet away, that only made the implicit threat all the more chilling.

The captain looked down at Sorley's body and took a deep, quavering breath. Looking up to meet Brannigan's cold, angry eyes, he spread his hands. "I don't know for sure what's going on, but I've seen enough over the last few years to guess."

Brannigan folded his hands over the buttstock of his rifle. "Well, let's hear your guess. Because from where I'm sitting, this looks like a setup and a half, and my boys and I aren't all that happy about it." He glanced meaningfully at the rapidly cooling meat on the deck that had been the late security coordinator.

**

El Salvaje slid out of the helicopter as soon as the skids touched and ran toward the *Lyubov Orlova*'s superstructure, keeping his head down to avoid the still-turning rotors, even though they were well above him. It was something he'd never quite gotten used to. He was always a little afraid that a helicopter's spinning rotor blades were going to take his head off.

The guards inside knew better than to stop El Salvaje for anything. They'd tried to keep him out when Cain had been busy, once. He'd forced his way through at gunpoint, conducted his business, and walked out.

That night, he'd slit the lead guard's throat as a warning. Cain hadn't said anything about it. He'd known the sort of man he'd hired.

He found Cain on the old cruise ship's bridge, converted into a command center. The old man was geared up and armed, and his face was bleak as El Salvaje came through the hatch.

"Tell me you got him."

El Salvaje shook his head. "He's not aboard."

Cain's eyes narrowed, and El Salvaje could almost read his thoughts. There was no way, given the fight that they'd faced—and Cain had been able to listen in on the radio calls, at least, even with the *Lyubov Orlova* over the horizon—that they'd had time to sweep the entire yacht. "You'd better be damned sure of that."

El Salvaje was a dangerous man, more dangerous than most of the pirates, even the special operations trained ones. He'd killed more people than even those men. Yet he was no fool. He knew just how deadly Cain was, and that while he might have made it clear that keeping him away from Cain was a bad idea, he had no doubt that Cain had enough backup to make sure that any would-be assassin wound up dead a few seconds after he decided to put a hit into action.

Presuming Cain, who had a special operations background himself, didn't just gun him down right there. El Salvaje had a pretty high opinion of his own abilities, but he'd seen Cain in action.

Moving very carefully to keep the man from getting the wrong idea and reaching for the SIG P226 on his hip, he reached into the utility pouch on the front of his plate carrier and pulled out a small camera. It wasn't a phone camera, if only because he suspected there were ways to track smartphones even at sea. He never used them. Holding it up so that Cain could see it clearly, he found the shots he'd taken just before ordering everyone still alive off the yacht. He handed the camera over.

"They had charges rigged throughout the hull. Enough explosives to sink this ship if we'd brought the yacht alongside. Now, I might be wrong, but Fontaine would never take that risk, if I read the intel about the man correctly."

Cain's eyes narrowed as he scanned the photographs. Finally, his lips tight, he handed the camera back, his eyes focused on nothing, anger written across his features. "No, he wouldn't risk himself. We got suckered." Finally, he glared at El Salvaje. "How many did we lose?"

The mercenary shrugged. "I haven't gotten a count. You don't pay me for that."

Cain's expression hardened further for a moment, but while El Salvaje had his own respect for Cain's abilities, that respect, to some extent, was reciprocated. Perhaps "respect" wasn't quite the right word; neither one trusted that they could make a move without being killed or seriously wounded in the process.

There was no love lost between El Salvaje and Cain. There never had been and never would be. They shared an interest, and certain risks were considered acceptable in pursuit of that interest. That was it. No more, no less.

"Do we need to return to the US?" El Salvaje didn't know their target nearly as well as Cain did.

The former special operator shook his head. "No. He wouldn't be there for something like this." He rubbed his chin, the graying stubble scratching like sandpaper. "I think I know where he is." His expression hardened again, and his eyes flashed. "Should have known it wouldn't be enough for him to just try to sic the Navy on us. Well, we'll see about that."

***

"I've been skipper of this yacht since Mr. Fontaine bought it." Brannigan had allowed the captain to sit down, though Wade, Flanagan, and Hank were still watching the rest of the bridge crew like hawks. "If he's taken her anywhere, I've been aboard. I signed an NDA when I first took the job, that doesn't expire for another fifty years, but…" He waved at Sorley's body. "Given this little game, and the bombs that are planted aboard this tub, I think that waives any obligation to keep his secrets."

"Probably." Brannigan was still on his feet, his arms crossed, his face impassive.

The captain sighed. "Look, I tried to look the other way. For years. I didn't know anything for *sure*, and I didn't want to know. But while Joshua Fontaine might have one hell of a shiny public image, he's not nearly as clean as everyone thinks he is. Not even close.

"I started to figure it out less than a year after he bought this yacht and brought me on as her skipper. We set sail from Key West and headed out toward the Bahamas, going about ten nautical miles into international waters before he ordered a halt

126

and had us hold position. We stayed there for most of a day before another yacht showed up.

"The party lasted almost three days, and I don't think I need to tell you what kind of entertainment was aboard both ships. It was international waters, after all. But I did recognize the man who came in the yacht. Have you heard of Felix Satarov?"

Brannigan nodded. Flanagan wasn't sure, but he suspected he could work out the rest from context.

"He was only the first. Over the years to follow, we came out here to meet with oligarchs, gangsters, spymasters, dirty politicians, and financiers. There was always plenty of chemical and sexual fun to be had." The look in his eye turned haunted. "Even when a few of the girls threw themselves overboard, the party didn't stop."

"What does he have to do with the pirates?" Brannigan asked.

"I don't know, not for sure." The captain's shoulders slumped. "Those trips with this yacht never came close to anything like them, until this one. But…"

"But you can guess." Brannigan's eyes were fixed on the captain, unblinking.

"I can guess." The skipper sighed. "I mean, between the drugs, the shady money people, and the human trafficking, it can't have been far off, can it?"

Brannigan just waited silently.

"It's possible that he just got wind that the pirates were targeting him. What it does look like to me, though, is that he was hoping to take them out, one way or another, and the bombs were his insurance policy. I knew that Sorley was looking for some kind of high-end shooters to ride security on this boat. From what I've seen so far, that probably means you guys." He looked around at the Blackhearts but got blank, vaguely hostile stares in reply. He seemed to shrink a little. "Whether he had gotten word that they wanted him, or they crossed one of his pals, he seems to have wanted to take them all out, permanently." For once, the captain's expression changed from weary fear to anger. "And he was willing to sacrifice not only a three-hundred-million-dollar yacht to do it, but also everyone on board."

"To give him the benefit of the doubt—not that I'm suggesting we do any such thing—from what we've heard about these pirates, maybe he figured that if it came down to using the explosives, then there wouldn't be anybody left aboard alive, anyway." Santelli had just come in and heard the last bit.

"There *is* another possibility." The captain seemed reluctant to continue, but he kept talking under Brannigan's stare. "I don't have anything solid to go on here. It's all circumstantial. But there was another big shot money guy named Howard. Fontaine was trying to buy him out on something, but he wouldn't sell.

"Next thing anybody knows, a bunch of vital shipments for Howard's interests start disappearing. Within a month, he's in so much trouble that he *has* to sell out."

Flanagan raised an eyebrow. "That definitely sounds fishy as hell. So, what? He got cozy with the pirates, pointed them at his business rivals, and now he wants to clean up after himself?"

"Sure sounds that way." Brannigan mused on the problem, then looked around at the rest of the Blackhearts. "Carlo, how are the engines looking?"

"For the most part, they're not in bad shape. Sorley over there just shut 'em down and disconnected some stuff that wasn't too hard to reconnect. Tom and Doc got them a little shot up, but from what I can tell, there's no serious damage done. Some frag and a couple of bullet holes, but they didn't penetrate the blocks, and didn't hit anything else vital. We'll have to keep an eye on 'em, but they should run okay." Santelli was still wiping his hands on a greasy rag. He'd offered his not-inconsiderable skill as a mechanic to try to get the yacht moving again.

The charges on the hull were another concern, but Burgess was down there working on them. He wasn't an EOD tech, but he'd learned a few things over the years, mainly in the world of contracting and mercenary work after he'd left the SEAL teams. None of them wanted to try to move without making sure that the considerable amount of PETN aboard wasn't going to go boom.

"Well, then." Brannigan studied the captain for a moment. "Carlo, you stay up here with the captain and the bridge crew. I want everybody else down in the team room, as soon as Tom's done with the charges.

"We've got some planning to do."

CHAPTER 17

"We've got a choice to make, gents." Brannigan looked around the compartment. It was just the Blackhearts, with the exceptions of Santelli and Hank, who were watching the remaining crew and their two captured pirates. "Maybe I'm paranoid, but it looks to me an awful lot like Fontaine set us up as bait. We got the firepower we needed to make sure all the pirates came knocking, at which point, Sorley was going to run for it and blow up the ship.

"Now, I don't like that. I know none of you do, either." Wade's murderous glare was enough of an answer to that. "It leaves us with three choices, though.

"One: we can cut ties, sail this boat back to the States, and walk. We won't get paid, but there shouldn't be too many more nasty surprises, either."

"Unless and until Fontaine decides to come after us, just in case he's dirty and he thinks we figured it out," Kirk pointed out.

"There's that," Brannigan conceded. "Option two is that we continue the hunt and try to take the rest of the pirates off the board, forget about the *potential* double cross—we don't actually know for sure that's what it was; maybe Sorley was acting on his own—and see if we can get paid afterward." While every Blackheart would be fine with killing pirates, nobody looked

131

entirely on board with the idea of just letting things slide. There were too many indicators that they'd been sacrificial lambs, and none of them were happy about it.

"Option three is that we go to that island the captain told us about and confront Fontaine. That might work out peaceably, or it might turn violent. If he's dirty, we might prevent later trouble down the road. Then we can coordinate with Chavez and Abernathy about going after the pirates later. Might even get paid twice."

"I'm all for Option Three, myself." Wade had his arms folded. "I agree; I think Fontaine set us up and figured we'd all get killed to cover his ass. I think we owe him."

"If we know about his island, and the pirates had good enough intel to think that he was aboard this tub, what are the odds that they'll be going there, too?" Burgess stroked his beard thoughtfully. "How long is it to this rock?"

"About a week, according to the captain," Brannigan said. "We might well cross paths with them again. You're right."

"Well, then." Flanagan sat up, planting his boots on the deck. "We'd better get a watch schedule and a recon plan worked up."

***

"Where would he be hiding?" El Salvaje asked. Outside, to the flanks of the *Lyubov Orlova*, the other pirate ships were spreading out again, dispersing over the ocean to avoid observation by satellites overhead. There was no *avoiding* it altogether, but a flotilla would attract attention. Fortunately, there was too much ocean and too few watchers for any state to have picked up on what was happening so far. They still had to be careful, though.

Cain had turned to his charts. "He doesn't think I know about it, but he has an island retreat just off the coast of Africa, south of the Canary Islands." He tapped a spot on the chart where there wasn't much of anything documented. "It's not much more than a rock, or rather, it wasn't before he took it over. He's had a lot of work done." He let out a gallows chuckle. "He thinks that I can't dig up any information I need, just because he fed us the intel for those first hits."

El Salvaje didn't mention that Cain hadn't managed to dig up the intel they'd needed about the trap set on Fontaine's yacht.

"He will have security."

"Oh, yes," Cain agreed. "The best money can buy. He can afford it, in no small part thanks to what we've done for him." He snarled, but he was thinking it through, rubbing his chin as he looked at the chart. Cain was a brutal sociopath, but he was still a thinker. That was what made him dangerous, and why El Salvaje was currently willing to play the paid retainer.

"I know where it is, and I know many of the details of its construction, but we are still going to need reconnaissance." Cain tapped the chart, his finger on the Canary Islands, north of where he'd marked Fontaine's retreat. "That island is too small for all the recreation that his security might need, and he needs to bring supplies in from somewhere."

"You are thinking about moving to the Canary Islands first and spying out the lay of the land from there." El Salvaje didn't phrase it as a question, and he didn't need to.

Cain nodded. "Like you said, he will have a lot of security. We already got hurt badly in that attack on the yacht." He stared down at the chart, and the angry man who'd launched that attack was gone, replaced by a cold, calculating killer. "We'll look around, find out what we can, and if we need to kidnap a few of his support staff and wring them out, we'll do it.

"Then we'll take his retreat, kill him, take everything he owns, and burn the place to the ground." A little of that temper leaked out again. "Set *me* up, will you, Fontaine? Wash your hands of *me*, after everything I've done for you? You'll pay for that."

He let out a long, angry sigh. "Oh, you'll pay."

CHAPTER 18

"The bird's about as ready as it's going to get." Flanagan stepped up next to Brannigan on the bridge. Only one of the yacht's two MD-500s was still operational, and even that one had taken a couple of rounds during the pirates' boarding action, so it had required a lengthy and careful once-over, which had taken most of the first day since the fight. "I'll take Mario, and we'll take her for the first circle once the sun goes down." Somewhat to their surprise, Fontaine had included night vision in their gear, which was going to be a help. They could fly blacked out and hopefully spot the pirates before the pirates spotted them.

Unless the pirates also had NVGs, in which case this was going to be a lot more of an even contest than any of the Blackhearts liked.

It wouldn't be the first time, though. The Humanity Front's experiments in Kyrgyzstan had forced them to assault the base there without radios or NVGs. And they'd conducted some of their other operations on a lot more of a shoestring than that.

Brannigan just nodded, watching the water, thinking. Flanagan was pretty good at reading their chief, so he could imagine any number of possibilities that the Colonel was thinking through.

He'd thought of a few, himself. "Depending on what we find, what do you think about trying to thin the herd a little?" He had almost hesitated to ask, given the disparity in numbers and firepower, but it had been nagging at him for a while. They *had*, after all, signed on to fight pirates, and Flanagan didn't think he was alone in his dislike of the idea of letting a crew of sophisticated sociopaths continue to prey on shipping, even if it was mostly high-end stuff being moved around for rich assholes who probably were none too clean, themselves. He knew that they'd discussed doing this anyway, but that had been after dealing with Fontaine.

"I know what you're thinking, Joe, and I can't say I disagree." Brannigan kept his eyes out on the ocean in front of them, still thinking even as he answered Flanagan's question, spoken and unspoken. "We're not in the best position here, though, and if they're still together in a flotilla, even with only four or five ships, that's going to be a tough nut to crack. As soon as we hit one, the others will be all over us. Remember, we still don't know exactly what kind of numbers we're up against here. They probably only pulled off because they found the explosives belowdecks, not because we had them outmatched."

"We *did* kind of have them outmatched, just judging by the body count," Flanagan pointed out.

"Doesn't matter, now that they're alerted." Brannigan had a lot of factors to consider, which Flanagan didn't necessarily share, and he was thinking things through carefully. He glanced over his shoulder at Flanagan. "I get that we all want to do some serious pirate hunting, Joe, but I can't ask the team to throw themselves into the lion's mouth pro bono, not without a lot more intel and a solid plan." He shook his head. "Conduct your recon, and we'll decide on a course of action once we've got a better picture of the situation."

Flanagan nodded. It was the best they could do under the circumstances, and he knew it. With at least four ships, mostly big freighters, the pirates obviously had them outnumbered. The Blackhearts had pulled off some pretty audacious ops over the years, but they weren't supermen. "We'll be back in a couple of hours, then."

Brannigan clapped him on the shoulder. "Good luck, and good hunting."

***

The drone of the MD-500 had almost faded into the background over the last hour, despite the fact that it was still too loud to talk except over the intercom. Fontaine's pilot had tried keeping up a constant patter over their headsets for the first few minutes, but he had given up when both Blackhearts had responded with monosyllables, when they'd responded at all.

Neither Flanagan nor Gomez were given to a lot of talk, and that was when they weren't focused entirely on watching the water beneath them.

Flanagan thought that the pilot was probably nervous, even more so than the copilot, who hadn't said a word since they'd climbed aboard, but had given both armed men sideways looks that were more than a little afraid. The support staff aboard the *Dream Empire* wasn't exactly made up of meat-eaters, and most of them had probably never seen the sort of violence that had left bullet holes and bloodstains all over the yacht.

The fact that the Blackhearts obviously didn't exactly trust any of them was probably making them even more nervous.

Flanagan kept an eye and an ear on the pilot and copilot as they circled the yacht, moving farther out to sea with each circuit. The pirate vessels had been out of sight within a couple hours of the fight's end, and they weren't sure where they'd gone, so they were being careful. He didn't want to suddenly overfly a pirate ship and get shot up. They'd all seen what even 5.56 from a short-barreled rifle could do to an MD-500 at close enough range. These were fragile machines, and they weren't designed to take fire.

He hoped that they *could* trust the crew that had survived. Especially the pilot and copilot. After all, neither he nor Gomez were helicopter pilots. If the crew got froggy, they weren't going to be able to fly the bird, or even land it safely.

He just hoped that, if these two were working for the pirates, or were part of Sorley's plan, they hadn't thought of that.

137

Scanning the ocean beneath them, he froze. Reaching over, he tapped Gomez on the shoulder and pointed. Hopefully the other man would see it, because he didn't want to risk taking his eyes off the contact in case he lost it.

It looked like a cargo ship as they got closer, though the image through his twin-tube PS-31s was grainy and blurred. There was no way to be sure, right off, whether it was one of the pirates' Ro-Ro ships or just an ordinary commercial freighter.

He reached forward and tapped the pilot on the shoulder. The man jumped a little. "Take us lower and move in toward that ship off to port." He thought about it a second. "Try to keep us at least a mile away, and *do not* overfly it."

The pilot acknowledged a bit shakily, and they began to descend.

It took a few minutes to close the distance. They'd been a bit too busy to note specific details of the ships that had launched the assault on the *Dream Empire*, but from its position, Flanagan thought it was probably one of them. When he looked across the fuselage at Gomez, who was watching over his shoulder, he got a nod. Gomez was pretty sure it was one of the same ones.

He expanded his scan, looking around at the horizon. There might be one more ship out there, a good twenty nautical miles away. The Ro-Ro was on its own, though.

Tapping his fingers against his MCX, Flanagan thought about it. The pilot was doing a good job of maintaining his distance, but Flanagan thought that he could see some activity up on the Ro-Ro ship's superstructure, which meant that they'd at least heard the helicopter, and someone down there was reacting to it. It was impossible to say for certain from a mile out what that reaction was.

Gomez leaned in close. When Flanagan twisted his head to look at his teammate through his NVGs, the half-Apache tapped his headset. Flanagan pried one earpiece away and Gomez put his mouth to Flanagan's ear.

138

"We can't see enough from up here. We're going to have to get closer." He was right, but a close flyby carried a lot of risk in an unarmored helicopter, if that did turn out to be a pirate ship.

That turned out to be unnecessary, however.

A flicker of light strobed from the Ro-Ro cargo ship's fantail. It might have just been a strobe light or a flashlight except that both Blackhearts had been around long enough to have seen a lot of muzzle flashes in the dark. They both knew exactly what that was.

The pirates were jumpy, too. And they'd just given themselves away.

"Get us out of here," he instructed the pilot. "Back to the yacht."

"Are you sure? We've still got half the planned route to cover." If he'd seen the flashes, the pilot hadn't identified them for what they were. The ship was still far enough away that the bullets were subsonic by the time they got anywhere near the helicopter, so the harsh *snap* of supersonic shockwaves wasn't there, and probably wouldn't have been audible over the roar of the bird's engines, anyway.

"See those flashes down there?" The pilot looked down and started a little. "They're shooting at us.

"We know where one of our targets is, now."

***

Dawn wasn't all that far off as the yacht's two launches skipped over the waves, heading north, following the captured cigarette boat.

It had taken a bit of time to get the helicopter back to the *Dream Empire*, land, brief the strike team on the target, and launch the boats. Now they had a limited time window in which to pull off this raid. Dawn came all too soon.

Determining who would go had almost been a fight. They couldn't leave the *Dream Empire* unguarded, though, so Flanagan, Wade, Gomez, Burgess, and Curtis had been selected to go. That gave them one machinegun and one fair-to-middling

139

doc, while leaving Brannigan, Santelli, Bianco, Hank, Kirk, and Doc Puller to hold the yacht.

The launches weren't silent, especially at the speeds they were making, but there was no avoiding that, especially if they hoped to hit the ship under the cover of darkness. They just had to hope that the pirates had relaxed their vigilance a little after having driven the helicopter off, and that Curtis could provide enough fire support from the second boat to cover their boarding action.

Gomez was driving the cigarette boat, leading the way by about a quarter mile. He'd be seen long before the yacht's launches. Which was part of the plan.

He watched the growing silhouette of the cargo ship ahead of him, keeping his head down almost directly behind the steering column, trying to gauge his timing. Somebody up there had to have noticed the oncoming boat by now.

They had. Muzzle flashes flickered in the dark along the gunwale and the forward rail, and bullets went flying over his head with hard, loud *snap*s, a few actually hitting the boat with loud *bang*s, though most went into the water or far out into the air.

He held his course, accelerating toward the ship. It wasn't *quite* time yet.

Another burst hit the bow with a quintet of crackling *bang*s, and then it was time.

Jamming the throttle all the way open and wedging the steering column in place, Gomez got up, turned, and dove off the boat's stern.

He hit the water hard, not quite managing the graceful dive that he'd hoped, between his body armor, gear, and weapon. It wasn't the most difficult swim back to the surface he'd ever done, but at the same time, it had been a long time since he'd spent any serious time in the water. He'd very much become a desert creature since returning to the family ranch in New Mexico.

Striking out, kicking hard to make up for the fact that he was in boots and fatigues instead of a wet suit and fins, he swam away from the speedboat, even as more fire converged on it, smashing the fiberglass and the Plexiglas windscreen.

Fortunately, he didn't have far to go. Burgess and Flanagan, at the tillers of the two launches, had accelerated as soon as they'd seen and heard the gunfire, and one of the boats was suddenly looming over him, Wade leaning out over the gunwale, a gloved hand extended to haul him into the launch. Gomez grabbed it gratefully, and Wade pulled him up until he could hook one boot over the side and roll into the bottom.

Flanagan was still aiming for the Ro-Ro's stern and had already sped back up to a good fifteen knots. They had to move fast, while all eyes were on the speedboat.

"Only counted four shooters," Wade commented, as they skipped and bounced across the waves, spray flying from each impact and a V-shaped wake practically glowing in their NVGs behind them. "Let's hope that's all of them."

None of them believed it would be, but they were ready. They sped toward their boarding point as the pirates kept pouring bullets into the abandoned boat.

CHAPTER 19

The Blackhearts held their fire as they got closer and closer, staying low while Flanagan and Burgess closed ranks and slowed down to reduce the noise they were making, hoping that the thunder of gunfire would cover the noise of their engines, even as they circled around toward the stern. The speedboat, undeterred by the bullets tearing holes through its hull, hadn't quite maintained a straight-line course, but it was still straight enough that it impacted the Ro-Ro's hull just behind the bow, hitting with a sickening *crunch* as fiberglass shattered and aluminum bent. The speedboat hadn't had a chance against the steel hull of the cargo ship, but the gunfire ceased for a moment, probably as the pirates ducked back from the side, expecting an explosion.

Wade and Gomez had, in fact, suggested turning the pirate cigarette boat into a Boat-Borne Improvised Explosive Device. While they'd had a few rockets—though they only had two more rounds for the Carl Gustaf aboard—and machineguns aboard the *Dream Empire*, however, there hadn't been any real supply of explosives, so they'd had to settle for what diversionary value they could get out of a collision.

They hadn't *quite* reached the stern before the bangs and scrapes of the collision had died away, and someone shouted that there was no one aboard the boat. Then another shout echoed from just before the stern, and a figure turned toward them, the bright cone of an IR floodlight streaming from the man's weapon.

Curtis was ready for it, down in the bow of the second launch with his EVOLYS, already braced and all but aimed in.

The FN machinegun roared, spitting fire into the night, and Curtis practically cut the pirate in half. They were less than two hundred yards away by then, and Flanagan cranked the throttle, driving the first launch toward the open cargo bay, where the pirates' own boats were staged, ready to race out to intercept their prey.

He didn't drive all the way into the well deck, but slowed just close enough that Wade could throw a grappling hook, snagging a rail on the starboard side with the first throw. Hauling on the line, hand over hand, he brought the boat into the hold while Flanagan killed the motor and Gomez covered him.

Curtis laid a couple more long bursts into the figures along the side of the mid-sized cargo ship, then Burgess was bringing the second launch in alongside the first.

Gomez and Wade were already out and onto the catwalk along the starboard side, guns up and looking for targets, as Flanagan finished securing the launch and moved to join them. Burgess did the same, while Curtis stayed where he was in the bow of the second boat, covering the well deck with his EVOLYS. The machinegun wasn't well suited to CQB, so Curtis would stay back and hold the boats.

They all just hoped that a four-man assault team would turn out to be enough.

The well deck itself was mostly empty, except for four speedboats, one of which appeared to have been partially broken down for parts. There wasn't anyone else there, at least until boots rattled on the ladderwell leading down from the upper decks.

Gomez didn't wait. He opened fire as soon as he had a shot at shins and knees. The SIG MCX's reports echoed like thunder in the steel-walled hold, and while two of his rounds sparked off the ladder and the rail with resounding *bang*s, at least one smashed through shin and calf, dropping the pirate to his

144

knees with a shrill scream, just before Gomez and Wade both shot the man through the torso and neck. The pirate crashed limply down the ladder, his weapon clattering loudly and hanging up halfway down, holding him in place by the sling around his neck.

The four Blackhearts moved forward carefully, weapons up, covering not only that ladderwell, but also the other three others that led down into the well deck from above. This wasn't the best way to tackle a ship like this, but it was the best way they could with what they had.

There was no space to circle wide around the ladderwell, thanks to the arrangement of equipment and boats on the deck. Muzzles rose to cover the hatchway overhead, just in case. The pirates would *probably* be more reluctant to use frag grenades aboard their own ship, but that wasn't something that any of the Blackhearts were all *that* confident about.

The hatchway was empty. If another pirate had been ready to come down that ladderwell behind the dead man, he'd reconsidered as soon as the first had been shot down.

That didn't mean that they weren't about to walk into an ambush as soon as they went up those steps, but it also didn't mean that they could hang out and debate the matter, either. While they were down in the well deck, Gomez had no doubt, the pirates were adjusting their defensive plan and maneuvering to hit them from a different angle.

A moment later, the stuttering roar of Curtis's EVOLYS confirmed that thought, the flickering muzzle blast lighting up the darkened well deck as he hosed down the figures attempting to come down the forward, portside ladderwell.

Gomez acted, then. His rifle pointed up at the open hatch, he started up the steps, slowing just enough to let Burgess catch up.

The hardest part was getting over the snagged corpse halfway up. He still moved fast, especially since it looked like that hatch was too small for the two of them to pop it at once.

Crouching just beneath, he paused for a moment, weaving back and forth to clear as much of the open space above the

145

ladderwell as he could without exposing himself. A couple more bursts from Curtis's belt-fed hammered through the hold, rocking the Blackhearts on the steps, and then Gomez was moving.

He surged up through the open hatch, hastily clearing aft before flipping around as he clambered up the last couple of steps to clear his back.

Just as he turned, a rifle thundered in the narrow passageway, and a blossom of fire flashed right in front of him. He felt a ferocious impact in his chest.

***

The man who told people to just call him "Bull" spat a vicious curse as Fish and Nail were cut down halfway down the ladder, spilling to the deck below in a limp pile of meat and blood. The intruders had the hold locked down. That was three men dead in less than ten minutes. Four, if you counted Shaft on the fantail. Whoever these guys were, they were good.

Bull had avoided the assault on the yacht. He suspected he knew why Cain had such a mad on for Fontaine, but he also knew the kind of money Fontaine had at his disposal, and the sort of security that money could buy. He'd been pretty sure from the get go that trying to take that yacht would be a suicide mission, and he'd been proven right.

Now, it seemed, the hornets' nest they'd kicked was coming for revenge.

It was possible that it was someone else. Navy SEALs, maybe. Out in the middle of the Atlantic, it could even be Royal Marines or French Commando Marine. He didn't think it was any of the above, though. SEALs would have at least a destroyer in tow, and probably wouldn't have crashed a speedboat into the hull. These guys had come out of nowhere. No, it had to be the mercs Fontaine had hired. The ones who had already kicked his fellow pirates' teeth in aboard the yacht.

He heard the gunfire from the other side. He'd managed to avoid joining the assault, but only because he'd wrangled himself a watch post. Now here he was, trying to defend the *Balearic* with the handful of pirates who were left after that bloodbath. There was a reason he had the crew holding back from the rest of the flotilla. He'd had twelve shooters and ten sailors. Now he was down to eight shooters and ten sailors, and most of the sailors weren't good for much in a fight.

"Back up." He'd had an idea. There were a couple of spots on the top deck where they could actually look down into the well deck, and they might be able to get a shot at that machinegunner from there. "On me."

***

Gasping for breath after taking that shot to the plate, Gomez nevertheless threw himself backward, dropping his muzzle to shoot between his knees, while two more rounds went past his face, so close that he could feel the shockwaves of their passage. He shot back, half blindly, hoping and praying that he wasn't about to put a bullet in Burgess's skull as the other man came up the steps to help.

His first shots went wild, but one of them still blew a chunk out of the gunman's arm, throwing his own aim off and making him drill two new holes in the bulkhead above Gomez's head. The next round was a little more on target and passed through the side of his neck. Blood spurted and the pirate dropped his weapon, letting it hang on its sling as he grabbed for the bleed.

Then Gomez shot him through the skull, painting the bulkhead behind him with a fine mist of red before he finished crawling backwards out of the hatchway, clearing it for Burgess.

Burgess popped out a moment later, twisting on the ladder so that his muzzle came out at the same time as his head.

Gomez dragged himself against the bulkhead, getting out of Burgess's way as he came the rest of the way out into the passageway, Wade and Flanagan on his heels. Rifles pointed fore and aft, clearing the remainder of the corridor, even as Gomez felt around his torso, searching for bleeds, and gasped to get some breath back into his lungs. That had *hurt*.

"Mario? You okay, brother?" Burgess turned to him as Wade and Flanagan took up security on the passageway, crouching over him.

147

"I'm alive," Gomez grunted. He accepted Burgess's hand and hauled himself to his feet. "I'm not sure this plate's going to be good for too many more hits, though."

"Let's try not to get shot, then." Wade was facing forward. "We need to move." Surprise was done, so now they needed to rely on speed and violence of action.

"On you." Flanagan stepped around the hatchway as Burgess took up rear security and Gomez fell in behind.

"Bridge?" Wade was already moving.

"Let's clear this deck first." Flanagan was right behind Wade, his weapon leveled over the bigger man's shoulder. "We don't have the charges to sink this sucker, so let's make sure there are no pirates left to use it."

"Fine by me." Wade moved to the first hatch forward. The cargo ship wasn't that large, so the clear shouldn't take all that long. Flanagan was covering the passageway past Wade, while Gomez watched the outer deck through the portholes along the starboard side and Burgess covered their six. There didn't appear to be much of any way for the bad guys to get at them from that direction, but it never paid to make assumptions.

Wade held on the hatch for the brief moment it took for Flanagan to give his shoulder a squeeze. "With you." Then he threw the hatch—little more than a light, hollow-core door, really—open and went in fast. Flanagan flowed in after him, even as Gomez took up coverage on the entire passageway.

"Small room. Clear." The two Blackhearts were already on their way out as Gomez took lead, moving toward the next hatchway.

Leapfrogging like that, they began to clear the lower crew deck. They got to the next compartment before more gunfire erupted astern.

***

"Why the hell did I agree to this? Hanging out alone while Joe gets all the action…" Curtis kept muttering to himself, complaining about holding security on the boats to distract himself from the fact that he was scared stiff. Solo operations were

148

one thing when he was slipping around the less savory parts of Vegas, but they weren't something he really wanted to mess around with in combat. Yet here he was, watching the boats with his EVOLYS—which was an awesome machinegun, he had to admit—all by himself, because they simply didn't have the numbers to do this otherwise.

It wasn't impossible to hold security as a lone wolf. Especially in this position, he had a good field of fire on all potential approaches, meaning the four ladderwells leading down from the upper deck. The only thing was, he was getting an itch on the back of his neck. They hadn't *seen* any other pirate vessels nearby on approach, but he had his back to the open ocean beyond the well deck, and that bugged him. He needed to protect the boats from a flank attack, but he also had to cover his own six. When a man's by himself, he has to cover *every* angle as best he can.

With a muttered curse, he slapped himself in the back of the head, just before hauling the EVOLYS up and scrambling over the gunwale, into the first boat. "Cover all the angles means reduce the number of angles you've got to cover, you freakin' meathead." He glanced up at the overhead as he crossed the lead boat and scrambled up onto the catwalk. "I hope Joe didn't hear that. I'll never hear the end of it." He got onto the catwalk and moved against the outer hull, fading back into the stern, where he had some cover—or at least concealment; he didn't necessarily trust the steel of the hull and bulkheads to stop bullets—from the rear and his right flank.

As he did so, though, he got a glimpse of movement out of the corner of his eye, high and off to the left. At the stern, where he wouldn't have seen it a moment before.

Pivoting, he dragged the EVOLYS around, bringing it up and snapping it into his shoulder. Where eyes go, muzzle goes.

A dark figure, silhouetted against the sky in his NVGs, was leaning over the rail behind a rifle, searching the entrance to the well deck. Looking for him. He thought he saw a second figure not far behind the first.

149

Curtis braced the machinegun against a slight projection of the bulkhead on the inside of the catwalk and leaned into the belt-fed, getting as low as he could just to bring the weapon to bear on the figures above, and opened fire.

The EVOLYS roared, flame strobing from the muzzle, and the long burst smashed the first man off his feet before chewing into the second. Curtis rode the recoil, using it to guide his shots rather than fighting it, and the line of bullets tracked across the first man and up into the second's neck and face.

He knew he needed to move after that. He'd cleared the targets he could see, but he'd also just revealed his position. The key to staying alive when solo was either to barricade himself thoroughly enough that none of the bad guys could get at him, or else keep moving, make himself impossible to pin down. Barricading wasn't an option in the open hold.

Turning forward, knowing that he was about to collapse at least one of his fields of fire, he headed for the bow, where he could hunker down and cover the boats from a position where he wasn't going to get shot in the back.

***

Flanagan was pretty sure that was Curtis's belt-fed he'd heard. The harmonics of the ship's structure made the sound a little hard to identify, but so far, the pirates had all used their R4s on semi-auto. That had been machinegun fire. He paused just short of the next hatch and keyed his radio. "Gambler, Woodsrunner. Status?"

"Still breathing, but it's kinda lonely down here." Curtis sounded a little short of breath. "Two more down."

Without knowing exactly how many pirates were aboard, that bit of information was only of limited usefulness, but it was still good to know. Two fewer bad guys to worry about.

The Ro-Ro wasn't all that big. Flanagan was starting to think that it had started its life as a ferry, not an oceangoing cargo ship. That was an advantage, since it meant that there could only be so many bad guys aboard.

He keyed his radio twice to indicate that he'd heard and understood, and then Gomez pulled the next hatch open, and they were moving through.

The next compartment confirmed his suspicions that this had been a ferry. Instead of another crew cabin or equipment room, they were in a large, open compartment that spanned the entire width of the vessel and stretched almost clear to the bow. There were only a few portholes, lining up with the exterior windows in the outer passageway. Even the benches were still bolted to the deck.

There was no one in the compartment. It took seconds to clear it and move on toward the bridge.

They had to backtrack aft to get to the steps up to the top deck. They moved quickly and smoothly, weapons up despite the emptiness and the lack of movement.

Clearing their way into the ladderwell, they moved up, Wade in the lead. Flanagan was right on his heels, so when they reached the hatch leading to the bridge itself, pausing to stack up, he could hear the voices on the other side.

"I'm telling you, Bull's dead. Everyone who was out on deck is dead. Fuck, who are these guys?" The man sounded close to panic, even though his voice was muffled by the bulkhead and the hatch itself.

"Doesn't matter. We've got a good position here. We can hold 'em until Cain sends somebody." Even though the second man was clearly trying to maintain his bearing, he sounded a little shaky, too.

Wade had his ear to the hatch, right at the hinges, and looked up at Flanagan with a raised eyebrow. Flanagan shrugged slightly and kept listening, though he motioned to wait for just a second. Something was going on here, and while every instinct, honed by years behind a gun, told him that they needed to make entry and take these bastards down, all the same, he'd survived long enough to know that storming a prepared position was often asking to get shot. And there were no hostages to worry about that he knew about. That reduced the urgency of the clear. The time

151

crunch lay with how long it would take the pirates to send reinforcements.

"You think he's going to get anyone here in time?" The first man actually sounded a little calmer. "We're already behind, and we don't have more than a handful of shooters left. He's not going to risk losing any more just to get our asses out of a crack."

It wasn't lost on either Blackheart that both men were speaking English, though only one had an American accent. The other sounded vaguely Australian.

There was a pause. "Just what are you thinking about, Colt?"

Another pause. "I think you know."

"What makes you think that I'm going to let you?"

A moment later, a series of gunshots hammered in the space beyond the hatch. Wade kicked the door open—it was another of the hollow-core doors, not a steel ship's hatch—and then Flanagan went through the opening fast, his eye just above his red dot, checking hands, looking for weapons.

All but one of the men in gray on the bridge, however, had dropped their weapons and thrown themselves on the deck, their hands out in front of them. The one man who hadn't was in the process, down on a knee, halfway to the deck, and froze as the Blackhearts burst onto the bridge. He slowly raised the R4 over his head by its forearm, before lowering it very slowly and carefully to the deck.

The man who'd been shot was sprawled on his back, staring sightlessly at the overhead, lying in a spreading pool of blood, still twitching. It looked like a burst had been walked up his torso, tearing through his guts, across his plate, and into his throat.

"We surrender!" The man closest to the corpse kept his face pointed at the deck, his hands stretched out in front of him, far from the rifle he'd dropped. "Don't shoot!"

For a brief moment, as he scanned the bridge over his rifle, Flanagan half thought that Wade was just going to waste everyone in the compartment anyway. Technically, there was

152

nothing stopping them. These were pirates, and the Blackhearts weren't cops.

Wade held his fire, though, even as Flanagan tallied what they'd found.

Crewmen in civilian clothes were huddled against the sides, down on their knees with their hands on their heads. There were about ten of them, which, when combined with the gray-clad shooters, made for a very crowded bridge. None of them *appeared* to be armed, but with pirates, looks could be deceiving. They'd have to be searched.

He keyed his radio as Gomez and Burgess made entry, letting his rifle hang but keeping his hand on the firing control. "Kodiak, this is Woodsrunner. We've got a little problem, here."

CHAPTER 20

It took a few minutes to get everyone on the bridge down into the hold, on their knees with their fingers interlaced behind their heads, facing the outer hull, with Curtis holding security with that EVOLYS and the very real threat that he could eliminate every one of them in one burst.

The man called Colt, who'd shot his interlocutor on the bridge and forced the surrender, was now sitting in the middle of the passenger compartment on the second deck, stripped of his gear and with his hands folded in his lap, Gomez standing behind him and just offset enough that he could shoot him in the head without accidentally overpenetrating and hitting Wade.

Flanagan and Wade had quietly discussed who was going to take lead on this, and Flanagan had bowed to Wade's intimidation level. Not that Flanagan wasn't plenty dangerous on his own, but Wade just *looked* the part.

The man in gray fatigues looked like he was in his late twenties, early thirties. His hair was longish and he was trying to grow an operator beard, but he hadn't been gifted with the genetics for it. Patchy hair covered his cheeks and the tip of his chin, and the caterpillar on his lip was nothing to write home about, either. Black haired and olive-skinned, he could have been Hispanic, Italian, or just well-tanned.

His hazel eyes were fixed on Wade as the big man loomed over him. Under different circumstances, it might have been good practice for an interrogator to look as normal and non-threatening as possible. Even in his shorts, though, Wade would have been hard-pressed to make "non-threatening" work. Still geared up, in plate carrier, helmet, and with his rifle held in front of him, he wasn't even trying.

He didn't sit down, either. "Okay, start talking."

"What do you want to know?" Despite the fact that he'd apparently been scared enough by the way the Blackhearts had gone through his companions like a buzzsaw to force a surrender, even killing one of his compatriots to make it happen, the guy was still wary, still looking for a way out.

"Everything." Wade kept his stare fixed and unblinking. The icy blue of his eyes was usually unnerving enough for most people. When he locked on and didn't blink, his hands on a weapon, it got worse. "From the numbers to the ops to the intel on Fontaine. Everything you know about this entire operation. Or else I feed you to the sharks." Wade smiled, and it was not a pleasant expression. "Nobody's gonna miss you."

The pirate looked a little more nervous at that. He'd probably figured out that, as a pirate, he had no rights, especially in international waters and in the hands of mercenaries who didn't have a chain of command beholden to some bleeding-heart politician somewhere.

And the odds that anyone would ever find out what had happened were *extremely* slim.

"I don't know that much. I was just a shooter." When Wade's expression hardened, his voice rose. "I'm serious! Cain always played things close to the chest. He only told us what we needed to know from hit to hit. We all got a big enough cut that nobody ever complained. Why would we? It was a good gig."

"Who's Cain?" Wade still showed all the emotion of a shark eying its dinner.

The man shrugged, though there was a hesitancy to the movement, and he sort of glanced over his shoulder toward

156

Gomez as he did it. He was clearly nervous about moving at all while the lean, wiry man with the rifle was behind him. "That's just what we've always called him. I have no idea if it's his real name. Like I said, it was a good enough gig that nobody asked too many questions."

"He's American?"

Another shrug. "If he's not, he's doing a hell of a good impression."

"How about you tell me a story?" If Wade was trying to be friendly all of a sudden, he wasn't fooling anyone, but Flanagan knew him well enough that he suspected the retired Ranger knew that and was just using it to ratchet up the intimidation factor even more. "Tell me everything you've done with this crew, from the beginning. Don't leave anything out."

The pirate swallowed. "I don't have to…"

"You're not getting it." Wade's voice had suddenly turned as cold as his eyes. "The only reason I'm not cutting parts off you right now is because answers start to get iffy under that kind of questioning. So, I'm giving you a chance to buy yourself some time. If you're not interested, then we can get right down to doing what gets done to pirates."

The pirate seemed to gather himself, then. "If you're going to kill me, anyway, then I don't have a lot of incentive to cooperate, do I?"

Flanagan sighed. This wasn't going according to plan, and while it seemed like the pirates didn't think that this Cain was going to come back for them, they still couldn't afford to hang out aboard this ship for long. "If you cooperate, we might leave you with some chance of getting recovered. Leave us with nothing, and we've got no reason to leave you alive at all."

The pirate dared look away from Wade long enough to look at Flanagan and searched his expression as if looking for any thread of hope. Flanagan saw a swirl of fears, hopes, and a sort of stubborn, angry pride in the man's eyes. He showed no reaction to any of it, but maintained his own stoic stare, until the pirate seemed to deflate.

"I got a call from a friend I'd worked maritime security with about a year ago. He said there was a new job, one that was going to pay a whole lot more than anything we'd ever made before. It was also going to be rad as fuck, he said. We'd get to do real cool board and seizure stuff and get paid for it."

He shrugged. "I wasn't going to pass it up. I'd been working these shit jobs with shit gear, for shit pay for *years*. I signed up. We had to sign an NDA and everything. Then we boarded a boat and headed out to sea.

"Turns out that Cain had found this old, derelict cruise ship. He'd fixed it up and was living aboard it, out at sea, never going into any country's territorial waters. That's the base." He paused. "It had to have taken a *lot* of money to get it fixed up like that. I guess it had been adrift for years."

"Are all the contractors Americans?" Flanagan felt Wade glance at him at his use of the term "contractors," but there was a certain balance to be struck here. He had no intention of letting these animals back out to prey on the innocent further, but he had to coax as much useful information out of this guy as possible, and as the pirate had pointed out, he had no incentive to talk except to prolong his life a little bit longer. If he felt somewhat more comfortable, he might talk a little more freely.

The pirate looked at Wade, then back at Flanagan, trying to read the room. Fortunately, the three Blackhearts present were probably the best poker players on the team. Or, they would be, if Flanagan ever played poker.

"No." He tried to relax, but it was obviously an act. "I mean, just judging by the way some guys talk, I don't think so. It's not like we're all that buddy-buddy."

"Really." Wade glanced up at the overhead, by implication looking toward the dead body on the bridge, which they still hadn't moved. "No honor among thieves, huh?"

"Hey, the people who owned the cargos we've gone after ain't exactly nuns, you know?" Flanagan thought it was a little strange that the pirate seemed to want to justify the attacks now, but he supposed it stood to reason. "They can afford the losses, anyway." He paused. "Well, I guess some of them could."

"What does that mean?" Wade had picked up on the same thing Flanagan had. There was more to this than just piracy. Otherwise, this Cain and his crew would have gone after easier prey.

The pirate seemed to have started to relax. Maybe he'd decided that Wade's threats had been bluster, and that he really was in the hands of Americans who wouldn't dream of stringing a bunch of pirates up to make an example of them. *Little does he know…*

"So, apparently one of the targets we hit first belonged to some finance bigwig. I never found out any details—except that it was a hell of a take; we could probably all have retired to the Bahamas or something with what we got from that one—but I guess it was even more valuable to the owner. He lost some big deal because of it."

The pirate suddenly froze as Wade's eyes narrowed. He must have realized that he'd just said a little too much.

"Any idea who this owner was?" Flanagan asked quietly.

For a moment, the man in gray just looked from one of the Blackhearts to the other, almost like he was looking for a way out. Wade shifted his position, just a little, his muzzle coming up only a fraction of an inch, but it was enough.

"The ship and the cargo both belonged to Mitsuo Takahashi. He wasn't on board, but the hit he took from losing that cargo almost bankrupted his company. Or so I heard."

Flanagan nodded. The pieces were falling into place.

As he did, boots rang on the deck, and he turned to see Burgess stick his head in. "The yacht's getting close, and the sun's almost up. We need to go soon."

"We'll be down in a minute," Flanagan assured him. "You get the mechanics taken care of?"

Burgess nodded with a faint grin. "All set. They had plenty of tools for it."

"Good." Flanagan looked at the pirate, who was getting nervous. "Well, you've lucked out. Because you cooperated, we aren't going to just line you up against the bulkhead and shoot you. The people you robbed might not be good guys, but that doesn't touch on the crews you murdered. By all rights, I *should* just shoot you all. But instead, we're going to leave you aboard this crate." He glanced aft. "There should be enough food and water in the galley to last you a while. We've just smashed all the radios and the transponder." The deck shuddered under their feet and a distant *boom* reverberated through the hull. "You don't have any engines anymore, either."

He turned toward the hatch. "If you're lucky, somebody will come along before you run out of food and water."

"Wait, you can't do this!" The pirate started to surge to his feet, until he felt the cold, hard touch of Gomez's muzzle at his back. He subsided back into the seat. "We're in the middle of nowhere!"

"You should have thought of that before you started raiding ships and killing crews." Flanagan paused in the hatchway and looked over his shoulder. "Maybe the ocean will have some pity on you."

Wade watched the man over his rifle as Gomez passed him, heading below, toward the hold and the launches they'd used to board. Only when he finally turned to follow, closing the hatch behind him, did he turn away.

The look on the pirate's face was a combination of rage and despair, the last any of the Blackhearts saw.

***

The pirates and the crew watched the Blackhearts get back into the yacht's launches, keeping their hands on their heads, fingers intertwined. There was more than a little resentment in those looks, not to mention quite a bit of fear. Not only had they heard the destruction of the engines, and could already probably feel the ship drifting, but they'd watched Burgess systematically disable every small boat in the hold except for the Blackhearts'

160

and transfer all the fuel to the launches. There would be no escape that way.

It might have been cruel, when Flanagan thought about it, setting these men adrift this way. If they weren't picked up, they were doomed to a slow, lingering death from hunger and thirst.

There was a chance that they might be picked up, though. A thorough sweep of the vessel had turned up what they hoped was all the weapons and ammo. Most of that was now aboard the launches, which was part of why the sun had now been up for nearly an hour. Whatever they hadn't been able to take, they'd thrown overboard.

So, at least if the pirates did get picked up, they wouldn't be able to take whatever ship found them by force.

Wade hadn't said a word about it, but he wouldn't have had any problem with just summarily executing the lot of them. Gomez probably wouldn't have, either, though despite his quiet violence, he'd never been as overtly bloodthirsty as Wade. There was something about it that meant Flanagan just couldn't bring himself to it, though. He was pretty sure that, if they'd caught the pirates in the act of slaughtering a crew, he probably wouldn't even have hesitated.

It bothered him a little, even as they pulled out of the well deck, leaving the cargo ship dead in the water behind them. Had he made the right call? Or had he just condemned fifteen men to a tortuous death rather than get his hands dirty?

He couldn't say for sure. A part of him thought that was exactly what he'd just done. Another part thought that they didn't have the numbers or the resources to secure that many prisoners, he couldn't just turn them loose, and he wasn't entirely convinced that just lining them up against the wall and mowing them down wouldn't be cold-blooded murder. Even in the old days, pirates had still gotten a trial, short and summary though it might have been.

Maybe Brannigan would have a different idea. But it had been Flanagan's call, and he'd made it.

They sped away through the swell, the pirate ship receding behind them, heading back toward the *Dream Empire*.

***

Brannigan scratched his head. "Takahashi?" He squinted at the yacht's captain. "Why does that name ring a bell?"

Captain Mills sighed. "Because Mitsuo Takahashi was one of Mr. Fontaine's main rivals in finance, back a few years ago when he was first becoming a powerhouse in the money world. Takahashi took some serious losses from some cargoes that never got where they were supposed to go and went bankrupt shortly thereafter."

Brannigan and Santelli shared a look. "Well, there it is." Santelli shook his head. "If that's not confirmation that Fontaine's trying to clean up after himself, I don't know what is."

"It certainly looks that way." Brannigan frowned, staring out through the forward windscreen at the ocean beyond. The *Dream Empire* was still only about midway across the Atlantic. There were still several days to go before they got near Fontaine's purported island getaway. He took a deep breath. "All the same…" He tapped a finger against his chin, thinking.

"There's still an awful lot we don't know. I want more intel before we go hammer and tongs after either Fontaine or the pirates." He mused for a moment. "We've got a couple of days yet. Keep the recon flights going. I want to know where the rest of those pirates are, if possible.

"In the meantime, I've got a couple of calls to make."

CHAPTER 21

El Salvaje might have started his life as a street urchin in a major city, but he'd learned from that experience, and he'd built on that foundation through all the operations he'd taken part in and then run over the years since. He was a chameleon now, a man who could blend in anywhere.

The Canary Islands were easy. There were plenty of people of his skin tone, and most of them spoke Spanish. He had to adjust his accent and dialect a little, but he'd been through the Islands before, so that didn't take long, either.

He'd flown ahead, establishing himself as a tourist from Spain a full day before Cain was due to arrive. After he'd cooled down a little, the pirate chief had allowed that El Salvaje would be better suited to conduct their advance reconnaissance. Cain and most of his shooters weren't exactly low-profile. They were doorkickers and killers, and few of them were practiced at the kind of gray man tactics that would be necessary to avoid detection, especially if Fontaine's security was on alert. And after the abortive attack on the yacht, plus the obvious fact that Fontaine had *expected* it, they were guaranteed to be on alert.

So, the shooters would wait out at sea while the short, slender, unassuming man who could have hailed from any country on either side of the Mediterranean did the groundwork.

He was pretty sure he'd spotted the boat from Fontaine's island the evening before. While it was nothing like the size of the *Dream Empire*, the yacht was still pretty big, sleek and fast. It had tied up on the wharf just next to the Los Cristianos ferry terminal, dominating most of the dock, and half a dozen men had gotten off and headed into the city, three of them obviously armed under their loose, light-colored shirts. Unlike the pirates, these guys weren't geared up in gray fatigues, or any kind of uniform at all, but El Salvaje had been both an infiltrator and a counter-infiltrator, depending on where he'd been working at the time. He could spot security with a glance, and these guys were it. They watched everything carefully, and the way they carried themselves was wary and ever so slightly tense, ready to move into action in a moment.

Not all security contractors acted like that. Even the elite, the guys headhunted from special operations forces around the world, weren't always on edge. In fact, the really good ones could be alert without ever looking like it. These guys weren't quite on that level.

El Salvaje reflected on it as he fell into a loose follow behind them, while the six men, far too bunched up to keep a low profile, headed into the city. The streets were narrow, overshadowed by close-set, multi-story buildings, but that group was obvious enough that he wasn't worried about losing them. Even if he lost contact for a few moments, it wouldn't be too difficult to intercept them again.

It was clear that Fontaine's people knew that the yacht had been hit. They also had to know that their trap had failed, despite the fact that it had gotten a lot of the pirates killed. If nothing else, that explained their knife-edged alertness on the ground.

Despite their state of watchfulness, they didn't practice the greatest of tradecraft. They didn't spread out at all, but maintained their almost-military formation as they made a beeline uphill, hardly changing direction at all as they went. They were still on foot, but they were heading somewhere deeper in the city, and they were going there with a purpose.

164

El Salvaje maintained contact, never quite looking directly at them. Reading his targets carefully, even while only observing them through his peripheral vision, he was reasonably certain that he hadn't been picked out of the crowd.

That was what he'd expected, but if he had been, he would have needed to step up his skills. It was good to know that he hadn't slipped over the last few months aboard ship.

He had learned never to try to predict the target's movements to the point that he would try to be clever and get too far ahead. So, he didn't bother to attempt to read where they were going, but just went with the flow, trailing them at a comfortable distance.

Still, it was getting late in the day. Almost as if they'd deliberately sailed in as the sun was going down to avoid notice. They'd failed, especially through their lack of tradecraft, but they'd tried.

So, he wasn't that surprised when they turned into the Oasis Bar and Bistro.

Smoothly, as if he'd intended to go there the entire time, he slid into the next-door Mendez and Montesinos Restaurant, finding a table where he could watch the Oasis without being obvious about it. He ordered some food and a drink and settled in to get comfortable.

Like just about any other tourist, he pulled a phone out of his pocket as soon as he sat down. He could watch the Oasis out of the corner of his eye while still reading the phone.

He didn't contact Cain, though.

Are you on the ground?

Si.

We need to meet. Where we talked about.

When?

I'll let you know. I'm watching some targets for current employer right now.

There was no reply. There wouldn't be, nor was one needed. They understood each other.

He lingered over the meal and the wine. He'd never been a heavy drinker, but nor had he been a teetotaler like some revolutionaries he'd known. There was something to be said for maintaining one's control, but if it came at the expense of standing out when one needed to blend in, it was a liability.

If he'd hoped to follow Fontaine's people to their final destination, and possibly separate one from the herd, he was doomed to disappointment. They stayed in the Oasis for hours, finally coming out just before midnight, the three non-security types obviously inebriated, the security just as obviously irritated and on-edge. They staggered up the steps and around the corner to the Casa Rosy, where they checked in and headed upstairs.

El Salvaje strolled down the street, watching and listening. One of Fontaine's people was loud when he was drunk, and he didn't appreciate having been dragged away from a pretty girl in the bar.

"We don't even have to be back at the boat until tomorrow night!" Judging by how slurred the man's words were, it was probably a miracle he could stand upright. "What's the hurry?"

He couldn't hear the security man's reply, but whatever it was, the man was clearly at the end of his patience. The drunk let out a yelp as an iron grip closed around his upper arm, and the security man propelled him rapidly and roughly inside.

El Salvaje carefully analyzed what he'd just seen and heard as he continued his stroll without a pause. Unless the security types were going out on mission after their charges were passed out, it looked like the group had gone to ground for the night. Possibly a good part of the next day.

He doubted that those security knuckle-draggers would be allowed to leave their charges. If he was reading them right—and he was pretty sure he was—they were babysitters, not operators.

That meant he had the rest of the night to get some things done.

It wasn't as if he slept much, anyway.

He continued downhill, but soon doubled back, heading north until he came to a salmon-colored apartment building on a

166

streetcorner, that would have overlooked the ocean to the west if it hadn't been for the equally tall building just across the street.

El Salvaje didn't care about the view. He let himself in and headed upstairs to the upper apartment.

The woman inside was shorter than he was, and downright petite. She could pass for just about any Mediterranean ethnicity, just like he could, at least at first glance, though his practiced eye easily saw the Mayan heritage in her features.

She was also armed, with an old Skorpion machine pistol on the table in front of her. She didn't relax when El Salvaje came through the door, but she didn't reach for the weapon, either.

As he stepped into the kitchen, she rose and stepped in close. "I was surprised to hear from you." Like their text messages, she was speaking Maya, rather than Spanish. No one in this part of the world was likely to understand it. "Is this job not working out?"

He kissed her. "It has been good, but things are happening. It will not last much longer."

She raised an eyebrow. "Inside or outside?"

He thought about it a moment. "Possibly both. Cain is not entirely stable." He didn't mention that few of the people he'd worked for over the years had been. It was an occupational hazard of working for revolutionaries and other non-state actors like cartels.

Not that any psychiatrist would ever consider the man known as El Salvaje to be especially stable. The same could be said for the woman who was currently putting her tongue down his throat as she melted into him, her arms around his neck.

He knew all of this, and he had never especially cared. He'd ended up in this life to survive, and he'd do what it took not only to survive but to get as rich as possible in the process.

It wasn't as if there was any other way open to him. He would be executed quickly if any of the legitimate authorities every found out who he was.

Of course, he knew enough about those legitimate authorities to know they were really no better than he was.

167

He disengaged himself, and she turned back to the table. "Fortunately, when I *did* hear from you, I thought that this might be the case." She tapped an envelope on the table. "Everything is set, *if* you need to make a sudden exit."

"I knew I could count on you." The two of them had been together, off and on, since both had been teenagers. She was as resourceful a woman as he'd ever known—and as vicious a killer when it came to it.

"When do you need to go?" The meaning in her words was evident in the look she gave him.

He smiled. "In a few hours."

***

"Thanks for getting back to me so fast, Hector." Brannigan leaned back in his chair. He'd hesitated to take the yacht's master suite as his own, but Santelli had all but insisted. Vehemently. Fortunately, being in the bow, the satellite phone had good reception. He *could* have used the yacht's considerable onboard communications suite, but that wasn't a risk he was willing to take. If *he* were Fontaine, he'd have backdoors on everything, just in case. Especially if he was leaving the yacht to someone else.

"Well, I *did* get you into this." It was early morning where Hector Chavez was, but he sounded awake. He also didn't sound happy. "It's the least I could do."

"Give it to me straight."

Chavez sighed. "Abernathy doesn't have a team anywhere in the region that could be there in time to make a difference. I've got a crew about two days away, and I can try to get them close to back you up, but they're younger guys on a milk run, and they don't have the kind of hardware that you'd need. They wouldn't be much more than a speed bump. They're aboard so the insurance company is comfortable, not because the client's worried about actual pirates."

"Doesn't seem all that wise, considering the ships that have been disappearing," Brannigan mused.

"That's why you do what you do, and generally stay out of this cluster, John." Chavez wasn't happy about it. "The red tape and bullshit in this industry is out of control."

"What *can* you get me?" He hadn't just asked if there was any backup available.

"Well, fortunately, while he might not be able to provide the firepower and manpower, Abernathy has plenty of access to information, and he's generally willing to share it with us. Especially, it seems, if it means you can put the hurt on a dirty billionaire who's been calling pirates in on his business rivals."

Brannigan raised an eyebrow as he stared out to sea. "That's confirmed?"

"Well, it's still mostly circumstantial, if we're being honest, but the sheer mountain of 'circumstantial evidence' is sure pointing that way. Especially since he apparently had a short-notice, high-pressure meeting with Claire MacAfee about a new prototype a month ago, left mad, and then said prototype disappeared along with the ship carrying it to France." Chavez sounded almost amused.

"That sounds awfully coincidental, all right," Brannigan allowed.

"So, yeah, we're fairly sure that he's dirty. Abernathy agrees. Furthermore, he's hired a ton of private security on his island, starting about two weeks ago, which also coincidentally was the same time that Navy anti-piracy task force went out looking for these pirates. The security on his comms is the best that money can buy, and even Abernathy's group hasn't been able to penetrate it. Not that they've been trying very hard; they've got bigger fish to fry, and this just became an issue." He heard Chavez moving some papers around. "Here we go. This is the big connection. Flanagan said that the pirates were using an old, derelict cruise ship as their mothership?"

"That's right."

"Okay, then. The *Lyubov Orlova*. Built in Yugoslavia in 1976, she was used for Antarctic cruises by the Far Eastern Shipping Company out of Vladivostok, then after the fall of the

169

Soviet Union, she was sold to Marine Expeditions, then Quark Expeditions. She passed through a couple more sets of hands after running aground, then was impounded for unpaid debts, and was being towed to the Dominican Republic to be scrapped when the tow line broke. She drifted off into the North Atlantic and is believed to have sunk after a couple months.

"However, it turns out that our friend Fontaine, through several shell companies, mounted a salvage expedition, one that most everyone else involved didn't want to risk. There are no records of the expedition's success or failure. We know it went out, we know the ships came back, and that they went out again, but that's it. No publicity at all. Best guess is that that's our pirate mothership."

Brannigan nodded, even though Chavez couldn't see. "So, Fontaine finds a derelict that nobody's looking for, fixes it up for his pirate buddies, then sics them on his business rivals, giving himself one hell of an advantage."

"At the cost of over a hundred people dead, now, by conservative estimates. Nobody has ever reappeared from any of the disappeared ships." A note of cold rage had worked its way into Chavez's voice. "Whoever he got on board, they're some cold bastards."

"From what Joe got out of that one on the Ro-Ro they took, they're mostly Americans, though I wonder how many are actual SOF guys and how many are the dregs of the maritime security industry. No offense."

"None taken." Chavez snorted. "I do my damnedest to select those guys out. Seen it too many times when I was getting started. They pull any rando with a DD214 they can get off the street, sell 'em to the client as high-speed Navy SEALs, and then rake in the dough while paying the undertrained meat puppets as little as possible." He sounded like he wanted to spit. "Again, be glad you're in the business you're in, and not this one."

"This is good info, but I need more." Brannigan and Chavez had known each other long enough that he could afford to be blunt. "What can you tell me about the island? And his security?"

"The island itself?" Chavez thought it over for a moment. "Not much. There are no plans available on any open source. I doubt even Abernathy has access high enough to get them. As near as anyone's been able to reconstruct, construction was an almost entirely compartmented affair, with a lot of the labor coming from offshore companies.

"As for security…" There was the sound of what might have been more papers being shuffled around. Chavez still liked handwritten notes, as long as he was somewhere that they wouldn't become a security risk. "Here we go. Unfortunately, I don't have solid numbers for you, there, either, but it's better than trying to find a floor plan. From what I've been able to dig up, it looks like he hired anywhere between a hundred fifty and two hundred new security personnel in the last two months."

"Hell." Brannigan leaned back in the chair and stared at the overhead. "Well, I guess that means a frontal assault's out."

There was a pause over the phone. "Don't tell me you were actually thinking of doing that."

"Not in the old Marine Corps way, no." Brannigan chewed on the problem, his eyes staring unseeing at the patterns on the overhead above him. "But just going in shooting might not work out that well. We might have to finesse this a little bit more. Play the game."

Chavez didn't answer right away, which told Brannigan that his old friend didn't think that was a good idea, either. "If he hasn't had contact with Sorley for hours…"

"Then he knows that he's probably blown." That had been a given since he'd intercepted Sorley, if he'd thought about it. "That's why the method we use to approach is important. If we come in shooting, he might be ready for it. If we sail in like babes in the woods, innocently believing that things just kind of went haywire…"

"It's a hell of a risk, John."

171

"So's everything about this job." Brannigan's mind was increasingly made up. "It's a gamble, but I think it's a better gamble than trying to commando raid our way in under cover of darkness. If we can throw him off, we might have a better chance."

"It's your hide, John. I just hope he doesn't decide to blow the charges as soon as he sees that boat."

"He can try." It was something he'd considered, which was why Hank was currently double- and triple-checking every one of them to make sure there wasn't a backup detonation system. "But I think we'll surprise him."

At least I hope we will.

CHAPTER 22

Cain met El Salvaje on the street just above the Casa Rosy, along with five of his hitters. That was probably plenty, and El Salvaje was just thinking about how much they stood out, even in civilian clothes and with their weapons in bags, when four more came up the steps from between the restaurants where he'd eaten and run surveillance only a few hours before.

Fortunately, it was still just before 0400 local time, which meant there really was no one out and about. The streetlights were still lit, though, casting their orange glow across the street and the hillside, which meant that if anyone happened to get up and look out one of the many windows in the stacked, whitewashed apartments and tenements above them, eleven men gathered on the street would look awfully strange.

"Do you know what rooms they're in?" Cain got right to the point.

"Of course." El Salvaje's reply was flat, without any of the resentment that another man in his position might have felt. Whether he felt it or not, he wasn't going to show Cain. He was fairly certain he could kill Cain and probably one or two of the others and escape to the safehouse, but it wasn't quite the time yet. This still might work out. El Salvaje had been around long enough to know better than to throw a good job aside because it *might* go sour.

173

He led the way into the Casa Rosy, acting like he was just coming in from partying and going to his own room as he walked past the reception desk. There wasn't anyone there at the moment, anyway.

The other pirates followed. If he'd been in charge, he probably would have specified that they had to enter in ones and twos, spread out over the next couple of hours. He probably would have gotten a room, but he wasn't going to do that with his own funds, and Cain hadn't provided him with the operational funds to do it. So, he had to deal with the pirates' somewhat sloppy and overconfident version of a surreptitious entry, as they gathered in the hallway outside the target rooms.

Fortunately, they didn't try to kick in the doors or otherwise make a lot of noise in the breach. Cain pointed at the first door, and one of the pirates, a wiry, sallow-faced man known to El Salvaje only as Victor, got down on one knee with a lockpick kit.

It didn't take long; Victor knew his business. El Salvaje knew next to nothing about the man, but that was par for the course with this crew. No one in such an organization had a vested interest in allowing anyone around them to know too much about themselves. None of them knew much of anything about El Salvaje either.

The lock disengaged with a click, and Victor eased the door open as the rest of the pirates drew weapons. They hadn't brought the heavy stuff, the rifles and submachineguns, but they all had pistols and plenty of reloads. So did El Salvaje, even though he'd stayed lighter and even more low-profile than the rest, with only his Star M-43 and three spare magazines. It would be enough.

Victor was being careful, just in case the targets had used the extra security lock, but the door opened without difficulty. Their prey must have thought that they were untouchable here, so close to Fontaine's island. El Salvaje was sure that Fontaine, with all his money and resources, had enough close contacts with the

Spanish government that he expected his people to have some special protection.

They padded quietly into the room as the door swung open, weapons in hand. The blinds were drawn and the lights were all out, and at least one of Fontaine's people was snoring loudly.

Cain motioned to El Salvaje, and the two of them moved on the figures on the big bed, pistols trained on them. Even the security man—there appeared to only be one in this suite—was out cold, sprawled on the couch near the door. He hadn't even stirred when the door had opened.

The two of them moved to either side of the bed. Cain's SIG P226 had a compact light attached under the barrel, and he flicked it on as they loomed over their targets.

The two men in the bed couldn't have appeared more different. One was grossly fat, pasty pale, and blond, and was sprawled on his back, breathing noisily through his fishlike mouth. The skinny one with the flock of seagulls haircut had almost been crowded off the side of the bed, but was also out cold, unresponsive to even the light.

El Salvaje nodded. These were definitely two of the support personnel. These were the ones they wanted. The security men would probably have more information, but he knew that Cain didn't think they were worth the risk.

Cain looked over at the two gunmen covering the security contractor on the couch. He nodded.

One of the gunmen quickly holstered his pistol and pulled a garotte out of his pocket. Two more pirates also returned their weapons to their belts and moved in on the man on the couch. In one sudden movement, they pinned him down as the first man wrapped the wire quickly around the sleeping man's throat, tightening it savagely.

The man woke suddenly, but his arms and legs were already pinned and the garotte was already cutting off his airway as the wire dug deeply into his throat. He tried to free himself, but he was outweighed and outmatched, and he couldn't breathe.

It was over very quickly. The pirate hadn't used piano wire or anything else fine enough to really cut into the target's throat, so there was no blood. He still held on, keeping the garotte tight as the man went limp, maintaining the strangulation until he was sure that the target was dead.

Cain and El Salvaje waited until the murder was finished. Neither of the men on the bed stirred while it happened. Only the slightest rustle of movement had betrayed the violence happening on the couch. The garotte had been tight enough that the dead man hadn't even gotten out a grunt.

Finally, Cain reached down and tapped the fat man on the forehead, hard, with the muzzle of his pistol.

The man must have had a lot to drink. He didn't stir. Cain hit him again, harder this time, hard enough to leave a mark. That woke the man up, and he squinted into the brilliant light shining into his eyes. "What?" He put a hand up to shield his eyes. "Carter, I fucking told you."

Cain took a hand off his pistol to punch the man in the gut. "Shut your fucking mouth. Get up."

The fat man still didn't get it. "I told you, Carter…" The smell coming off the bed suggested that not only was he still half-asleep, but he was also still half drunk or better.

Cain snarled and grabbed the man by the pressure point behind his jaw. "Get up." He turned to the men standing over the dead security guard. "Bring the fucking corpse over here where this blimp can see it."

The pirates hauled the dead man up and dragged him across the suite while Cain pried the fat man up to a sitting position with the pressure point, now holding his pistol near his sternum, still pointed at his prisoner. El Salvaje, meanwhile, grabbed the skinny man, rolled him off the bed and onto his face on the floor with a jarring impact, dropping a knee into his back and pressing the muzzle of his M-43 into the base of the man's skull. "Not a sound," he hissed.

The pain of the pressure point had finally gotten through the fat man's mental fog, and he now recognized that the light

176

shining in his eyes was attached to a weapon. He whimpered a little as Cain hauled him to the foot of the bed, but another tap to the head with the pistol silenced him.

The man who only called himself Rock was holding the dead man up with the garotte. The man's face was already turning blue, his tongue bulging out of his mouth and his eyes staring and empty. Cain pointed to the corpse. "If you make one wrong sound, or even *look* at anyone we pass, that's going to happen to you. Do you understand?"

The fat man nodded, his lips flapping a little, his mouth still gaping open. El Salvaje only spared him a moment's glance, being focused on his own prisoner. The skinny man had soiled himself, and was now shaking violently underneath him. He whispered almost the same instructions as Cain had given the fat man, though he was half tempted to simply stab the little man in the neck and let him bleed out. One captive was probably going to be enough of a burden as it was.

"Move." Cain shoved the fat man toward the door. The man was still in shorts and a t-shirt, though barefoot. They only had so far to go, though, and Cain probably had decided that the discomfort might make the man cooperate more willingly once they got out to the *Lyubov Orlova*.

El Salvaje hauled his own prisoner up off the floor. "This one's going to need to change if we're not going to alert someone." The stench was already enough to make a man with a weaker stomach gag. Fortunately, El Salvaje had no such weaknesses anymore. He'd been up to his hips in blood and guts more times than he could count.

Cain glanced over with barely disguised contempt. "He's drunk." He stared at the cringing man with the flock of seagulls haircut. "Look at me." The man did as he was told, though he flinched violently when he looked into Cain's eyes. "You've had too much to drink. That's it. That's why you pissed yourself." He sniffed and wrinkled his nose. "*And* shit yourself. So act like it if you want to live."

The man nodded spasmodically, and then they were moving into the hall. So far, not a shot had been fired, and they were still in the clear. If they moved fast enough, they might well be back at sea before anyone figured out what had happened.

El Salvaje was mostly concerned with the local *Policia*. By the time Fontaine's support network got involved, they would be far away. He was reasonably certain, from what he'd seen, that no alert had been triggered, and no message had gotten off to Fontaine's people.

The other group of pirates were coming out of the other suite as they came back into the hallway, dragging one of the security men. They didn't have anyone else, which meant they'd killed the other security contractor and the protectee, and had taken this one despite Cain's earlier decision. Whatever had gone down in there, at least it had been quiet, but the pirates hadn't wanted to come out empty handed. Cain saw it too, and his scowl deepened, but he didn't say a word. That would come later.

Hurrying down the hallway, guns still out just in case, they headed for the street.

***

Cain's pirates might have been far better assaulters than infiltrators, but they weren't quite so unprofessional at it that they moved out of the Casa Rosy in a big formation, weapons obviously visible and captives in the center. Instead, they spread out in pairs and singletons, with Cain dragging the fat guy like he was helping a drunk friend, even though they were moving *away* from accommodations.

Fortunately, it was still early enough in the day that the street looked just as empty as they filtered out of the foyer as it had just before they'd gone in. The streetlights were still on, even as the sky got lighter in the east, but the street was deserted.

It stayed that way as they made their way by different routes toward the wharf where the boats were docked. El Salvaje broke off early, moving through a narrow alleyway with his charge.

178

If the scrawny man hoped that he might have a chance at escape since he was now alone on a shadowed street with the small, wiry man who'd thrown him out of bed, El Salvaje quickly disabused him of any such ideas with an iron grip on his tricep that practically drove him to his knees. "Keep walking, keep quiet, and you get to live. Otherwise, you will become one more crime statistic." He was sure that Cain intended to kill their prisoners once they were done with them, but there was no point in panicking the shrinking, cringing *maricon* with that information.

They moved quickly down the hill, as quickly as the close-packed cityscape allowed. He hadn't gotten more than a couple of blocks before he noticed that the other pirates were beginning to converge already. He had just turned aside, intending to swing around to the east, when a shot rang out.

The sound was a warning as it echoed across the city and the mountains behind. El Salvaje cursed. He knew exactly what had happened. One of the pirates had just crossed the local cops.

Propelling his charge ahead of him with a tightening grip on his arm, El Salvaje broke into a run. It was entirely possible that the local *Policia* might not be prepared enough to lock down the city before they could get clear, but he wasn't going to chance it. Even if the rest of Cain's little strike force got rolled up, El Salvaje intended to be on that boat.

If he had to murder his charge and fade back into the city, taking up his contingency plan, he could do that, too. Even if it meant killing more of the pirates to get clear.

He'd done it before.

They ran through the narrow, twisting streets, his captive stumbling a couple of times. El Salvaje deciding to take a more direct path rather than the serpentine, more elusive route that he'd wanted. Several more gunshots *crack*ed in the early morning quiet, and he knew that he had to get to that boat, fast.

If he didn't make it there in time, he was sure that they'd probably cast off without him.

He'd have to take his revenge if that happened, but it was better not to miss the boat.

179

They came out onto the beach past the Burger King, and then they were running flat out for the wharf. His prisoner had apparently decided that if he didn't keep up, El Salvaje was going to kill him, which was a reasonable expectation. He certainly wasn't going to slow down, nor was he going to leave this little worm behind to potentially identify him.

The number of people still breathing who could identify him could be counted on one hand. The pirates could identify him, sort of, but they would come after him themselves, and they also knew enough to be aware that he could easily make that a losing proposition.

The sand was relatively hard packed, since high tide hadn't been that long ago. It was an easy enough run to the wharf. They weren't alone, either, as a growing formation of pirates, guns in hand, converged on the boat.

Cain was in the lead, hauling the fat guy by main strength. For his part, the fat guy was slowing down, dragging at Cain, and looked like he was pleading for his life. He knew that there was no going back once he was aboard that boat.

One of the last of the pirates came out onto a small brick-paved plaza just above the beach, next to the Cafeteria Bahia Restaurante, and turned back for a moment. He dumped the remainder of his pistol's magazine at someone uphill. The bark of the weapon was achingly loud, despite the rising voices shouting about the violence that had been unleashed on the quiet streets of Los Cristianos.

The fat man was down on his knees, blubbering. Cain, his face a mask of frustration and rage, suddenly turned, put his P226's muzzle to the man's forehead, and pulled the trigger.

It happened too fast for the fat man to shake his head or try to dodge. Red spray spattered from the back of his skull as the 9mm bullet punched straight through, and he collapsed, the puckered hole between his eyes smoking faintly.

Cain cursed as El Salvaje closed in with his own prisoner. The pirate chief looked at his top mercenary with burning eyes.

"That one had better be worth it." Then they were running down the wharf toward the boat.

El Salvaje quickly suppressed the flash of rage at Cain's redirection. *He* hadn't been the one to pick the fat guy, nor had he been the one to just murder him. El Salvaje didn't know any of Fontaine's personnel, but he knew that Cain did. If this was a dead end, it was on Cain, not him.

Not that the man would ever accept that.

They got aboard the boat without any further engagements. In fact, no one followed the last man down onto the plaza. El Salvaje hoped that meant that the man had killed his pursuer, rather than the other possibility, that he'd simply been shooting at shadows.

As the boat roared away from the pier, sirens beginning to wail in the city behind them, Cain turned to the captured security man.

"If you want to live, you're going to tell us where exactly Joshua Fontaine is, and every detail you can remember about his island, his mansion, and the current security he's got on it." He pulled a karambit from his belt. "Make damned good and sure you don't even give me the *impression* that you might be lying."

As the boat bounced over the waves, leaving the city and the island behind, the man began to talk.

CHAPTER 23

"Come on over, Joe." Brannigan had moved to the bow and was leaning on the rail, staring out to sea, thinking as the sun came up.

Flanagan moved to join him. None of them had dressed down since they'd first taken contact, and he was still in his plate carrier and carrying his MCX Virtus. He scanned the ocean, then turned and leaned against the rail, taking up a position where he could watch the deck behind them. Flanagan hadn't quite reached the point where he trusted any of the crew they still had aboard. "What's on your mind, John?"

Brannigan filled him in on the conversation with Chavez. The Blackhearts' second in command scratched his thick, black beard thoughtfully.

"Sounds like a plan to me. We've certainly gone ahead on thinner intel. So, what's bugging you?"

Brannigan chuckled grimly. "Maybe I'm getting old. There's no way forward that doesn't look like a suicide mission."

Flanagan thought about it. "What else is new? Just about every place we've gone into, we shouldn't have been able to get out. This is no different. We scope the place out ahead of time and figure out the lay of the land. If it looks like they're alerted, then we sneak in commando style. If not, then we do the Trojan Horse thing we talked about."

Brannigan shook his head. "Whichever way we go in, if we're going to try to take that island, it's going to be tough, regardless."

Flanagan was thinking, though. "We don't really have to *take* the island." His eyes were narrowed, staring off at nothing, though they would sharpen to focus on any movement coming from the superstructure in a heartbeat. "I mean, Fontaine doesn't *know* that we're onto him. Sorley didn't exactly get any messages off before Wade smoked him in the head."

"What are you thinking?" Brannigan knew when his younger second in command was onto something, and he knew to encourage it when he saw it. Not that Flanagan needed the encouragement, but it was a habit that Brannigan had cultivated as a Marine officer, especially after having seen far too many of his brother officers do the opposite while he'd been an NCO, himself.

"I'm thinking that the Trojan Horse plan might be best, regardless." Flanagan turned to Brannigan as he spoke, the idea becoming more fleshed out in his mind by the moment. "He hasn't heard from Sorley, and we just say that Sorley was killed when the pirates hit the yacht. It's not *technically* a lie, provided we just say it was the same day. He didn't leave any follow-on instructions—which he didn't—so we figured that we'd done our part of the job and continued on. If he's really desperate about these pirates, he might just accept it and put us into the security rotation. Then we have a little bit of a chance to snoop around. Worst case scenario, we take the pirates out, get paid, and go home with enough intel to bring Fontaine down legally."

"I know for a fact that's not the worst-case scenario you cooked up." Brannigan turned back toward the ocean.

Flanagan laughed quietly. "Well, no. The worst-case scenario is we all end up dead. Naturally. This is worst-case *success.*"

"And what if he *did* try to detonate all that PETN belowdecks?" It had been bugging Brannigan since Burgess had found them. "He's going to know something's off."

184

"He'll suspect." Flanagan had thought of that, too. "But maybe something went haywire. Like I said, if he thinks that the pirates are coming for him, is he really going to turn aside eleven shooters who already killed a bunch of them?"

"You've got a point," Brannigan allowed, "but you're also assuming that he's going to act rationally. If he's scared enough, he probably won't. And how many of these billionaires are you familiar with who are actually sane?"

"Precious few," Flanagan admitted. "Still, he's got enough brains to cook up this whole scheme, and the fact that he's trying to eliminate the pirates he stood up—presuming that's actually what's going on—means that he has enough of a sense of self-preservation to do anything to save his own ass. We can take advantage of that."

"You hope." From the tone of his admonition, Flanagan could tell that while Brannigan was leaning toward his suggested course of action—it *was* a sound plan—he wasn't *entirely* convinced. It *was* kind of a wild card plan, and a more straightforward clandestine infiltration might be safer. "We don't know anything about this guy except for his carefully groomed public profile and what we've found out from his people and Chavez. If he really did intend for us to get killed, he might accept our story at face value to draw us in. Then this whole thing will blow up in our faces as soon as we sail within sight of that island."

"Could be." Flanagan shrugged. "In which case, we kill everybody and run. It's worked before."

Brannigan chuckled dryly and clapped his second-in-command on the shoulder. "So it has." He sobered as he turned back toward the water. "I just hope that we can get ashore and look around a bit before it comes to that."

Flanagan nodded grimly. He was probably thinking the same thing.

Thinking about just what kind of weapons a man with Fontaine's resources could buy, and if he'd already considered the yacht expendable, what else might he do if he felt threatened?

***

185

Brannigan watched the island through binoculars from the bridge as they got closer. It was nearly nightfall, the sun having disappeared behind a line of clouds to the west, over the ocean, and the island was shrouded in shadow.

Not that it was dim. Bright lights spilled actinic white beams onto the lawn in front of the massive estate that covered almost half of the rocky island itself. It was still early for such lighting, which suggested that Fontaine was worried.

Of course he was worried. He had just turned on a particularly advanced group of pirates, and something had already gone wrong.

"Well, there it is." Captain Perkins sounded nervous, as well he might. He'd sailed halfway across the Atlantic on a floating bomb that had been rigged up by his employer, who apparently considered everyone aboard expendable. "He's calling."

"Answer it." Brannigan took a deep breath and turned to watch the captain, keying his radio as he did so. "Stand by. This could get real in a second."

The captain lifted the phone. It was less a phone and more a satcom station, but it worked as a phone when need be. "This is the *Dream Empire*." He paused, going a little pale. "Yes, sir. Yes, sir. Uh." He glanced at Brannigan, who nodded. "I'm afraid Mr. Sorley isn't aboard, sir. He… uh…"

Brannigan tensed slightly, feeling every nerve suddenly on edge, his hand ready to snatch that MCX up in case the captain sold them out. If he told Fontaine that the Blackhearts had killed Sorley…

But the captain knew what was at stake. "He was shot, sir, sometime around the pirate attack. He didn't leave any instructions past that point, so, well…" He took a deep breath. "We continued on, since the pirates broke contact after they took significant casualties." Captain Perkins wasn't military, to the best of Brannigan's knowledge, so he must have practiced that line.

He listened for a moment. "Yes, sir. No, he was the only one. Yes, sir." He finally put the handset down with an explosive sigh. "Well, he wants us to bring her in. There's a special spot at the end of the quay just for the *Dream Empire*."

"Did he buy it?" Captain Perkins had been read in on his part of the plan, at least, and Brannigan decided he could trust him that far. He'd played his part. Of course, he'd probably been afraid that Wade would shoot him if he didn't, but still.

"I think so. He's hard to read at the best of times, but he didn't really *sound* suspicious." Perkins had become increasingly comfortable with voicing his own suspicions that Fontaine had bankrolled the pirates, and he was at least doing a good job of playing the role of a man who was all in for the sake of his own vindication.

"Well, I guess we'll see." Brannigan turned and headed below. "If his people start shooting as soon as we come into range, we'll know he didn't buy it."

He found Flanagan, Wade, and Burgess already at the side, though they were standing behind the raised gunwale, watching the approaching quay through the portholes in the hull. It wasn't *cover*, but concealment by itself could present an advantage if the enemy didn't know they were there.

It took a while to bring the yacht in. The monstrosity of a vessel was nearly the size of a naval destroyer, and it took a delicate hand at the helm to make sure she didn't smash into the quay with enough force to sink her and permanently damage the pier itself. The Blackhearts, now lined up along the port side, except for Hank and Doc Puller, who'd drawn the short straw and had to watch the starboard side, just in case there was any trickery in play, watched and waited in silence, weapons ready. Just in case.

A small welcoming party was already on the quay, watching the yacht approach. Several of them were clearly support personnel, but about half were just as obviously security, geared up and armed the same as the Blackhearts, with plate carriers, helmets, and MCX Virtus carbines. Apparently, either Sorley or whoever had been above him in Fontaine's security hierarchy really liked that loadout.

As the yacht slowed and finally came to full stop right next to the pier, and mooring lines were tossed out, another figure came striding briskly down the quay, flanked by two more shooters with MCXs. Those looked shorter, Brannigan saw in the light over the quay. Probably Rattlers, the super-short SBR version of the MCX. They were also suppressed, which the Blackhearts' rifles were not.

In that brief pass under the light, Brannigan had also seen that the man in the middle was Joshua Fontaine. *So, he* is *here.*

The gangplank was run out, and Brannigan, his rifle slung but his hand on the firing control, led the way down. Fontaine was standing off to one side, flanked by his security detail, his arms folded.

As the Blackhearts filed down the gangplank, alert and ready without really *looking* like it, Brannigan studied their employer. Fontaine was clearly trying to look imposing and in control, but he was nervous, his foot tapping and his mouth working a little. He probably hoped that it wasn't obvious, but to someone with Brannigan's experience, he might as well have been screaming.

"Who's in charge?" Fontaine at least kept his voice level as he stepped forward.

"I am." Brannigan was watching the billionaire's security detail as much as he was watching the man himself. They were younger men, all noticeably younger than the Blackhearts except for Hank, and they were just as clearly on edge as Fontaine was. No, not quite. They were professionals, that much was clear. One of them, the youngest in appearance by far, was downright relaxed, but it was that kind of alert relaxed that Brannigan had only seen in the most consummate professional warriors. He let his eyes linger on that kid for a moment. That one could be a serious threat.

Or an asset, depending on how this fell out.

"I'm Joshua Fontaine." The billionaire entrepreneur—and possibly international criminal—stuck out his hand. Brannigan shook it, unimpressed by the limp, cold clamminess of the man's handshake.

"John Brannigan." He motioned to the men behind him, who had spread out quietly and casually across the quay, relaxed but ready for action if it came. They were all entirely too aware of just how expendable Fontaine had apparently considered them. "This is the rest of my crew, minus a couple who are still on security aboard."

Fontaine looked around the group of them and his eyes widened a little, even as Brannigan saw the calculation going on behind them. "This is it? You must have taken some serious losses in the attack."

Brannigan shook his head. "Not exactly. Sorley was it."

He saw Fontaine freeze, just for a split second. "About that. What happened?"

Brannigan had been thinking about just how to deal with this for a while. Finally, he'd decided to be up-front and honest and see what that shook loose.

"He turned on us, shortly after we'd repelled the pirates. Tried to jump Wade." He jerked a thumb over his shoulder at the big man looming behind him. "He paid for it."

If Fontaine had been thinking hard before, now he was seriously reconsidering his options. He was good at hiding it, but Brannigan could tell that there was a lot of cold, emotionless calculation going on there. This man was dangerous.

"Is that right?" He rubbed his chin. "Well, that does put a new spin on things. I knew that the pirates had my organization infiltrated, but that it was Sorley..." He shook his head. "Well, I'm glad it worked out, then. If Sorley was working with the bad guys, then he got what he deserved." He turned back toward the mansion, which sprawled across the center of the island. "We're on somewhat high alert here, considering the attacks on my assets and now the yacht. As you might have suspected from the fact that I hired a body double, this has been a concern for a while now. As long as those pirates are out there—and have apparently decided to target me—we have a problem. I'm happy enough to have you

189

and your men here, and I'll gladly extend your contract for a while, until this calms down."

He glanced over his shoulder, a faint frown furrowing his brow. "I'll admit, I expected there to be more of you. The contract with Mr. Chavez stipulated a high-end security force."

"It doesn't get higher-end than my boys, Mr. Fontaine," Brannigan assured him. "Don't let the numbers fool you."

Fontaine looked back at him with open curiosity at that, but Brannigan wasn't about to tell this man about some of their previous missions. He only wanted to get him thinking about the inadvisability of crossing them.

"Well, I'm glad to have you here. I'll introduce you to the island's security coordinator, and we can get you settled in." He glanced at the *Dream Empire*, his expression unreadable even under the direct glow of the light above the quay. "I don't think it'll be safe to have you leave for a little while, given some of what's happened."

As they continued toward the massive stone house, Brannigan reflected on what exactly that meant. *Safe for us? Or safe for you?*

CHAPTER 24

The island's security coordinator was a sour-faced man by the name of Farah. He didn't look all that happy about having the Blackhearts on the island, contrary to Fontaine's eager welcome.

"Security quarters are here. It's already pretty full, so you're going to have to grab a bed where you can." He glanced over his shoulder. "You seem to already be pretty well loaded out, but there's ammo in the basement." He paused just short of the stairs that led down. "I'll show you where the armory is, but you need to make sure you stick to the armory and the other places I show you, you understand? There's some sensitive stuff down there that Mr. Fontaine doesn't want anyone getting into." He searched Brannigan's blank face, his eyes narrowed, tired, nervous.

Brannigan decided to probe a little. "Seems like an odd place to keep sensitive materials." He kept his expression neutral and his voice casual, watching Farah out of the corner of his eye. "Most financial bigshots keep their sensitive stuff in big-time banks and such."

If anything, that seemed to make Farah even more nervous. "Well, not Mr. Fontaine," he snapped, leading the way down the stairs. "He's got his reasons."

191

The man suddenly looked over his shoulder, and Brannigan saw the ghost of a haunted look flit across his face. "I'll be honest with you." His voice dropped to just above a whisper. "This ain't a good time. You'd have been better off just turning around and heading back to the States aboard that yacht."

"We haven't been paid," Brannigan said mildly. "Besides, I thought that you and Mr. Fontaine could probably use some extra security."

That seemed to shake Farah even more, and he clammed up. "Yeah, well, I guess we do." He turned away and continued down the stairs, turning onto the next flight at the landing. "We got probed by a helicopter yesterday." He sighed. "If Sorley was working for the pirates, then he probably told them something about what's down there. Now they want it, and they've got the guns to come and get it. Wherever they got those."

Something about the stiffness in Farah's voice told Brannigan that he was reciting a rehearsed story, not what he really believed. *Interesting.*

At the base of the stairs, Farah turned sharply right and led the way through a narrow doorway into what looked like a U-shaped hallway. The door directly in front was labeled "Technical Room," and Farah turned right once more, toward a blank steel door just around the corner. He tried to shield the cipher lock as he tapped in a code, but Brannigan could see enough to spot the numbers and commit them to memory.

That could well become useful, soon.

Swinging the door open, Farah ushered them inside, flipping the lights on as he went. The armory was set up almost identically to the arms room aboard the *Dream Empire*, if larger.

Since the Blackhearts were already decently well-armed, they simply went to the ammo crates against one wall and started breaking out belts and boxes of 5.56. No one said much, and Brannigan stayed near the doorway with Farah.

"If we're going to help secure this place, we're going to need a full familiarization tour," he observed.

Farah shook his head. "After talking with the captain—who had nothing but good things to say about your men and your skill, by the way—Mr. Fontaine and I agreed that your group would probably be best utilized as a quick reaction force. Why waste you guys patrolling the grounds when you might be a lot more effective as a unit to stop an incursion?"

While on the surface, that might have been common sense, or even a compliment, Brannigan thought he saw the game at work. Fontaine didn't know them and didn't trust them, and so he wanted them all held in a central position, just in case they were more than just relatively uninformed mercs.

He wasn't playing, though. "Even if we're going to act as a centrally-located QRF, we still need to know the layout of the house and grounds as thoroughly as possible." He wondered if Farah had the military experience for this gig, or if he was just being purposely obtuse *because* Fontaine didn't trust the Blackhearts. "If we get lost on the way, we're not going to do Mr. Fontaine or anyone else any good."

Farah didn't even blink. "I'll have to talk to Mr. Fontaine about it. He was pretty specific."

Of course he was. "Maybe Sorley was working for the pirates," my ass.

As soon as Santelli nodded that they had all they needed or could use at the moment, Farah ushered them out, securing the armory behind them. "I'll show you to the central security station. That will be your post until I get word otherwise from Mr. Fontaine."

Brannigan just nodded, though he noted a couple of dark looks from Wade and Santelli. Flanagan and Gomez were calm and stoic, but both men were alert, eyes checking every corner and every doorway as they passed, noticeably memorizing every square inch of their surroundings. Bianco looked nervous, and if Curtis thought he was being surreptitious about his distrust, he was failing miserably. Kirk's face was stony, not quite as hostile as Wade, but neither relaxed nor casual, either. Burgess almost mirrored Flanagan.

193

Brannigan was momentarily glad he'd left Hank aboard the yacht. The kid was good, but he was good at the kinetic side of things. They hadn't had a lot of practice in this sort of skullduggery, and he wasn't sure how well his son would do at disguising his distrust and willingness to kill everyone in the room if things went sideways. Farah was already nervous enough with Wade glaring at him.

And Fontaine clearly suspected something.

Well, I suppose fair is fair. We do, too.

Farah led them up to the top floor and out into the central hall, which was more of a gallery surrounding a central opening that looked down two floors at the main reception area, lit from above by a massive skylight. Farah led them straight to a large room on the north side of the mansion, through a pair of double doors made of some kind of blond wood.

In a normal house, that room might have been a playroom or something, but here it was a fully-equipped ready room, with two banks of monitors displaying camera feeds from all around the island, as well as what appeared to be a radar screen with a range several hundred miles out to sea. That was interesting. They'd known that Fontaine had money, but that kind of a setup required government sort of money.

He remembered what Chavez had said about Fontaine having friends. This could get tricky.

The man at the monitors wasn't wearing any kind of uniform, but was instead dressed in cargo shorts, sandals, and a Hawaiian shirt. When he pivoted around in his swivel chair, however, the Glock 19 in his waistband was clearly visible. He was a younger man, maybe in his late twenties, with long reddish hair and beard. Full sleeve tattoos covered both arms. "What up?" He eyed the Blackhearts as they filed in. "New meat?" He grinned. "Well, your timing is either perfect or terrible, depending on your perspective. Pay's gonna rock, if we live to spend it."

"Cody, these are the guys Mr. Fontaine hired to ride the *Dream Empire* out here." Brannigan took note of Farah's choice of words. "Ride" the *Dream Empire*, not "protect." If they hadn't

194

already known that the yacht had been bait, that probably would have confirmed it. "They're going to be our QRF for a while, at least until this thing with the pirates blows over. They'll stage here when they're not down on rest plan." That turn of phrase told Brannigan that Farah at least had *some* military experience.

The man called Cody looked them over appraisingly. "You want me back out on the patrol schedule?" The tone of his voice sounded a little conflicted, as if he wasn't sure if he wanted to give up his comfortable chair in the CP.

"No, you'll still be here until Eben comes to relieve you." Farah glanced at Brannigan, who gave no sign that he'd noticed. "These guys need to be ready to move fast if we get hit."

Given the fact that Fontaine's security had radar that would tell them the pirates were inbound a couple hours before they could really hit the place, that was a pretty transparent cover story. The reality was getting clearer.

They were being put where they could be watched. Fontaine hadn't bought the whole story.

Not that Brannigan had expected him to. He was increasingly convinced that Fontaine probably *had* tried to trigger the charges on the *Dream Empire* after losing contact with Sorley, and the fact that it had failed had him scared. This was already, based on the intel, a man trying to cover his tracks after he'd created a monster in a ruthless attempt to eliminate his rivals. Now he had unknown shooters, who had apparently defeated the pirates and killed Sorley, right inside his refuge. He was nervous, all right.

Farah pointed to the couches along one wall and the TV and snack bar along the opposite. "Go ahead and make yourselves comfortable. I'll get you a floor plan so you can familiarize yourself with the layout." The attempt to transparently deflect the problem of assigning a QRF without allowing a walkthrough would be laughable if the situation wasn't so dangerous. "You know where the sleeping quarters are." He checked his watch. It was getting close to an hour after sunset. "I'd only ask that at least half of you are up here at any one time."

Brannigan nodded lazily. "As per." He turned to Santelli. "Carlo, work up a watch roster, will you?" He glanced at Gomez, locking eyes with the dark, taciturn man.

Gomez's nod was infinitesimal, but Brannigan saw it. Santelli did, too.

Farah muttered something about making the rounds and slipped hastily out of the room. Cody seemed in a mood to talk, but none of the Blackhearts were. It wasn't just that it was getting late after they'd crossed the Atlantic in a week. The time change wasn't nearly as brutal as when they flew, but it was still going to be a factor for a couple of days.

Santelli finished the rotation roster. Gomez was one of the first on the sleep schedule. His face was utterly impassive as he, Burgess, Kirk, and Bianco headed out the door and for the stairs.

***

Gomez wasn't sure how easy it was going to be to slip away while inside the mansion. He felt like a trapped animal, right in the middle of the enemy's den. He knew they were being watched, and wished like hell they could have tackled this some other way. Infiltration from off at sea, using the launches, would have been far better.

He knew why Brannigan had opted for this approach, and while they were prisoners, at least they were armed prisoners. Fontaine's people probably thought that the disparity in numbers would keep the Blackhearts out of trouble.

The only question was how this was going to resolve itself. The bad guys had to assume that the Blackhearts knew too much. That was the only reason Gomez could imagine that Fontaine had welcomed them into his lair.

"Lair." If he'd been slightly more careless about his thoughts, he might have shaken his head. He'd never imagined he'd be in such a James Bond sort of scenario that he'd be in the middle of a bad guy's "lair." It was a good enough word for it, though.

He kept his eyes open as they moved down the stairs. There were security contractors, mostly in civilian attire like them,

196

but geared up the same way, sitting at each floor. That was going to make it difficult to get past and check out the basement, where the "sensitive" stuff was.

Mario Gomez was a hunter and a woodsman, as good as Flanagan, if not better. But his preferred environment was the desert and the woods, not the middle of a posh mansion on a tiny rock in the middle of the ocean. If he was going to be in a place like this, he'd rather hit it hard, fast, and with a maximum of violence.

Still, he wasn't the only one who knew the score, and he wasn't the only one looking for an opening.

Kirk stopped in the doorway as they reached the ground floor, just short of the sleeping quarters. "Hey, don't I know you?" He leaned on the door frame, looking down at the contractor sitting in a chair that he'd kicked back to lean against the wall, reading something on a tablet.

The man, dark haired and with a narrow, chinstrap beard, looked up with a frown, searching the bearded face looming over him. Kirk would be a thoroughly nondescript, utterly normal looking guy if not for the ZZ Top beard. He didn't stand out, and Gomez suspected that about half of the men he'd worked with over the years probably wouldn't remember him if they saw him in a crowd. Which was why he was currently making this guy doubt his memory.

"I don't know." The contractor put the tablet down, frowning, his head tilted as he studied the man standing over him. "Were you ever at Coronado?"

Great. A SEAL. Gomez dismissed the rest of the conversation as he surreptitiously slipped down the stairs behind Kirk's back, heading for the basement.

Unfortunately, there was another man at the base of the stairs, in a similar position as the guy Kirk had just distracted. Gomez wasn't nearly as gregarious and didn't think he'd be able to play the same game, but he had to get past this guy somehow, preferably without knifing him, which he was still entirely ready to do.

197

The man looked up as he came down the steps. "Wrong floor, bud. Sleeping quarters are up there. Nothing down here except all the machinery."

"Just looking around." Gomez kept coming. The contractor stood up and blocked the doorway.

"You must be new here. There's no 'just looking around' around here." He pointed back up the stairs. "Head back on up. Trust me, it's not worth losing the paycheck."

That alone would have confirmed Brannigan's suspicions, but he'd been tasked with scoping out the mansion, and that was what Gomez intended to do. He took another step closer. "How the hell are we supposed to secure this place when we don't know the layout?"

"The best we can." The guy wasn't having it. He held up a hand to stop Gomez in his tracks. Which was exactly what he shouldn't have done.

Gomez grabbed the extended hand as fast as he could, twisting it around and bending it the wrong way, forcing the man to turn halfway around as he gasped in pain. Gomez kicked him in the knee, driving him toward the floor as he wrenched his arm around, then landed a solid hammer fist to the base of his skull. The man went limp, just for a moment, long enough that Gomez had his opening. He let go of the hand and wrapped the man up in a triangle choke, holding it until he was good and sure that his quarry was out cold. Then he carefully returned the unconscious man to his chair, trying to prop him up as naturally as possible, not without a few glances up the stairs and out into the basement, just in case he'd been heard.

He paused, then carefully and quietly unloaded the guard's rifle and pistol, and then relieved him of his knife.

As he headed deeper into the basement, he reflected that the safer course of action probably would have been to kill the man, but he was pretty sure he was about to find something that was going to turn this into a fight, anyway.

The lights were on in the hallways, so he did what he could to look like he belonged there, despite every nerve screaming at him to hide, to move from cover to cover. He was sure he was broadcasting his nerves to the world, even though a casual observer would have simply seen another security contractor doing the rounds.

The armory was still locked, and unlike Brannigan, he hadn't seen the combination. He didn't need to check that, though. Whatever Fontaine was up to, he doubted it involved arms trafficking, though there was clearly *some* of that going on, just to equip the pirates.

Most of the doors down there were cipher locked. He knew how to get past those locks, but without knowing what—or who—was on the other side, it wasn't quite worth the risk. He listened at a couple of them, but either the doors were too thick to let sound through, or there was no sound to be heard.

He worked his way across the basement, after glancing in the pool room and then passing locked door after locked door. Some of the doors weren't cipher locked, and they proved to be storage or equipment rooms, just like the man at the base of the steps had said.

He still smelled a rat.

Another steel door, cipher locked like the rest, stood at the end of the short hallway. He'd moved carefully through the shadows at the wall, since there was an opening to the main reception area above, and anyone up there could have looked down and seen him. Fortunately, there didn't appear to be anyone up there at the moment, and if the basement was as off limits as Farah and his cronies had made it sound, then the other contractors probably avoided that opening, just to keep their jobs.

As he neared the door, he thought he heard voices. Without a sound, he moved up to the door and put his ear close to the crack, listening.

"I don't trust them." He didn't recognize the voice. The man spoke with a faint lisp, and Gomez was certain he hadn't heard him before.

199

"I *did* hire them to hunt pirates. They'll get to hunt pirates. As long as we pay them enough, they shouldn't ask questions." That was definitely Fontaine.

"Do you really believe that?"

Fontaine sighed. "No." There was a pause. "Sorley wouldn't have made a move unless he thought we were blown. The fact that they got him…" Another pause, and when Fontaine spoke again, he sounded scared. "Who are these guys? Sorley was the best. They *shouldn't* have gotten the drop on him."

"It doesn't matter." The man with the lisp seemed to be thinking. "We've got a couple of options. We keep our noses clean while they're here, and hopefully they won't have an excuse to move until it's too late. We get somebody back aboard the yacht and rewire the charges. Better yet, move them so they don't find them again. That was sloppy, and I blame Sorley for that entirely.

"Then, we wait for Cain to get here and throw them into the most untenable position on the beach we can get, and hope that that takes care of both our problems. These guys are obviously professionals, but Cain won't make the same mistake twice. He'll be ready the next time."

"And if that doesn't work?" Fontaine was getting impatient. "That many shooters should have been overwhelmed by Cain's strike force. That was the whole plan; to get that floating bomb alongside the *Lyubov Orlova*. Instead, they didn't take a single loss, apparently killed a bunch of Cain's people, defused the charges, *and* killed Mark Sorley, which wasn't easy, I'll let you know."

"If that doesn't work, then we pay them off, make sure that we have a kill switch on all the *Dream Empire*'s comms, let them get halfway across the Atlantic, and blow the ship. Tragic loss. Probably happened because a pirate ship slipped through the net."

Gomez's first thought wasn't about getting back to the rest of the Blackhearts to warn them. Instead, like the predator he was, his first thought was how to get into that room and kill both Fontaine and the man with the lisp.

Fortunately, however, he'd gotten pretty good at suppressing that animal urge to find the nearest threat and rip its throat out. Easing back from the door, his weapon ready, he padded quickly back toward the stairs.

Despite the fact that he was still moving deliberately and stealthily, he was now on alert and carefully clearing each corner and doorway as he neared it. He now had confirmation that this was a hostile environment, and while it wasn't clear that the rest of the security contractors on site knew the score, he couldn't take chances now.

Especially not after he'd already choked one of them out.

He reached the stairs without seeing or hearing anyone else. The basement was still quiet and the man he'd choked out was still unconscious in his chair.

For just a moment, he looked down at the man he'd incapacitated. It would take the matter of a moment to kill the man, silencing him forever. He'd never be able to tell Fontaine that one of the newcomers had penetrated the basement.

Except that killing him would tell the same story, and if he woke up while Gomez was cutting his throat, this could get messy, fast. He decided, grudgingly, to leave the man and get back to the security center to warn Brannigan.

He didn't dare put this on the radio. They were using Fontaine's radios, which meant they were compromised. Bianco might be able to work something out to get them off Fontaine's net, but Gomez would be the first to admit that he had no idea how to do that. So, this had to be communicated in person.

Reaching the ground floor, he kept his weapon leveled, wishing he had a suppressor, though he knew that even then, a gunshot would wake the entire floor. He carefully rolled his feet on the steps as he mounted higher, keeping his muzzle trained on the doorway leading toward the sleeping quarters. Kirk had covered for him on the way down, but he didn't hear voices, which meant that the other Blackheart's distraction had played itself out, and the man was back on watch. If he found Gomez coming up out of the basement, then the entire op was compromised.

The man was leaning back in the chair, however, his back to the stairs, engrossed in whatever he was reading on his tablet. He probably didn't think that he needed to worry about the stairwell so much as keeping the new mercs *out* of the stairwell.

Gomez moved like a ghost, hardly daring to breathe as he continued up the steps, rotating to keep his back to the wall and his muzzle on the man in the doorway, until he'd moved far enough toward the next landing that he had to shift to cover up the next flight of stairs. The man in the door hadn't reacted at all.

It was only a matter of time, but he'd stay soft as long as he could.

In a matter of seconds, he was out of sight of the ground floor doorway, and while he didn't *relax* exactly, he lowered his weapon and tried to move normally, casually. He wouldn't be questioned from here about being in the basement. Until the alarm was raised, he could just act like he belonged there. All he had to do was keep from alerting the rest of Fontaine's security just long enough to get the Blackhearts alert and ready to fight.

The man at the doorway on the top floor looked up as he stepped through. "What are you doing up here?"

Gomez shrugged. "Couldn't sleep. Thought I'd come up and let somebody in the security room go down."

If the blond man with the wispy mustache was suspicious, he didn't show it. He just nodded. "Fair enough. I gotta ask. Everybody's jumpy as fuck around here right now."

Gomez shrugged. "If it's because of those pirates that hit us out there, I can see why."

The man looked up as Gomez walked past, out into the gallery. "You guys really fought pirates aboard that yacht?"

While he really didn't have time for this, something drew Gomez to pause and look back over his shoulder. The man had put down the magazine he'd been reading, and he was studying Gomez with some uncertainty. "Yeah. Got a little hairy there for a minute."

"Huh." The man sat back in his chair with a slight frown. "I thought all the hysteria about pirates was just somebody reading too much into the news." He picked up the magazine again, but then paused and looked up at Gomez once more. "You think there are enough of them that they'll try here? I mean, that's what Farah's been saying, but they'd have to be nuts to try to hit this place."

Gomez shrugged. "I just get paid to carry a gun and shoot bad guys."

The blond man chuckled a little and turned his attention back to his magazine. The cover girl was deeply tanned, with a whole lot of that tan visible, her highlighted hair flying across the top of the page. "I hear that."

Gomez turned back toward the security center, his expression impassive but a faint, nagging doubt in his mind.

If that guy was emblematic of the rest of Fontaine's security force, then these guys had no idea how dirty their employer was. Which meant they were going to die without knowing why.

There was no doubt in his mind, as he tapped on the door, that a lot of Fontaine's security contractors were going to die in the next hour or two. There was no getting around it. Fontaine had decided to kill the Blackhearts. That meant anyone who got in their way on the way out was getting smoked. No ifs, ands, or buts about it.

He knocked again, and the door cracked open. Flanagan peered out for a moment, then pulled the door open and ushered him inside.

The long-haired guy named Cody glanced over at him but didn't seem to pay him any mind. So, Gomez nodded to Brannigan, and tilted his head toward the corner.

Brannigan joined him, leaning in to listen. "Fontaine knows. They're going to kill us, either by a sacrifice play with the pirates if they show up, or if that doesn't work, by letting us go back on the boat with a new set of charges."

Brannigan's eyes flicked over his shoulder at Cody, but the other contractor wasn't paying attention. His eyes were riveted on the radar screen. A moment later, he snatched up the radio.

"We've got incoming! Twelve to fifteen contacts, inbound from the north! Code Red, Code Red, Code Red!"

Then another voice came over the radio. "Confirm Code Red. Be advised, the contractors who landed with the *Dream Empire* are pirates." The voice was the man with the lisp, but his voice was icy cold despite it. "They are to be neutralized immediately before their friends arrive."

CHAPTER 25

Kirk had kept his radio on and turned up, even while he and the other Blackhearts who'd gone down to their sleeping quarters tried to get some rest. So, while he'd been dozing, the back-to-back calls, announcing first that the pirates were indeed on their way, followed immediately by the declaration that it was now open season on Brannigan's Blackhearts, brought him fully alert in an instant.

Burgess was already out of bed, his feet on the floor, reaching for his weapon and gear. Bianco wasn't far behind. None of them had dressed down except to shed their plate carriers and helmets. They'd all been expecting trouble.

Kirk immediately moved to the door. Fortunately, none of the other security contractors had been in the same room; they'd had this one to themselves. He quickly locked it, keeping his muzzle trained on the opening, while Burgess and Bianco got their gear on.

None of the three of them spoke or made any more noise than necessary. Meanwhile, he could hear movement outside. These guys had moved fast.

Burgess touched his shoulder, and he stepped back, ceding the cover position to his old friend while he quickly shouldered into his own plate carrier and pulled his helmet on. Meanwhile, someone tested the door handle.

A low voice sounded outside. They still hadn't heard any movement from inside, so hopefully they thought the Blackhearts were asleep and oblivious.

Then gunfire echoed through the mansion, the sound deceptively quiet as it filtered down from two floors above, and it was game on.

Something hit the door, hard. It cracked and shook in the frame, but it didn't open and it didn't break. Kirk was about to tell Burgess to go ahead and open it and get clear when Bianco took matters into his own hands.

"Clear." He hefted that EVOLYS, leaning into it like it was no bigger or heavier than the others' MCXs, and laid into the door with a long burst.

The roar was deafening. Flame flickered from the muzzle as Bianco tore through the door—and anyone on the other side— with a long burst. Farah probably shouldn't have let them rearm, because Bianco had enough ammunition to cut through most of the mansion.

He didn't just sit in place and hose down the doorway, though. He moved as he held down the trigger, angling to one side to clear the fatal funnel, throwing himself against the wall to finish the burst as close to where he could imagine the stack might have been waiting to make entry. When he ceased fire, screams of pain came through the ravaged door, just before Burgess reached out, unlocked it and threw it open.

Kirk followed Burgess out, turning sharply left to cover his back as Burgess went right. He found himself in a corner and cursed. He should have remembered that. The only place the bad guys might have stacked up was right where Burgess had gone, and he quickly turned, even as gunfire hammered in the small, enclosed hallway behind him.

***

Hank leaned on the rail, fuming. He understood that someone had needed to stay back on the yacht, but he couldn't help but feel like he'd been picked for babysitting duty. Doc Puller hadn't been trouble, not really, but he was also the new guy, and

206

hadn't yet proved himself. It felt good, to some extent, not to be the noob anymore—even if he probably never would shed the callsign, especially since he'd let on how much it bugged him—but that didn't mean he wanted to be minding the FNG while everyone else moved headed inside to where the action was probably going to go down.

He knew that the yacht was still probably on the pirates' target list, and that his father didn't play favorites, but that didn't help him shake the feeling that he wasn't measuring up, somehow.

The radio on his belt squawked. He looked down with a frown and pulled it off, turning up the volume. He hadn't quite caught that.

He held it to his ear just in time to hear the man with the lisp announce the death sentence on the Blackhearts.

"Shit." He spun away from the rail, hastily shoving the radio back into his back pocket instead of wrestling with the belt clip, and snatched up his MCX. He could see some movement on shore, but so far, no one was moving toward the yacht.

That didn't mean he or Doc were safe. He headed back toward the superstructure, his rifle held at the low ready, just in case. The crew had behaved themselves on the rest of the voyage to the island, but all the Blackhearts had been aboard and alert at that point. He had no way of knowing for sure that none of them had just been biding their time.

The arms room was supposed to be secured, but he'd seen "supposed to be" before, and he didn't trust it.

He realized, as he made entry into the master cabin, quickly clearing it solo, like he'd had to learn to do *after* he'd gotten out of the Marine Corps, that he couldn't trust the radio, either. He'd heard Fontaine's people on it, which meant anything that the Blackhearts sent could be heard, too, and any moves they broadcast on that net could be quickly countered. They were outnumbered, on the bad guys' turf, and they had no comms.

Which meant that he had to find Doc, somewhere aboard the yacht, and get to a defensible position.

Where is he? He's supposed to be in the arms room, watching the cameras, but, again… "supposed to be." Puller had already wandered out of the prescribed areas once. He knew that Flanagan had some history with the guy, but Hank wasn't that impressed. Puller didn't have the self-discipline that most of the rest of the Blackhearts had, even Curtis.

He worked his way aft, clearing as he went. Most of the crew had gone ashore with the rest of the Blackhearts, so the yacht was all but abandoned, so he could move quickly.

Just aft of the theater, though, he spotted one of the younger support staff, waiting crouched around the corner. He leveled his rifle at the young man, who flinched, throwing his hands up with a startled curse. "Hey, man, I was just gonna sneak a movie! That's all!"

Hank studied him for a second. It was possible that the kid was sneaking around to try to catch one of them off guard, but that was real fear in the young man's eyes, and he was dressed in shorts and a t-shirt, with nowhere he could easily conceal a pistol or even a knife. He lowered his weapon.

"You'd better get somewhere more secure than the theater. The pirates are coming in."

If the kid had been frightened by having a rifle pointed at his face, he looked positively sick now. "Really?"

"Yeah. Get to your quarters and lock the hatch." It probably wouldn't do him much good if the pirates boarded and systematically cleared the yacht, but it would keep the kid out from underfoot.

With a spasmodic nod, the kid got up and scrambled aft, glancing over his shoulder once at Hank before disappearing through another hatch. Hank, for his part, continued to the next ladderwell and headed below.

He was almost to the arms room when he heard something. He couldn't quite place the sound, so he slowed. He'd turned his radio down, just in case, and for a moment, he thought about turning it up so he could listen in. With a shake of his head, he kept moving down the corridor, his MCX in his shoulder, listening carefully.

Someone up ahead was murmuring with some frustration. As he got closer, taking each step with exaggerated care to avoid making noise, he thought he heard the clink of a tool on metal. If he had the layout right, whoever was making the noise was right at the hatch leading into the arms room.

He came around the corner, to see the first mate trying to get the arms room door open. The man looked up as Hank cleared the corner, and right as he did, Hank saw the warning in his eyes.

He shot the first mate just as the man dropped his lockpicks and grabbed for the pistol in his waistband. It was a perfect shot, right through the sternum, and the man staggered backward and fell on his ass. For a fraction of a second, realization dawned in the first mate's eyes, and then they went empty as he collapsed onto his back on the deck.

Hank swept the passageway aft before he moved to the hatch and knocked, hard. "Doc! It's Hank!"

The hatch cracked open, and Doc Puller peered out over a drawn Glock. As soon as he saw that Hank was alone and armed, he pulled the door the rest of the way open, and Hank slipped inside.

"I heard the radio, but I didn't think I should risk calling you." Puller motioned to the body on the deck outside as he shut the hatch and locked it again. "What do we do?"

"We've got to expect them to come after us, now. Whatever just happened, we're targets." Hank pointed to the monitors. "Fortunately, we can see what's going on, at least until they figure out how to disable those." He scratched the back of his head while he thought. "Damn. I think we need to stay here for now and watch the cameras. Without comms, going into that shitstorm is going to be suicide." He hated himself even as he knew that it was the right call. "We need to hold the back door for the rest to get out and get away."

"What about them?" Puller pointed to one of the video feeds.

209

Hank followed his gaze and swore.

Three helicopters were speeding toward the island, skimming just above at least a dozen speedboats.

***

The radio call had just ended when Brannigan pivoted around toward the man called Cody. He was just barely too slow, though. Wade already had his weapon leveled at the long-haired contractor's head.

Cody had half turned around as the radio had squawked, and now he froze, his hands held at shoulder level. "Look, fellas. No need for things to get stupid, here."

"That's entirely on you." Brannigan was somewhat glad that neither Curtis nor Wade had spoken first. "You can get down on the floor, hands on your head, and live. Or you can make a grab for that smoke wagon you've got there and get your brains spattered all over the desk."

Cody slowly and carefully got out of his chair, keeping his hands up, and got down on his knees, intertwining his fingers on top of his head. Then he looked down at his waistline. "Uh." He looked up at Wade. "I carry appendix."

Wade didn't move, didn't even blink. Curtis sighed, put his EVOLYS down on the floor, and moved to disarm the contractor. "Leave it to me, then. Hell's bells."

"Somebody had to be ready to shoot him." Wade wasn't apologizing. He didn't take his eyes off Cody. "You going to flex-cuff him or something?"

"I gotta do all the work." Curtis looked around for a moment, then yanked a power cord out of the wall, cut it with his multitool, then started tying Cody's hands behind him.

"All right." With Wade and Curtis keeping tabs on their prisoner, Brannigan could turn back to the problem at hand. Unfortunately, while the cameras provided a view of the grounds, and some of the security contractors running to defensive positions, there were none on the inside of the mansion. Probably because Fontaine didn't want any record of some of the things that

210

went on inside. "We need to link up with the others and get back to the yacht."

"What about Fontaine?" Flanagan asked. He was covered down on the door along with Santelli and Gomez. "If he's trying to clean house, we can't just leave him loose. He'll come after us. Somehow."

"I know." Brannigan was thinking about it. He glanced at the monitors and saw the helicopters and speedboats coming in fast, showing up on the grayscale IR cameras set high on the mansion's roof. "Let's get everybody together and into a better position before we start worrying about taking down an HVT while we've got pirates knocking at the back door."

"I'm guessing that means you're not really pirates yourselves?" Cody had craned his neck to look up from his position on his belly on the floor.

"Shut up." Wade was still standing over him, rifle leveled.

"No, we're not." Brannigan figured it wouldn't hurt, despite Wade's hostility. "Your boss is, though. Seems he helped put together that little wrecking crew out there, profited handsomely off their operations, and is now trying to bury his skeletons. Except they're coming back to bite him in the ass."

Cody squinted up at Wade. "Look, man, I don't know shit about that. It was a paycheck, and a good one. It's not like he ever confided in any of us."

If he was trying to argue to be let loose—or just not get shot—he was interrupted by the first blow to the door.

Whatever they'd hit it with, the door and the jamb both cracked, though they held. The Blackhearts spread out to the walls, weapons leveled on the doorway.

The second blow didn't quite open it, either, though the door shook and the *crack* was even louder. So was the curse outside. With the third strike, the ram smashed the latch through the jamb and the door shuddered open. A flashbang sailed through, but in the split second that it took for it to hit the floor, the Blackhearts had either turned away or squeezed their eyes shut. There was nothing they could do about the noise.

211

The blast rocked the room, the concussion ringing through the structure. Brannigan felt his hearing immediately go slightly dead, every sound muffled except for the ringing in his ears. He hadn't buried his head in his arm, but he'd closed his shooting eye and looked down with the other, so he hadn't gotten the full brunt of the flash. When he opened his eye, bringing the MCX's red dot up to cover the doorway, he still had a green blotch in his off eye, but he could see just fine out of the other.

Which was all he needed to hammer three rounds into the first man through the door as he loomed through the still-rising cloud of smoke from the bang.

The man staggered as the bullets tore into him. Brannigan had aimed high, knowing he was going to have to shoot around body armor. Even if one or two of his rounds hit the man's plate, at least one went through his neck or face, and he fell back into the doorway and the man coming in behind him.

Then Curtis opened up on the fatal funnel with the EVOLYS from where he'd dropped to the floor next to Cody.

Even as the number two man in the stack tried to disentangle himself from the one man and get through the fatal funnel, Curtis's burst chopped through his legs and he fell, already dead or dying from two more rounds in his head and neck, even as Curtis shifted to send another burst out through the door, chewing up the splintered and cracked jamb near where the latch had been, just to dissuade anyone else from trying to push the room.

Of course, that wasn't going to stop anyone from tossing in a frag, if they had them, and Brannigan wasn't willing to take that chance.

He knew the chance he was taking as he jumped the stack, brushing past Flanagan who lifted his muzzle at the last moment with a curse, and plunged out the door.

He practically ran right into the number three man, muzzle thumping him in the chest before lifting his rifle just far enough to put a bullet through his teeth. It was low for a headshot, but he was in a hurry. The round tore through larynx and spine, came out the other side, and hit the next man back in the shoulder. He jerked as Brannigan stepped out slightly, past the falling number three man, and shot him again, this time through the left eye.

That was the last one. For the moment. He pivoted, scanning the gallery. Flanagan had followed him out and killed one more who had been coming out of a doorway on the east side, and since he was still aimed in, Brannigan suspected that there was still another shooter in that room.

They didn't have the time to clear the entire floor. First things first. "On me," he barked, even as more gunfire thundered from somewhere downstairs.

CHAPTER 26

El Salvaje rode in the lead MD-500, his R4 across his knees, watching the island mansion get closer with startling speed. Below, the speedboats skipped over the waves, their wakes forming light streaks on the black water as the coxswains kept their throttles wide open, if only to keep up with the helicopters.

He was in the lead bird for a reason. He got to take down the mansion by himself. Cain had stayed back on the *Lyubov Orlova*.

The man known as El Salvaje kept his thoughts and feelings hidden behind his usual mask of stoic indifference, but he was thinking. He really should have disappeared in Los Cristianos. He'd had the plan worked out. All he needed to have done was take off with her. It might have taken a couple of days, but if he'd wanted, there would have been no way Cain could have found him.

There was still a chance that he could cash out of this job, though, so he'd stuck it out. He was now questioning the wisdom of that course of action. There were plenty of other jobs in the global underground where his skills and talents would be welcome.

Not the time. He shook off the reverie as they swooped in toward the quays and the sloping front lawn before the mansion. The boats were moving in fast toward the pier and the beach next

215

to it—which was probably artificial, knowing what he knew about Fontaine—while the helicopters circled overhead to provide top cover.

No gunfire met them, though he saw figures running toward the mansion or the landscaping around it, which might or might not serve as defensive positions. Even as he tried to draw a bead on one of them, he saw two more run inside through the front doors.

Something was going on down there, and he wondered at the presence of the massive superyacht docked at the quay. That was an added complication; presuming that the bombs had been disarmed, they were going to have to secure that ship to make sure Fontaine didn't escape.

He keyed his radio, hoping he could be heard over the noise of the helicopter, not to mention the gunfire that was finally starting to flicker out of the landscaping toward the boats. "Section Three, move on the docks and secure them." He scanned the mansion, but while there was a helipad on the north side, there was no good way onto the roof. They were going to have to take the building from the bottom up, floor by floor, room by room. Not ideal, but none of the operations he'd undertaken since he'd first hired out as a *sicario* in Cuidad Juarez ever had been.

The pilot was circling around toward the flatter part of the lawn just between the docks and the mansion, cutting off his shot on one of the running security men. Three of the boats were on the beach now, the pirates aboard trading fire with the men hunkered down behind some of the landscaping. Flickers of muzzle flash strobed through the night, even as the lights inside the mansion went out.

With a roar, the rotor wash flattening the grass, the pilot touched down, just as another muzzle flash was followed by the harsh *bang*s of bullet impacts through the acrylic windscreen. The pilot jerked and spasmed, and the helicopter lifted partway off the ground and threatened to tip over as the copilot yelped and tried desperately to switch over the controls before the pilot's death throes crashed the aircraft into a fiery ruin on the lawn.

El Salvaje threw himself out through the open door and went flat on the grass, searching for the source of the gunfire. He ripped off a quick burst of fire at the front of the mansion, then he was up and scrambling for cover among the rocks artfully arranged off to the flank.

All concerns about Cain and the end of this job were now subsumed by the sheer need to survive. Survival being dependent on killing everyone in that mansion, he got to work.

***

Kirk pivoted around only to find that Burgess had things well in hand. The last of the security contractors crumpled against the wall, blood painting the plaster behind him, as Burgess swept his muzzle back to clear the rest of the small hallway.

Realizing he was breathing harder than he might have expected, Kirk followed suit. "Nice work, Vinnie. Not exactly doctrine, but that's probably why it worked."

"Now what do we do?" Bianco had moved up to the doorway and was now barricaded on it, since there wasn't a lot of room in the hallway. "We're cut off and we can't exactly afford to use the radio."

Kirk thought it over. He'd been in some tight spots as a Special Forces soldier, especially in a profession where "green-on-blue" incidents were so common. This one kind of took the cake, though. Even that mission in the Central African Republic hadn't put his team in multiple positions within an enemy stronghold.

"I think we should probably strongpoint here." Burgess was holding on the opening to the main reception area, his eyes fixed on where his muzzle was pointing even as he tilted his head so that he didn't have to raise his voice enough to broadcast their plans to everyone on the ground floor. "We've got fewer numbers…" He was interrupted for a moment by another burst of gunfire from somewhere above them, even as a close pass by a helicopter rattled the mansion. "And it sounds like the Colonel's already moving. I don't know about you guys, but I'd rather sit tight and have them link up with us here rather than try to move and risk a blue-on-blue in the hallways, especially with no useful comms."

He'd barely finished speaking when a storm of gunfire sounded outside, slightly muffled by how deep inside the mansion they were. It sounded like the pirates were now on the ground, and that explained why they hadn't already gotten hit by more of Fontaine's security.

Kirk nodded. "Back inside, barricade on the door, and hold the hallway, then. I don't want to give *that* up."

As he and Burgess moved back inside, Bianco lifting the machinegun's muzzle as they passed before shifting to cover Burgess's sector, Kirk hoped that Fontaine didn't have some kind of escape plan that he could put into action before they could get at him.

The pirates aside, Kirk wanted a piece of their erstwhile employer. There had been some reasonable doubt before, even after they'd found the bombs on the yacht. Even after Sorley had tried to kill Wade—or maybe he'd been trying to kill Fontaine's body double—there might have been some other reasoning behind it. Now, though, with the bald-faced lie that they were pirates being disseminated to Fontaine's security, he *knew* down to his bones that the worst-case scenario was true.

If Fontaine got away, Kirk knew that it would be next to impossible to make him pay for this. Which was why he wanted to get after him *now*.

Hurry up, Colonel.

***

Flanagan pushed up to get ahead of Brannigan as they headed for the stairs. If Gomez was right—and things hadn't suddenly changed in the last five minutes—then Fontaine was in the basement, which meant they needed to get down to the ground floor, link up with the others, and then head down to the basement before anything else. Which meant they had to move fast, bypassing any room and floor that they could be reasonably sure didn't contain their target. All the same, if the security contractors thought they were pirates, they were probably going to try to converge and eliminate the Blackhearts before doing much more than holding the doors to the outside, even as the actual pirates descended on the island.

As he reached the stairs, a distant, slightly detached part of himself couldn't help but feel a little sorry for the contractors. The fact that Fontaine had gone with the "pirates" accusation meant that most of the men on his payroll had no idea what game Fontaine was playing. Which meant that they were going to die for nothing, thinking they were just doing their jobs.

Brannigan must have thought the same thing. As soon as they started down the stairs, leaving the abandoned chair where the security guard on the gallery had been sitting, a man who was probably lying dead on the floor behind them, he keyed his radio.

"This is Colonel John Brannigan. I don't know any of you, but I can tell by the fact that Joshua Fontaine just called me a pirate that most of you don't know exactly what's going on here. The truth is that we were hired by Mr. Fontaine to protect his yacht against pirates. Turns out, he had put a bomb aboard the yacht, and hoped that we could kill a few pirates before he blew up the ship himself. After all, if the pirates were going after him, then he couldn't possibly be connected to them, could he?"

Brannigan paused as they started down the stairs, letting Gomez move up to back Flanagan as he moved carefully toward the first landing, muzzle trained on the next landing down while Gomez covered through the gap between flights, aimed down at the bottom floor below. "The truth is, your boss bankrolled the pirates who are knocking on your front door, and now he's trying to distance himself if he can't clean house. And you're going to die for it."

There was another pause. So far, the gunfire inside the mansion had fallen silent, though the noise of the firefight outside was getting louder. Flanagan didn't know if that meant the message had gotten through, or if there were just nastier surprises waiting for them.

"Nice try, whoever you are." The voice was utterly cold, and somehow menacing despite the lisp. "All personnel, you are

219

not to communicate with the pirate who calls himself Brannigan. Shift to the Charlie channel." The radio went dead.

"Well, it was worth a try," Santelli said from somewhere behind them.

When they reached the ground floor, however, there was no sign of the man who'd been holding security on the stairs. Maybe he'd decided that Brannigan had been telling the truth. Maybe he'd been hauled into the outer defense as the pirates hit the mansion. Maybe he'd been one of the men who'd tried to storm the sleeping quarters and been killed.

Flanagan paused just short of the doorway, then he and Gomez went out fast, clearing the hallway before Flanagan kept pushing, the rest of the team falling in behind him.

The room they'd been assigned was just around the corner, and he paused at that corner, just in case. Since Fontaine's mercenaries had switched channels, hopefully they weren't listening in, and even if they were, deconfliction was a matter of life and death at this point. "Lumberjack, Woodsrunner. We are at the corner, just outside the stairs."

"Roger that, Woodsrunner. We're strongpointed in the room, but we have eyes on the hallway. Bring it in."

Flanagan lifted his weapon and moved around the corner. He was unfazed by the bodies lying in the hallway and the door, though even he felt a jolt of adrenaline when he saw that Burgess was on the door, his rifle aimed in at the corner. Burgess dropped his muzzle toward the floor as Flanagan came into the hallway and was identified, but there for a moment, he'd been looking down that barrel, and it wasn't a comfortable feeling.

He supposed it could have been worse. Bianco was covering the other direction with that big EVOLYS belt fed.

"Coming in." Flanagan led the way inside. With nine men in the room, it was crowded, and they couldn't get more than two guns on the hallway, but it was better to reset in a room than hang out in a hallway.

"What's the call, bossman?" Kirk was standing back from the door, his MCX pointed at the ceiling.

220

"We go after Fontaine, then we worry about the pirates." Brannigan had made up his mind. "This son of a bitch turned these animals loose and then tried to get us killed to cover it up. He goes down first." He glared up toward the outside. "I want that Cain bastard, too, but Fontaine comes first."

"Sounds like a plan to me," Burgess said. "On me."

"With you." Burgess and Bianco went out into the hallway in one smooth movement, Bianco holding on the hall while Burgess flowed toward the corner and the stairs, Gomez and the rest on his heels.

Outside, the roar of gunfire only intensified.

CHAPTER 27

El Salvaje dumped an entire magazine into the landscaping in front of the mansion, which was still brightly lit by the outside floodlights despite the fact that it was under attack. Anyone else might have thought that was insane, but as he squinted into the glare, El Salvaje had to admit that he thought it made some sense. Fontaine's security could see pretty clearly, while the assaulters were partially blinded by the floodlights.

That wasn't going to stop him. This wasn't the first such mansion he'd assaulted and secured. There were a number of Latin American and African politicians and other public figures who had thought they were well defended until he'd come knocking.

He wasn't sure he'd hit anything, but the fire from the bushes and rocks had slackened, giving him and the four pirates who had made it to the boulders with him a breather. "Move." He pointed toward the rear of the mansion. The island rose somewhat there, though the entire rock never got much more than a few dozen meters above the waves. He had enough intelligence on the layout, however, to know where they needed to go.

Despite the playboy aspect to the place, he knew that Fontaine had made preparations for emergencies, and that if they didn't move quickly, their target might just manage to slip through their fingers. Cain would be furious, though that carried considerably less terror for El Salvaje than it might for some of the men in storm gray who ran with him, half crouched over, behind the cover of the line of rocks.

A ferocious storm of gunfire erupted from the beach, as the pirates laid down what cover fire they could with their R4s from the boats and tried to get off the beach to close with the handful of security contractors who were holding the front of the mansion. El Salvaje paused, just for a moment, and peered over the rocks before passing the corner of the enormous stone house.

He could see better from there. There were about a dozen men with SIG MCX carbines crouched behind the massive planters that flanked the walkway leading up to the huge front doors from the beach and the docks. They had good cover there, and they were still successfully keeping most of the pirates pinned down. The helicopters had pulled off, most of them having taken at least a few rounds, and were now circling, trying to get shots at the security contractors. The landscaping provided good cover, though, even from the sky.

Except that Fontaine's guards had apparently not planned on anyone getting into the rocks on their flank. They were exposed from that angle.

Time was pressing, but he turned, laid his rifle across the boulder in front of him, steadied his position, and opened fire.

His rifle thundered, the muzzle flash bright in the dark, as he cut down three of the defending contractors in the first three seconds. He might not be the dead shot that some of the pirates were—mostly former American special operators, which had definitely put them on opposite sides once or twice—but he was good enough. He expended an entire second magazine, raking his fire up and down the front line before the mansion's façade. A lot of his rounds smacked off concrete and stone, but enough plunged into flesh and bone that in moments, half of the defenders were down, dead or badly wounded, bleeding out onto the landscaping. The fire from the beach redoubled in ferocity, and then the pirates were bounding forward as the defenders ducked for any cover from the flank, desperate just to avoid getting shot.

224

El Salvaje reloaded as he ducked back behind the rocks and continued on toward the rear. The target's escape route still needed to be cut off. Even as he moved, the defenders out front opened fire yet again, and he was pretty sure that several more of the pirates had gone down. However this night ended, he doubted Cain's group would ever be the same.

Two of the pirates had moved ahead of him as he'd engaged the defenders, and he let them go. Better to have someone else out front if Fontaine's personal security detachment was on point.

The rocks formed a low wall along the eastern flank of the mansion, somewhat sheltering the outdoor pool and courtyard on that side. The pirates worked their way around. The pool was as lit-up as the rest of the place, but there was no one on or near the courtyard. They still stayed low, just in case Fontaine had shooters in the windows.

Beyond the pool, the island fell away in a ten-meter cliff above a deep cove. Judging by the patio furniture on the ledge at the top, it was often used as another party spot, probably with guests diving off the cliff and into the cove. That wasn't all, though.

Stepping to the edge, he scanned the cliffside below. There. It was hard to see from that angle—which was probably the result of engineering rather than nature—but there was a cave leading into the cove from beneath the mansion. That would be Fontaine's escape route.

He quickly began looking for a way down, but it appeared that whoever had designed their target's retreat hadn't intended for anyone to climb down to meet the escape craft. Still, unless the billionaire intended to escape in a submarine—which was still a possibility; the yacht was purported to have its own submersible in the bay aft—they could bring any boat that attempted to get out under fire.

Still, it wasn't El Salvaje's way to just settle in and wait. He kept looking, determined to find a way down. There was a chance that Fontaine might still escape even if they shot his boat full of holes. He wanted to get to that secret dock and intercept the billionaire before he could even board his escape craft.

Not that he was doing it for Cain's sake at that point. There were a number of possible courses of action that would become viable if he had Joshua Fontaine as a hostage.

With his weapon held ready, he started to move around the lip of the cliff, looking for a way—any way—down.

***

Burgess took the stairs carefully. Stairwells are nightmares in close quarters battle, and making entry with flights going up and down made it more complicated still. He had to make a call to cover up or down, and since they were going down, he moved in and snapped his muzzle toward the downward flight while Gomez moved in right behind him, almost touching the back of his shoulder, weapon trained on the landing above.

The gunfire outside was getting more intense. They needed to move fast, preferably without getting shot to ribbons because they were moving *too* fast and missing things.

Gomez moved up, covering the landing and the stairs above, making room for the rest of the Blackhearts to move down. Burgess paused just long enough to be sure that Brannigan was behind him—the Colonel had moved up in the stack quickly—and then started down.

He rotated around the landing as quickly and carefully as he could, leading with his muzzle, pieing off the angles as he went. He knew that Gomez had incapacitated the guard at the base of the stairs, but that man had obviously been found, since the alarm had been raised.

Sure enough, he spotted movement just before he cleared the corner. There was someone at the base of the stairs. Possibly more than one. And if they had replaced the man that Gomez had hit, then they were going to be ready for someone to come down after Fontaine and the man with the lisp, whoever that was.

Burgess might have hesitated. A man with less experience almost certainly would have. Would have taken the cautious way, easing out and trying to spot the enemy without exposing himself too much.

Might have stuck his head out right in front of a leveled rifle muzzle.

Instead, he threw himself across the landing, slamming into the wall even as he pivoted to square his plates with the bad guys and bring his own MCX to bear.

The gunmen at the bottom of the steps hadn't quite been expecting that. The first round smacked concrete off the wall behind him, showering him with grit. His finger had already been tightening on the trigger as he moved, though, and he hammered a tight pair of shots into the first gray-clad silhouette that blossomed in front of his sights.

Training worked against him a little. Even as he fired, he realized he'd just slammed both shots into the man's front plate. He shifted his aim, smashing a third round into the guard's collarbone, and a fourth through his nose, even as the contractor put a pair into his own front plate, handicapped by the same training scars.

Burgess staggered a little under the hammer blows, hitting the wall again as it felt like he'd been punched in the sternum with a loaded fist. He gasped for breath as he desperately tried to transition to the second man, but Brannigan had beaten him to it. He hadn't even noticed the shots as gunfire had raged in the enclosed staircase, but as soon as he'd moved, drawing both men's attention, Brannigan had stepped out onto the landing just far enough to shoot the second contractor between the eyes.

Then Bianco was moving in front of him, covering the opening with that EVOLYS. "I've got you, Tom." A moment later, Kirk was checking him for bleeds.

"Kirk, Joe, John, Mario, and Carlo, with me. Kevin, you stay here with Tom and Vinnie. Cover our backs." Brannigan was already at the base of the stairs, standing over the two dead men, covering what he could see of the hallway outside the stairwell. "We don't have time. Everyone else, on me."

He barely waited for Flanagan to join him, and then he was through the door and moving.

Burgess waved Curtis off as the shorter man started to take over from Kirk to do blood sweeps. "Both rounds hit the plate. I'm fine. Just got the wind knocked out of me a little." He looked up the stairs. So far, no one had tried to come at them from that direction, but even if they were off the cameras—which he doubted—any of Fontaine's security men that were trying to get to the front of the mansion to help repel the pirates outside would have to come past them. "Let's concentrate on keeping the back door open."

Even as he said it, he wasn't sure just how well that was going to work. They had Fontaine and his security on one side, and pirates on the other, and this wasn't the only stairwell.

The night's work was going to require a *lot* of killing.

***

Hank watched the camera feeds with a growing sense of helpless rage. *Why did I get stuck aboard the damn boat while the rest went ashore?*

He couldn't tell exactly what was going on. The field of view for the *Dream Empire*'s cameras was simply too limited. All he could see was the firefight at the front of the mansion and the helicopters circling overhead.

So far, no one had moved on the yacht, but that was only a matter of time. How long until one of those MD-500s strafed the deck or landed someone to disable the yacht?

He'd barely thought it when the aft camera picked up an oncoming helicopter. *Great minds think alike, I guess.* He turned toward the hatch. "I'm going to the aft helipad. Stay here and watch my back."

"I can't watch your back from down here," Puller protested.

"Yeah, you can. Just watch the cameras and warn me if somebody's trying to come up behind me." Hank didn't have time for this. "There's only two of us, and one has to keep an eye on the cameras in case they land forward or come up the docks.

228

You're the FNG, so you get the duty." He shrugged. "Sorry, that's just the way it is."

He ducked out through the hatch before Puller could respond, though he still heard the loud curse behind him as the hatch shut.

He'd barely gotten a handful of yards aft when Puller's voice crackled over the intercom. "Hey, Hank? What are we supposed to do about comms?"

Hank swore, skidding to a stop just before the hatch leading out onto the stern and the aft helipad. He had to think about it for a moment. His dad and the others hadn't been on the radio since the attempt to appeal to the contractors to abandon their employer. But if the contractors had switched channels to keep the Blackhearts from listening in, maybe they couldn't listen in on the Blackhearts, either.

A moment later, he heard Flanagan call Kirk. That decided him. If the others were more concerned with effective comms than the security of those comms, then he'd follow suit. He keyed his radio.

"Doc, this is Hotep." It was a weak callsign, he knew, but it was better than just a bland "Hotel" for his first initial, while he figured out something better than "Noob." "Just use the radio."

"Roger." Hank got moving again, closing on the hatch astern, waiting with somewhat more trepidation for the inevitable call from one of the more experienced Blackhearts, insisting that he didn't get to pick his own callsign, than he was for the inevitable firefight that was about to erupt.

He barricaded himself on the hatchway, dropping to a knee as he braced his support hand against the bulkhead. Under other circumstances, the lower position might make for greater stability, but he really just wanted to make himself a smaller target.

This was nuts. He felt naked, exposed, and he was scared stiff. His hackles were up on the back of his neck, and he just *knew* that someone would somehow manage to sneak up behind him and execute him while he was focused on the stern, all by himself.

Never go anywhere alone. He'd drilled that into his platoon and then his company as a Marine officer, and now here he was, his only battle buddy a dozen yards forward and below, watching cameras but unable to provide him with covering fire.

It is what it is. You did *insist that you wanted in on this team. They work lousy odds. Always have, probably always will. So deal with it.*

He still glanced over his shoulder once at the deserted passageway behind him, just before the bird came in to flare above the helipad.

For a moment, he was tempted to open fire while the MD-500 was still airborne. Maybe he could kill the pilot and copilot, kind of like Gomez had done off the side when the pirates had boarded the first time. In the dim light, however, he wasn't nearly that confident in his marksmanship, and he didn't want to risk getting gunned down by a pirate in the side door because he'd missed.

He had only his rifle and one eye exposed as the helicopter came down. The pilot wasn't coming in straight-on, since they were still taking some fire from the front of the mansion, even as one of the other birds made a pass along the façade, a shooter in the door hosing down any position he could see. Hank could only hear the gunfire, the snarl of the rotors, and the distant sound of shattering glass. But the bird that was heading for the yacht was still coming in from off to the starboard flank, which reduced his own visibility while keeping him hidden for a few moments longer.

The rotor wash swept across the pad and through the hatch, battering him with the wind, and then the bird was down in front of him, the nose pointed toward the forward port corner of the pad.

The pirates couldn't have lined it up for him any better.

He leaned out just slightly and opened fire. Bullets smacked through aluminum, acrylic, flesh, and bone. He saw a dark spatter on the windscreen just before he dragged his muzzle

230

toward the tail, catching one of the dismounting pirates in the throat just before he shot yet another one through the armpit.

The pilot hauled back on the collective, pulling off the pad and turning hard away, even as two more pirates threw themselves flat on the deck to avoid both Hank's bullets and the spinning skids. One fired blindly back at Hank, but they were close enough that he still had to duck back to avoid the rounds that punched through the bulkhead with loud *bang*s. The yacht wasn't exactly armored.

As soon as he'd ceased fire, the incoming got more intense, as the pirates pushed the fight. They might be thugs, but they were also professional gunfighters, and when survival is on the line, professionals will respond accordingly.

More bullets tore through the metal of the bulkhead and ripped in through the open hatch to smack into the bulkhead forward. Hank was forced to fall back as one of the pirates went full-auto, ripping long bursts through metal and fiberglass to keep him back.

It wasn't exactly standard CQB doctrine, but it was doing the trick.

Wishing for a frag, he fell back, deeper into the superstructure, past the aft lounge, looking for the next spot to barricade.

This was going to be one hell of a game of hide-and-seek.

CHAPTER 28

Brannigan stepped over the bodies at the base of the stairs, taking the right, his muzzle pointed deeper into the basement, while Flanagan pivoted to cover his back. He waited just long enough to get a squeeze from Kirk, and then he was moving, pushing deeper in, hunting for Fontaine.

The lights had been dimmed in the basement, just like they had been upstairs. He couldn't tell if that was because it was supposed to be unused, despite the fact that Gomez had already been down there and scoped it out, or if Fontaine's people thought that the low light would be a tactical obstacle to the Blackhearts. If that had been the idea, then they probably shouldn't have provided them with NVGs.

It struck him, as he moved deeper in, checking doors as he went, that Fontaine's plot hadn't been all that well-thought-out.

As they worked their way past the armory, they still hadn't taken contact, or even seen any further movement. It was almost as if the basement really *was* abandoned. Had Fontaine gone upstairs while they'd been consolidating on the sleeping quarters and the security station?

Maybe he had. Brannigan moved out into the long hallway that ran down the rest of the length of the basement. If that was the case, though, they might just have him bottled up, between them and the pirates.

Something made him think otherwise, though. Fontaine might not have fully thought out his entire plan, but he was a survivor. This entire pirate scheme suggested that he was far too ruthless to just break down and cower when things got rough. He never would have gotten as rich as he was if he was that weak.

Still, it was eerily quiet down in that basement. With all the commotion above, on the grounds and the upper floors, if Fontaine was down there, they should have heard *something*.

He moved to the next door, his feet rolling silently on the carpeted floor, and reached for the knob as Kirk covered down the hallway beside him. It wasn't locked, which was a first since they'd gotten down to the bottom floor.

He threw the door open and went through fast, Gomez on his heels. They cleared the immediate opening quickly, then took a moment to look at what they were facing.

The entire room was piled with luggage. No, not luggage, not exactly. The cases stacked in the relatively small space were hardened and locked, except that the locks Brannigan could see had been drilled out. Every one of them had a packing slip taped to it, as well.

Gomez moved to the nearest stack, carefully clearing behind it, just in case, and looked down at one of the labels. "I don't understand what's supposed to be in it. It's all in some sort of code." He straightened, looking around the rest of the small storage room. "Something valuable, though."

Brannigan checked and saw that Flanagan, Santelli, Wade, and Kirk had entered and were covering the hallway through the door. Hallways were death traps, and so they wanted to strongpoint in a room where they could. Then he moved to inspect the same case that Gomez had just checked. Tilting his head to see the label better, he studied it with narrowed eyes.

Sure enough, it was just an alphanumeric that didn't say anything to anyone who didn't know the code. He reached up and opened it, carefully. It was doubtful that there was anything explosive inside, but you never knew.

Shining a light in under the lid, he saw rows of what looked like hard drives set in black foam. He let the lid down. "Probably stuff the pirates took from his rivals, that they weren't interested in."

"Or maybe it was part of the deal from the beginning." Santelli peered at the cases. "He has to have been getting more out of this than just killing his rivals' businesses. Remember Chavez said that some kind of prototype went missing."

"Maybe." Brannigan turned away from the stacks. "Whatever this stuff is, it's not why we're here. Let's keep moving."

Wade glanced over his shoulder at the cases, and for a second, Brannigan could see the calculation behind his eyes. If they couldn't expect Fontaine to pay them—which was kind of obvious at this point—was there a paycheck to be had in the cases?

There wasn't time to grab any of them, though, and Wade was professional enough to know it. He shook his head slightly with a faint snarl and got back to the problem at hand.

Flanagan and Kirk gave each other the nod, and then they were moving out into the hallway. Flanagan took the lead, and Brannigan slipped out just ahead of Santelli, getting a quiet snort of disapproval from the balding fireplug of a man. Santelli had been his Sergeant Major just before both of them had retired, and he'd been occasionally annoyed by Brannigan's intense lead-from-the-front style then. With the Blackhearts, it had only gotten worse, in a way.

He knew he was stack jumping more than he was wont to, but Fontaine's treachery had truly infuriated him in a way that he hadn't been pissed in a lot of years. He was out for blood, and he knew it.

He just had to make sure he didn't get any of his boys killed in the process.

There were half a dozen more doors on that hallway, and they were going to have to clear each of them. Flanagan was starting to move toward the next, across the hall from the storage room, when one on the near side, down at the far end, opened.

Four gunmen in gray came out fast, weapons leveled, the first two facing him and Flanagan.

***

El Salvaje thought he saw the way down, but it was going to be tricky. All the same, if he wanted Fontaine, he was going to have to take some risks.

Fortunately, rock climbing down a spray-slick cliff in the dark, in the middle of a firefight, was not one of those risks he was going to have to take.

Slinging his rifle behind him as he took a couple of quick steps, he leaped off into space.

It wasn't something he necessarily would have thought of before this job. He'd certainly done *some* piracy in the Caribbean, but that had been small-time stuff, the sort of jobs that didn't require a great deal of maritime knowledge or skill. Working with Cain's pirates, most of whom had some maritime special operations training, and working on considerably larger craft, both pirate vessels and their targets, he'd had to learn a few things. Abandoning ship, jumping ten to twelve meters into the water, was one of those skills, and he'd gotten good enough at it that he wasn't going to hit the surface on his back or his belly.

Holding onto the rifle's muzzle to keep it from coming up and hitting him in the back of the head, he stared straight ahead for a brief second before the warm water of the Atlantic closed over his head.

Kicking to the surface, wishing he was a better swimmer—or had better gear for this—he held his position for a moment, as two of the other pirates splashed into the water on either side of him. The third was up there still, either hesitating or covering them.

It was all the same to El Salvaje. One more man he wouldn't have to either cut in or eliminate.

Not that he had any intention of cutting anyone in.

The three of them swam for the cave, a black, yawning mouth in the cliff face. It was considerably larger up close than it had looked from above. It was a well-camouflaged escape route, but one that would allow for a speedboat with easily enough legs to reach the Canary Islands to get out.

He just had to get inside before that speedboat came out and ran them over.

The other pirates were off to either side of him, the younger man with the decidedly North African heritage pulling ahead. He was a much better swimmer. He was also out in the middle of the channel, even as El Salvaje paddled toward the side of the passage through the rock.

The passage curved sharply, which accounted for the darkness. The walls were smooth, blasted rather than naturally formed. A lot of work had gone into this place; more than even the enormous mansion above. Fontaine had wanted not just an escape route, but one that was not easily seen from either sea or air.

Unfortunately for him, Cain had quite a spy network of his own. He'd never trusted Fontaine, and recent events had borne that suspicion out. First there had been the sudden lack of communication, then the near miss with the Spanish Coast Guard, that shouldn't have been anywhere near the target area. Finally, the US Navy counter-piracy task force that had haunted the North Atlantic for almost a month had decided Cain that Fontaine had turned on them, repudiating their lucrative arrangement. El Salvaje didn't pretend to understand why. He didn't need to. He'd spent his entire life in the global criminal underground. He knew how these things went.

Coming around the curve, he started to see light ahead. Staying low in the water, he looked for a way up onto dry ground, where he could maneuver and fight.

The walls were still sheer, though, as he came all the way into the massive, brightly lit, artificial cavern underneath the mansion. Concrete docks lined the walls, and no fewer than three massive speedboats were tied up alongside. Low, dark, and sleek, they were no nonsense designs without any of the opulent flair of most of Fontaine's possessions. These were designed to get places fast, and with as little notice and fanfare as possible.

Figures swarmed over one of them, and the throb of the engine reverberated through the chamber. Sure enough, Fontaine intended to make a break for it. They were too engrossed in their task, however, to look toward where the three pirates swam against the wall, the younger man having figured it out and joined El Salvaje and his companion. They must have expected the camouflaged entrance to keep them safe until the last moment.

Fortunately, it looked like there was a spot where they get up on the dock at the end, only a few meters away. He swam toward it, looking for a ladder or steps.

There weren't any. If the dock had been a meter taller, they never could have climbed it. As it was, it stood about a meter above the water level, which was going to be a difficult climb, but not impossible. The hard part was that the men in the water would have to keep treading water and couldn't cover the man climbing up onto the dock.

For a moment, he considered just sending the younger man, who had almost beaten him to the dock, up first. But only for a moment. He didn't trust the pirate not to get them all killed. So he slung his weapon again and kicked himself up to grasp the lip of the concrete pier, dragging himself up toward the top of the dock.

He wasn't as fit as some of the pirates. His stock in trade was viciousness, not the kind of over-the-top fitness that the American, Australian, and British special operators specialized in. It was more of a struggle to haul himself up onto the dock, weighed down by the water soaking his clothing and his gear. He didn't so much climb up onto the pier as he dragged and rolled his body over the lip, making entirely too much noise as he scrabbled on the concrete, shoving himself up into a kneeling position and bringing his rifle around.

Fortunately, even as the two pirates who had accompanied him climbed up with rather more ease, the crew on the speedboat didn't even look in their direction. They were thoroughly occupied with their tasks, the shadows were just deep enough that the pirates' presence wasn't immediately attention-grabbing, and the rumble of the engines covered most of the noise they made.

El Salvaje held out a hand to forestall the North African pirate from opening fire. These were support personnel. He didn't even see any weapons. That didn't have any bearing on his decision making, but that meant they weren't an immediate threat, and he didn't want to start shooting and warn Fontaine off. They needed to wait.

Still, after a moment, he changed his mind. Not about killing the crew. That would come later. But better to hold the boat itself and wait for Fontaine out of sight aboard his escape craft.

Rising to his feet, his rifle in his shoulder, he started toward the boat, water squelching from his boots as he moved. The other two pirates flanked him.

Neither was willing to step in front of him. That was probably wise.

They moved fast, and in seconds they were at the side of the boat, weapons leveled. Only then did several of Fontaine's people look up, their eyes widening at the sight of the dark, dripping figures pointing rifles at them.

"No one do anything stupid." The tone of El Salvaje's voice and the leveled weapon communicated just what he meant. "Continue what you are doing. We will just wait here." He climbed down into the boat, followed by his companions. "I do not think I need to tell you how unfortunate it would be if you attempted to warn your employer about our presence."

He and the other two pirates spread out through the large speedboat, getting low enough that they shouldn't be easily visible to anyone coming down the metal steps from the mansion above, at least not at first.

The crewmen on the deck were clearly uncomfortable, and just as clearly were just sort of fiddling with this or that. El Salvaje watched them coldly, unsure at the moment whether they were finished with their preparation and were just trying to appear busy so that they didn't have to confront the reality that they had just been hijacked by pirates, or if they were up to something.

239

He didn't have time to make that determination before a door opened with a *clang* that reverberated through the cavern, considerably louder than the distant thunder of gunfire that was still raging across the island above. Boots clattered on the steel steps as he turned his eyes toward the stairs, to see two men in civilian clothes and gray combat gear moving rapidly down toward the docks, with Fontaine behind them, dressed in casual outdoor clothes. He looked harried and scared. Three more security contractors were behind him, turning away from the door and heading down the stairs.

El Salvaje had hoped to lie low until Fontaine reached the boat, seize him, and then get off with his hostages. However, those two men in gray plate carriers and helmets in front were more alert than he'd counted on.

Both of them stopped dead, MCX carbines snapping up to their shoulders, even as one of the crewmen in the back shouted an alarm.

El Salvaje shot that man in the back of the head, just on general principles, spattering the transom with gore, then transitioned to open fire on Fontaine's security detail almost without aiming.

His bullets smacked off of steel rails and stone walls and ceiling. He hadn't intended to do much more than keep them from getting accurate shots on him and the other pirates, but he succeeded in hitting at least one of them, sending the man staggering back against the railing with a grunt.

Then all of the contractors were shooting, raking the speedboat with barely aimed fire, even as the two closest to the door reached down, grabbed Fontaine, and hauled him up the steps and back through the door.

True to what El Salvaje knew about Fontaine, that door slammed behind him as soon as he and the men who'd grabbed him were through, leaving the other three contractors, including the wounded man, on the exposed stairwell behind.

The other two pirates were shooting now, paying little attention to whether or not any of the speedboat's crew were in the way. Two more of them fell, even as the pirates crouched below the transom and sprayed bullets up at the landing.

One of them, the younger North African pirate, fell into the bottom of the boat with a sudden, limp finality. Blood flowed over the deck plates, and he didn't move.

El Salvaje shot the wounded contractor again, with a bit better aim this time, walking his rounds up the man's torso. Several were probably stopped by his plates, but the one in his guts and two in his throat would finish him off.

The second pirate was slightly more disciplined with his fire. He kept hammering at the two remaining contractors, even as they pushed rapidly down the stairs, presenting their weapons and their plates toward El Salvaje and his remaining companion, trying to cover their advance with fire. Bullets smashed into and through the transom with loud *bang*s, one of them ricocheting off into the dark above with an angry whine.

El Salvaje and the pirate had a better position, though, and those two might have been fast and accurate, but they were still exposed. The other pirate hammered pair after pair into the man higher up, while El Salvaje flipped his R4 to auto and leaned into the recoil, sending the remainder of his magazine at his target in one long, stuttering, rattling burst. Only about half the rounds hit, but the first exploded the man's knee with a burst of blood and smashed bone. As he crumpled, the rest of the burst ripped through his leg, his arm, and his shoulder.

The leg wound was the fatal hit, as his femoral began to spurt blood across the steps. He struggled to bring his weapon up, and then the pirate next to El Salvaje put a single bullet through his skull, just beneath the rim of his helmet.

The gunfire fell silent as El Salvaje reloaded. Then, without hesitation, his face blank, he turned and fired two rounds into each of the speedboat's crew that were still alive. There were only three of them left, and the first two were dead before the shock of what was happening penetrated the fear that had already reduced the third to the fetal position. That one lifted his hands, his mouth gaping wide in fear and pleading, just before El Salvaje put a bullet through one hand and into that open mouth. The man fell back against the gunwale, blood leaking from the hole, staring in horror, even as the light left his eyes.

Then El Salvaje was out of the boat and moving for the stairs. Fontaine was his ticket out. He was not letting the man get away.

CHAPTER 29

Hank felt the second helicopter set down more than he heard it, and he cursed under his breath. That meant more pirates had just boarded, and he was even more outnumbered than he had been before.

Take it easy, Junior. Just because the others might think that you got too used to sitting in a command truck or a TOC, directing a bunch of grunts who did the real fighting, doesn't mean you've lost it entirely. Remember how your old man brought you up.

The truth was that he *had* gotten awfully used to command, or at least to having a platoon or company at his beck and call when trouble loomed. That did not, however, mean that he was any less his father's son, nor that he was any less a Blackheart.

Let's show these boys a good time, shall we?

He almost slipped into the closet just off the game room forward of the lounge, but there was only one way in or out. He had to be able to move, to keep them guessing, even as he picked them off.

He desperately wished for a frag or two, or even a few flashbangs. Those would make things a bit more interesting, and even the odds a little. He had to make do, though.

243

There. Just in front of the hatch that led forward. The deep lounge chair wouldn't provide a lot of cover, but he just needed it to provide enough concealment to allow him to spring his ambush and move.

There simply wasn't a lot of cover, strictly speaking, aboard the yacht. He would have to rely on movement and concealment.

He'd done that before.

Crouching down behind the chair, he carefully adjusted his position, gauging angles and distances with a quick glance, and then he went completely still and waited.

"Hotep, this is Doc. You've got three coming to you. Four more moving up the port side."

He could hear the scrape of a boot outside the hatch. He didn't dare make a sound to acknowledge Puller's warning, but the new doc didn't follow up. He could probably see the situation better than Hank could.

Footsteps entered the game room. They were trying to be quiet, though it was the quiet of assaulters clearing and searching rooms. With one eye just barely peeking around the back of the lounge chair, Hank could see the first man in gray fatigues, plate carrier, and helmet, his R4 leveled toward the center of the room, where the Ping-Pong table stood. Even as Hank watched, he bent to clear underneath the table.

Hank moved.

Punching his MCX out, he tucked it into his shoulder, his finger already tightening on the trigger. The pirate was close enough he almost didn't have to aim.

Two shots thundered in the game room, the muzzle blast tearing the fake leather upholstery of the lounge chair and blowing bits of stuffing into his face. The pair of 5.56 rounds caught the man right at the juncture of shoulder and neck as he bent to clear under the Ping-Pong table, one of them ripping a bloody exit wound out through his hip. His heart and one lung shredded, he dropped like a rock.

Hank popped up over the top of the lounge chair then, already tracking toward his next target. The other two pirates were spread out along the aft bulkhead, in a classic L-shaped clear. He shot the first one as his red dot passed him, the bullet skipping off the top of the man's plate and into his neck, then he was dragging the muzzle toward the second one. He'd practiced this drill a lot, and he got the second round off before the pirate could quite draw a bead on him. His second, third, and fourth rounds slammed into plate, shoulder, and jaw, blowing the side of the man's face out with a spray of blood and smashed teeth. The pirate's finger closed spasmodically on the trigger, his rifle barking as he put a round into the overhead above Hank's head.

Hank knew he'd hit, but he couldn't stay put and he didn't dare stop shooting. Transitioning back to the pirate on the left, who was holding a hand to his throat, red gushing down over his plate carrier, letting his rifle hang as he reached for a pistol. Hank shot him again, this time through the bridge of the nose, even as he drove for the aft hatch where the three pirates had made entry, then he shifted and blasted the other man, dying though he was, through the temple. Red spatter painted the bulkhead as both pirates fell on their faces.

Then he dove through the hatch, turning sharply to his right to clear his blind spot. There was no one in sight. Moving fast but quiet, he moved toward the port side.

Hopefully, they thought he was falling back, heading farther forward. If he could get in behind them…

The younger Brannigan got back on the hunt.

***

None of the Blackhearts hesitated. There were no friendlies in that mansion, even if some of the contractors might have been working for Fontaine in good faith. And there's no such thing as a "friendly" pointing a rifle at you, unless he deconflicts and puts that weapon down *really* fast.

With a crash of gunfire that roared deafeningly in the hallway, Flanagan, Wade, and Brannigan all opened up. Their targets were too close together and too well armored for each man

245

to carefully pick his quarry and engage with controlled pairs. They just hammered rounds into the mass of gray-clad mercenaries, dragging their muzzles from side to side as they fired as fast as they could squeeze their triggers. Flame danced in the dimly lit hall, and blood flowed and sprayed as the fast-moving 5.56 rounds tore through flesh where they didn't meet armor. One of the contractors got a shot off, and Flanagan felt a fiery impact to his shoulder, but he gritted his teeth and pushed forward, keeping up the fire until all four men were rapidly cooling heaps of gray-clad meat on the floor.

The Blackhearts didn't miss a step but pushed over the bodies, muzzles dipping to check them quickly before moving back toward the door the dead men had exited. Hardly waiting until Santelli gave his shoulder a squeeze, Brannigan led the way in through the door. Flanagan fell in behind Wade, with Kirk, Santelli, and Gomez behind him, as they flowed into the room.

The brightly lit room was dominated by a massive entertainment center. The TV had to be six feet wide. Dark wood shelves lined the other three walls, set with enormous speakers and various curios and souvenirs. Deep, leather upholstered couches were arranged around the room, facing the TV.

There was no one inside. The TV was dark, the speakers silent. Flanagan, from his point of domination next to Brannigan, scanned the room for anything that the contractors might have been doing in there. The firefight had started a relatively short time ago, but he wouldn't have expected even the least professional security contractors to be still hanging out and watching a movie while all hell broke loose. The darkness of the TV suggested against it, too. No, there was something else going on in here.

Gomez, predictably, spotted it first, though Flanagan mentally kicked himself for missing it. He and Childress had been the top woodsmen on the team before Gomez had joined, and until Childress had been shot in the spine, the three of them had been quietly competing for that top spot. There was no prize, no reward, but the competition was there, nevertheless.

Gomez lifted his muzzle with a curt, quiet, "Moving," and circled quickly around the couches on the side of the room. He got about halfway down the wall before he reached for the shelf that was ever so slightly out of place. Giving it a tug, he swung a carefully camouflaged door open. Dim, slightly bluish light illuminated him as he dropped his MCX level and began to pie off the opening. Flanagan was already right there with him, having cut in front of Brannigan before the Colonel could jump the stack again.

As soon as he'd cleared most of what he could see of the next room, Gomez was moving, Flanagan going through right behind him, dropping his own muzzle to cover his teammate.

They were in a safe room. That much was obvious from the thickness of the steel door behind the bookshelf that Gomez had pulled open. The interior was every bit as lavish as the entertainment center had been, with wood paneled walls, two plush couches, and a massive TV hanging in the corner, which was currently playing some superhero movie. Of course, there were other screens underneath it, with camera feeds showing much of the mansion and the surrounding grounds.

The feeds weren't complete. Several monitors were dark, suggesting that the cameras had been shot out. A ferocious firefight was still going on out front, though it appeared from what they could see that Fontaine's security had fallen back into the mansion itself, though not without leaving some bodies behind them. Pirates were crouched behind some of the massive landscaping, trading fire with security contractors inside, the muzzle flashes brilliant in the slightly grainy digital footage.

"He was here." Gomez was looking around the room.

"How can you be sure?" Brannigan asked.

Gomez pointed to the almost invisible outline of a door across from the one they'd used to enter. "That's where I was listening to him and that dude with the lisp."

Nobody questioned him. It was Gomez. He had a sense of direction that seemed eerie even to Flanagan.

"Well, he's not here now, and I don't think he went up." Santelli was blunt. "Yeah, there's another staircase, but if this is the high-security part of this place, he's not going to abandon it while there's a firefight going on upstairs."

"How much you want to bet he went down?" Kirk pointed at the floor. "What if he's got another bunker under this one? Or an escape route?"

"How very Cobra of him," Wade quipped.

"There's nothing on the cameras." Santelli was eyeing them with a squint. "There wasn't on the ones upstairs, either."

Kirk snorted. Flanagan realized that Kirk, being a retired SF dude and never having had Santelli as a Sergeant Major, could get away with that a lot more easily than he or Curtis could. Or Doc Puller, now. "If he's bankrolling pirates and has a super-secret bolt hole, do you really think he's going to tell his stooges that?"

"I'm sure they prefer 'henchmen,'" Brannigan said dryly. "Let's go."

Guns up, they moved back into the entertainment center. There had to be another way out of the basement.

***

Stuck here holding security on a damned stairwell, while Joseph goes and sticks his head in the lion's den. Figures. Curtis was almost—*almost*—willing to consider the fact that his insistence on never accepting a rifle instead of a machinegun just might be a factor in why he more often than not got stuck on security or a support by fire position. It didn't make him fume any less. He'd cleared buildings with a belt-fed before. He was that good at it. He didn't need to be stuck here watching the back door.

The fact that he was worried about what the others might be facing without him wasn't something he'd ever admit, even to himself. After all, they were big boys. So was he. He just wanted a piece of the action.

He did worry, though. Especially about Flanagan.

His discontent was forgotten a moment later, as he heard voices and footsteps on the stairs above. He hefted the EVOLYS as if it weighed nothing, the muzzle trained, unmoving, on the next flight up.

The man in jeans, a polo shirt, and the same storm gray combat gear as the Blackhearts were wearing, came around the corner quickly, saw the machinegun pointed at his face, and reared back, letting his rifle drop to dangle on its sling as he threw his hands up. "Whoa, dude, don't shoot me!"

For a moment, Curtis was ready to lean out and rake the landing with fire anyway. There were no friendlies here. He'd heard the radio transmission marking the Blackhearts as pirates.

Except, he realized, they were using the same gear and weapons as Fontaine's personal security detachment. Which was an oversight if Fontaine had really wanted to do them in, but it was one that he was more than willing to take full advantage of. He started to pie his way out into the stairwell, his finger on the trigger, hoping he wasn't about to expose himself to the door too much.

The guys up on the landing weren't playing hide and seek, though. They had vacated his line of sight with a quickness. "Dude! Don't shoot!" There was a pause. "You guys are with that Brannigan guy, right? The ones who came in on the yacht?"

"Nah, bro, we're with you guys." Curtis was trying to find just the right angle to get a burst up that stairwell without turning his back on the door.

Burgess put his hand on Curtis's shoulder. "Hold up a second, Kev." He had his other hand on his rifle, but he was looking up the stairs.

"Damn it, Tom." He lowered the machinegun, but only marginally.

The guys up on the stairs either saw the movement, or else they figured that the lack of fully automatic fire tearing up the stairs, the wall, and themselves was a good sign. "Look, we don't buy the whole story that you guys are pirates, okay? Makes no damned sense. We just don't want to get shot by good guys while the real pirates are kicking in the door and Fontaine's throwing us at his problems while he runs for the hills."

Curtis and Burgess shared a quick glance, without ever *quite* taking their eyes off the stairs. "Kinda figured that was the case for most of these boys," Burgess admitted.

He turned up the staircase. "Come on down, real slow, with your hands where we can see them and away from your weapons. You get froggy, and Kevin here's gonna cut you in half."

"Why'd you tell them my real name?" Curtis demanded.

Burgess wasn't Flanagan though, and just sighed slightly. "It's your first name, Kev. You're hardly the only Kevin out there. I'd be willing to bet there's at least one other Kevin on this island."

Curtis was slightly disappointed. Flanagan's response would have been far more derisive, and far more fun. Then the contractors were coming down the stairs, their hands plainly visible.

"Dude, what the hell is going on?" The man in front was short, lantern jawed, bowlegged, and with long, curly hair. He looked from one man to the other, noticing quite clearly that neither Blackheart had relaxed or taken his hands off his weapon. "Look, guys, while it doesn't surprise me at all that that greasy fuck was up to no good, we were just here for a paycheck. We didn't get read in on any shady shit or get any pirate booty bonuses."

The two men behind him had still had their hands on their weapons until they'd gone eyeball to muzzle with Curtis's EVOLYS. They were keeping their gloved hands well away from anything that might be considered threatening.

"Well," Burgess drawled, "seems like your boss made a deal with the devil, and now he's trying to break it and clean house before it comes back around to bite him." He glanced overhead as another roaring storm of gunfire thundered across the front of the mansion. "Seems it's a little too late."

"Yeah." The mansion shook under the hammer blow of an explosion. "Are you guys it?"

If this guy had been a pirate, Curtis thought, then there would have been some kind of cold calculation behind that

250

question. If there was, then this dude deserved an Oscar, because his tone was more of concern. "'Cause as near as I can tell, there's a shit-ton of bad guys out there still, and they're pushing inside as we speak." He frowned. "There should be more of us to defend this place, but…"

"But your boss is probably surrounding himself with as many guns as he can get, and probably looking for a way out." Bianco was just around the corner, and he didn't turn his head away from his sector, but he could hear and be heard.

"Sounds like him." Apparently, there was no love lost between these three and their employer. "Dude's a prick."

"Look, don't take this the wrong way." Burgess was as laid back as ever, but he still had a hand on his rifle's pistol grip. "We can't be sure about you guys. So, you either put your weapons down, back up while we collect them, and wait this out against that wall with your hands on your heads, or you go out that door, and if we see your faces again, they get a bullet."

The three of them traded a glance. It was pretty obvious that neither option seemed like a good idea. But the long-haired guy shrugged, then unclipped his sling, carefully holding onto his rifle by the buttstock. "Okay, I guess that's what I'd probably do in your place. But if things go sideways, don't just leave us to die, huh? We can cover each other's backs. Fontaine paid well, but not *that* well."

"We'll see." A renewed storm of gunfire was accompanied by the sound of shattering glass and a panicked call over the radio to fall back to the safe areas on the ground floor.

The pirates had penetrated the mansion.

CHAPTER 30

Brannigan led the way back into the hallway. He'd jumped the stack *again*, and he knew that he was on the thin edge of letting his fury lead him to make mistakes. Being set up had him mad clear through, though, and he wanted Fontaine's head. The pirates were still targets, but they had faded into secondary status. Fontaine was the source of this trouble, and so he was going down.

He forced himself to slow down a little as he moved into the hallway, clearing the way they'd come before he turned toward the last door in the corridor.

He didn't *know* that it would lead to Fontaine, but it had appeared to be where the dead men at his feet had been going before they'd run into the Blackhearts in the hallway. It was the logical place to start.

The trouble was, the mansion was huge, and Fontaine really *could* have slipped past them. They simply didn't have the numbers to cordon the place off and perform a thorough sweep. And there hadn't been time for the sort of careful reconnaissance that would have allowed them to do a quick, in-and-out, targeted strike.

A moment later, though, even as an explosion out front rocked the mansion, he heard the muted *thump*s of gunfire from the far side of that door.

Except… who was shooting?

He paused, stacked on the door while Gomez covered his back, in case some of Fontaine's shooters had gotten past the boys on the stairwell. After a moment, he heard movement on the far side of the door, and a muffled voice. He couldn't make out words, but he could hear the nearly panicked tone in the voice, anyway.

Whoever it was, they were right on the other side of the door. He quickly motioned for Flanagan, Kirk, and Santelli to move back into the entertainment center, while he eased back from the door, though not so far that he couldn't act quickly when the door opened. He just wanted to keep himself and Gomez far enough out of the fatal funnel that they weren't immediately targeted when it did open. Wade didn't move, but kept covering their backs.

Kirk and Flanagan were barricaded on the entertainment center door just behind the dead bodies in the hallway. Santelli had disappeared inside, probably grumbling about being upstaged by the youngsters.

The door flew open, then, and a gunman in a plaid shirt and gray combat gear started to come out, but stutter-stepped in the doorway as he spotted the bodies on the floor.

Flanagan didn't wait for Brannigan to move. He shot the man through the skull from six feet away. The gunman dropped like a puppet with its strings cut, and then, with a panicked yell, whoever was on the other side of the doorway fired back wildly, bullets smashing into the doorframe and the ceiling, forcing Flanagan and Kirk both to drop to the floor to avoid getting shot.

Brannigan wished he had a flashbang, but wishes weren't going to solve the problem at hand. He threw himself through the still-open door, stepping over the dead man on the threshold and crossing the opening quickly, pivoting to bring his weapon to bear as fast as possible.

He was in a small storage room. Stacks of boxes lined the walls, and he almost ran into one of them as he got out of the fatal funnel of the door as fast as he could. A bullet still smacked a hole through one of them, showering the floor with shredded paper and cardboard.

The shooter wasn't right there in the room, and wasn't exactly aiming all that precisely, fortunately. He'd fired through the gap between the hinges on a partially closed, camouflaged door set against the back wall. He'd shot at movement and missed.

Brannigan threw himself onto the floor, looking for a target, even as the shooter on the other side of the door sent a burst tearing through the door itself, showering fragments of wood and plaster onto the floor and shredding several more boxes. The guy didn't have a target, but whatever was going on over on the other side of that door, he was desperate enough to fire blindly in the hopes of suppressing the Blackhearts.

The burst ended, and then, before Brannigan could pick himself up off the floor, Gomez moved in front of him, stepping over him and yanking the door open, his rifle leveled.

Gomez fired twice, and then Brannigan was up and moving in behind him.

Another of the gunmen in gray gear and civilian clothes was slumped against the wall on the landing of a metal staircase leading down into what looked like a tunnel carved out of solid rock. He was still alive, but not for long. One hand was clamped to a gushing wound in his throat, trying unsuccessfully to staunch the bleeding while his face turned gray, and Joshua Fontaine tried to pull the MCX loose from the sling around his upper body.

"Put it down, Fontaine." Brannigan's own rifle was barely inches away from Gomez's, pointed right at Fontaine's head. The billionaire didn't look at either of them for a moment, still trying to get the rifle loose. As Gomez stepped forward, though, and the door one flight of stairs down rattled under a sudden hammer blow, he froze.

He still didn't look at either of the Blackhearts, but he let the rifle slip out of suddenly motionless fingers. "Look, I can make this right. If you get me out of here alive, I'll make you so rich that you'll never have to work again."

Gomez didn't say a word. The muzzle of his MCX didn't move even a fraction of an inch.

"Get up." Brannigan wasn't even going to engage with the man's offer. It was an offer to buy off the men he'd tried to have killed. Furthermore, there was probably an implicit agreement not to talk to any authorities about any of this attached to the money, too. "Keep your hands where we can see them."

Fontaine rose slowly, though he looked over his shoulder as the door below shook again. "Please. I can make all of this go away. Just get me out of here."

For a brief moment, Brannigan considered just shooting him in the head. How many murders had this man bankrolled? Still, he wasn't a murderer himself, and there was a possibility that, if they got Fontaine back to the States, they could turn him over to Abernathy or someone else with the resources and the ruthlessness to pry every dirty little secret out of him without being deterred by his money.

That was the concern, even as he stepped forward and gripped Fontaine—none too gently—by the arm, Gomez maintaining his stark, unmoving coverage with his weapon, Wade looming behind him. "What's down there?" He pointed toward the door, which shook again under another impact. The doorframe was steel, so it didn't look like whoever was on the other side was going to get through anytime soon, but if they found the right tools, it was only a matter of time.

"I had an escape route." If he felt remotely apologetic about leaving his security to die for him while he bolted, Fontaine didn't show it. "But someone must have talked. Sorley must have told them about it. They got to it before we could get out."

Brannigan didn't believe for a minute that Sorley had been a mole for the pirates. Not after everything that had happened, never mind the intel he'd gotten from Chavez. He didn't bother to say anything about it, though, instead propelling Fontaine toward the door.

It was a cause for care, though. It meant that as scared as he appeared to be, Fontaine was still trying to play them all.

Keeping his voice low and deadly calm, he said, "You've got one chance to keep your miserable life. The pirates hold the front of the mansion now, so if there's another way out and around to the docks, that's your only hope."

He dragged Fontaine out through the door, calling ahead, "Coming out!"

Fortunately, the billionaire had the sense not to struggle as the Blackhearts closed in around him and hustled him back toward the stairs.

Meanwhile, the gunfire overhead redoubled again, and another explosion shook the mansion.

***

El Salvaje cursed, allowing himself the moment of passion as his sole remaining teammate slammed his boot just underneath the latch again. Kicking the door wasn't doing anything, and neither of the men they'd killed on the stairs appeared to have the key. He'd checked.

Leaving the pirate to continue fruitlessly slamming his wet boot against the unyielding door, he hustled down the steps toward the toolboxes and the storage cages next to the docks. There had to be some tools he could use down there. A wrecking bar or a hammer. Something.

He moved fast, pushed by the urgency of the task. Fontaine was getting away. Even if the other pirates had the mansion locked down, it would do him little good if Cain's loyalists got their hands on the billionaire. Then his exit plan would be set back considerably. Sure, he could still use the original plan, but getting a good chunk of Fontaine's money before he killed the billionaire and severed that last thread connecting him to the pirates would be considerably better for him. Instead, if Cain captured Fontaine, he might have to stay on for a while.

Cain might not realize it, or might not want to admit it, but as soon as Fontaine had turned against them, the operation was effectively over. They'd been as successful as they had been because of Fontaine's information and logistical support. Without that, the pirates' lives were going to be considerably more complicated.

There. The prybar wasn't nearly as good as a purpose-built breaching tool, but he'd had to improvise more than once in his line of work, particularly when he'd been coming up through the ranks of the cartels. He snatched the tool up, keeping his R4 tucked in at his side, and ran back up the stairs toward the door.

***

Hank moved quickly but carefully, staying low and behind the furniture as he crossed the fatal funnel of the hatch that led out onto the aft helipad. He got a glimpse of at least two men still on the MD-500 sitting on the pad, one of them behind a machinegun in the side door, the muzzle trained on the superstructure.

He just hoped that they didn't decide to hose down the yacht and forget about their buddies who were still aboard.

Just as he moved across the lounge toward the port side of the yacht, though, he spotted something that almost made him pause. Almost. He cataloged it in his head and kept moving.

A ship was getting closer and closer to the island. A big one. It looked almost like a cruise ship.

The pirates were closing in for the kill.

He slipped around behind the bar and headed forward again, his rifle in his shoulder, clearing each opening and bit of dead space as he went, careful to turn around and check his six o'clock every few paces, though always in a spot where he could avoid exposing his back to anyone who might still be ahead of him. He listened to the radio, which was fairly quiet since Fontaine's people had changed channels, but Doc Puller was holding his peace.

Hank wondered about that for a moment. Puller had struck him as a little bit of a flake when Flanagan had brought him in, and it had been clear enough that Flanagan had shared some of the same worries about his old corpsman.

But the more he thought about it, even as he paced up the side of the ship, straining his ears and eyes for any sign of the other

258

pirates, he realized that it actually made a lot of tactical sense. They knew their comms were compromised. If the pirates had been working with Fontaine, did the pirates have a backdoor to the same radios? It was a possibility. If Puller was watching the cameras, he could warn Hank if he was about to walk into an ambush, but too much chatter risked warning the bad guys.

At least, Hank hoped that was what was going on.

He stalked toward the theater, his boots rolling quietly on the deck, his weapon up. He thought he could hear some movement and voices ahead, possibly inside the theater itself. His ears were ringing with how hard he was trying to listen, despite the crackle of small arms outside the ship, on the lawn and inside the mansion.

He was three steps away from the hatch when the first pirate stepped out into the passageway.

Dressed in gray fatigues, gray plate carrier and helmet, and gray balaclava, the man might have been a maritime special operator from any number of affluent countries, if not for the South African rifle in his hands, and the fact that Hank knew these were pirates.

The man had cleared forward, and the man right behind him was just a hair too slow. And all Hank had to do was lift his muzzle a couple of inches.

It took two shots. The first took the number one man in the back of the head, knocking him forward as his lights went out. Hank was already shifting right, and he put his second bullet through the number two man's eye, even as that one came around the edge of the hatchway and shot him in the front plate.

The impact was savage, almost like he'd been hit in the chest with a sledgehammer. He staggered back a step as the wind was knocked out of him, and he felt one knee start to buckle. Then the number three man was coming through the hatchway, and his rifle was offline.

Except another shot took that pirate in the ear, blowing a chunk of skull out the other side with a spray of red, and he dropped like a sack of rocks.

259

"Friendly." Puller appeared in the hatchway, his rifle lowered. "That was the last of them except those assholes on the bird." He slung the weapon to one side and went down to a knee, holding out a hand to Hank as he sagged against the bulkhead, gasping for breath. "You okay?"

Hank nodded. "Just got the wind knocked out of me." His voice was a hoarse wheeze. "Never took a contact shot to the plate before."

Puller quickly checked him for bleeds anyway. "Come on. We've still got those assholes on the stern to worry about."

Hank grabbed him by the sleeve, though. "We've got more worries than just them. I think the pirate mothership just showed up."

CHAPTER 31

Burgess watched the contractors with half an eye, while still maintaining his vigilance over Curtis's shoulder. He hated sitting here in a stairwell, stationary and exposed, waiting, while the assault outside got closer and closer.

Movement caught his eye across the foyer, and he lifted his rifle, but the long-haired contractor called out. "Hold on, man! Those are ours!"

Burgess held his fire, though he wasn't sure he should. It was true that these guys were in civilian clothes under their plate carriers, and only one was wearing a helmet. One was in shorts and his plate carrier, and that was it. But they'd already killed quite a few of Fontaine's security contractors, and he wasn't convinced that that fight was over.

The long-haired contractor was turned halfway around from where he'd been facing the wall, looking over his shoulder. "Please. Let me link up with them. Fontaine might be a dickbag, but those pirates are gonna kill all of us if we don't team up. I swear, nobody here knew what was going on."

Curtis glanced up at him, even as a long, roaring burst of gunfire tore through the door on the far side of the foyer and sent one of the contractors spinning to the floor, gouts of blood spewing from the side of his head. The other two spread out, trying to return fire, but they were cut off from the gunman on the other side of the door by the geometries of the room.

Curtis leaned out just far enough to bring his EVOLYS to bear and shot back. The ultralight machinegun roared and bucked against the doorframe as he leaned into it, flame strobing in the dimmed lights of the foyer, red tracers chewing into whoever and whatever was on the far side of that door.

Still, Burgess hesitated to call the beleaguered contractors to come join them. That would mean the Blackhearts on the stairs would be outnumbered, and as much as the guy with the long hair was trying to be friendly, that didn't necessarily make him a good guy.

Then the flashbang sailed into the foyer and detonated. He was far enough away that he wasn't blinded or even rocked by the detonation. It was still loud, painfully so, but not disorienting. For the two guys on either side of the door, however, it was going to be a hammer.

Curtis was equally unaffected, and as far as he was concerned, while the contractors were a maybe, the pirates were instant dead men. So, he laid into that belt-fed again, chopping down the figures that suddenly loomed through the flashbang's smoke with a long, stuttering burst.

The survivors immediately rolled out of the fatal funnel, even as the first couple of men in the stack tumbled to a bloody heap on the carpet. Curtis ceased fire, having no further targets, and Burgess decided. He'd probably regret it. Hopefully he lived long enough to.

"Bring it in!"

***

Flanagan paused at the base of the stairs. "Friendlies!"

"Bring it in!" Bianco's shout came right on the tail end of a burst of full auto fire. Things were getting dicey upstairs.

Flanagan led the way up, clapping Bianco on the shoulder as he went. Brannigan was right behind him, one hand on Fontaine's shoulder, his grip tight enough that the billionaire was wincing every few steps.

He was kind of surprised to see five of Fontaine's security personnel, weapons in hand, barricaded on the steps leading up as well as the foyer beyond. One of them must have been asleep when this started, because he was barefoot, in shorts, and had his plate carrier thrown over his naked torso.

"My call." Burgess had seen his look and his raised eyebrow. "The pirates are in the main building now, and they're pushing toward the stairs. For all we know, they're already on the floor above us."

Fontaine didn't seem to be listening, though. "Raford! You've got to help me..." He winced again as Brannigan's grip tightened, practically driving him to his knees.

The long-haired contractor he'd called Raford, however, turned to look over his shoulder with an expression that could only be described as contemptuous. "Yeah, that's not gonna fuckin' happen." He nodded toward the Blackhearts. "Consider this our notice. We don't work for you anymore."

"We've got to get out of this building and back to the docks." Brannigan's voice was grim, his vise grip on Fontaine not giving an inch. He looked at Raford. "If you want to fix this, find us a way out. Just understand that one of my boys is going to be behind you with a gun every step of the way."

Raford might have looked a little uncomfortable at that, but another contemptuous look at Fontaine seemed to steel him. "Roger that. On me."

He didn't try to move into the foyer, but instead headed across the hall, into the kitchen at the back of the mansion. He moved fast, but not so fast that any of the Blackhearts might suspect him of trying to run.

Curtis stayed barricaded on the foyer while the rest moved behind him. Flanagan heard one more long burst as he neared the back door, opening up onto another porch overlooking the cliffs at the back of the mansion. He and Kirk stopped, each man kicking a table over and taking a knee behind it. They weren't cover, but they'd provide just enough concealment that they should be able to get the first shots off without the enemy managing to hit them.

"Kev! Turn and go!" Flanagan kept his muzzle trained on the door between the dining area and the foyer, careful to have leaned around the outside end of the overturned table, rather than popping over the top. He clamped his hand around the MCX's forearm, bracing it against the heavy wood tabletop, as Curtis came sprinting through the door, the EVOLYS pointed at the floor, his legs pumping hard.

Both Flanagan and Kirk held their position until Curtis was past and diving through the back door. Then, as Kirk got up to move, another flashbang bounced off the doorframe and dropped into the middle of the floor, only a couple feet inside the door.

Flanagan squeezed his eyes shut for a moment. The bang went off with a deafening *wham*, and he saw the flash through his eyelids. He immediately opened them, his finger already tightening on the trigger as his eye searched for the red dot.

Two pirates were already through the door, clearing their corners and pivoting quickly toward the center of the room. They weren't quite fast enough, and even though his head was already starting to ache abominably from the concussion of the flashbang, Flanagan was already practically aimed in. He knew where they'd be coming from. They didn't know for sure where he was.

He shot the man on the left through the armpit, the follow up shot coming almost unconsciously as his finger felt the reset and squeezed again as the dot settled from the marginal recoil. The rifle barked again, and the man fell against the wall, the strength already leaving his legs and his arms, the R4 slipping from his fingers as he slid toward the floor, leaving a red streak on the wall behind him.

Instead of going over the top, Flanagan leaned farther out around the side, but Kirk had beaten him to it. Kirk *had* gone over the top, though he'd laid his MCX on its side, staying crouched down so that only his helmet and barely one eye were exposed over the top of the table. He dumped the second man with a fast five shots, just hammering rounds into the shooter's silhouette until he went down.

264

Sometimes "shoot it until it stops moving, changes shape, or catches fire" is a viable tactic.

They needed to move. He heard a helicopter pass by, too close. That probably explained why the pirates had pushed the fight so hard and so fast. They had eyes in the sky, and they'd seen Fontaine moving. But there were more of them coming from inside the mansion, and more flashbangs followed the first, sailing deeper into the room.

Even as the bangs went off with tooth-rattling concussions, Curtis opened fire from the porch, raking the doorway and that front wall with fire. He paused just long enough to yell, "Turn and go," and then he laid into it again.

Flanagan turned his head to check the angles. He didn't want to just turn and run right into Curtis's fire. But his friend wasn't in the doorway. He was in one of the windows, off to the side, leaving a clear path to the porch.

Pivoting on his heel and toes, he lowered his head and sprinted for the door, Kirk already two steps ahead. Curtis ran the rest of the belt out on the pirates that were still trying to get into the dining room.

Then they were through, ducking beneath the windows, turning to the right where Santelli was crouched behind a rock, his weapon pointed up toward the windows above. The stout Bostonian pointed down the length of the mansion. "We're moving. Let's go."

***

El Salvaje slammed the prybar into the joint just below the latch. The steel door was a bit of a problem, but he was getting through it, one way or another.

The first blow didn't quite get far enough in, and as soon as he wrenched on the bar, it slipped out. He slammed it in again, this time twisting his body to kick at the back of it, trying to drive it deeper into the gap. That hurt; he wasn't a young man anymore, and the scars on his body pulled as he tried to contort himself to get some force behind the kick. It went deeper, though, and this time, when he hauled on the pry bar, the jamb gave a little with a creaking *crack*.

His movements almost frantic, he reset the prybar, slammed it deeper in, and pried again. The jamb gave a little more.

As the sounds of gunfire faded into the distance above, he kept at it, determined to get that door open and get after Fontaine before he escaped.

Or fell into Cain's hands.

CHAPTER 32

The footing on the ground along the back of the mansion wasn't great, at least not where there was some marginal cover from the windows. More flashes flickered inside those windows, accompanied by the muted *thump*s of gunfire, but so far, few of those shots had been directed at them. The pirates who had survived the bloodbath as the Blackhearts had broken contact inside the dining room had to have sent word over comms that Fontaine was getting away, but they were still in a fight with the remaining contractors, and those guys who had stayed on their feet were putting up a hell of a fight from the sounds of it.

Unfortunately, where they were covered from the windows, they were exposed to the sea. And the air.

Two more of the pirate vessels were visible on the water to the north, not all that far away. A long shot even with a machinegun, but they were a threat, nevertheless. Much more of a threat was the single remaining MD-500 circling overhead.

Flanagan wasn't far behind Brannigan, Wade, and Burgess. Brannigan was still hauling Fontaine along by that crushing grip on his shoulder and collarbone. Bianco and Gomez had pushed ahead, and even as that MD-500 spotted them and banked to come around toward them, he was already setting up.

His back was to the windows, but Gomez had taken a knee to cover him, and Gomez could react almost as fast as anyone

267

could appear in one of those windows. Flanagan hustled up to join them, even while Wade took point and the cluster of Blackhearts around Fontaine kept going toward the northeast corner.

They didn't go far, though, not with that helicopter coming for them. Wade found a pocket in the rocks, sheltering a small sitting area with plush lawn chairs set out to overlook the ocean, and they all went flat, Brannigan practically sweeping Fontaine's legs out from under him, even as the MD-500 bore down on them.

Bianco was ready. With the bipods braced against a rock, his own body, large as it was, as low as possible, he leaned into the EVOLYS and opened fire.

The belt-fed spat flame with a roar, red tracers sailing out to intersect the oncoming helicopter, hitting high on the windscreen and walking up into the engine. With four ball rounds between each tracer, that was a lot of metal hitting the helicopter.

The MD-500 was a civilian helicopter. It wasn't armored, no matter how many guns the pirates packed aboard it. Bullets chewed into the exposed machinery of the driveshaft, and a moment later, the rotor was shaking dangerously, threatening to tear the aircraft apart even as smoke began to belch from the engine. The helicopter dropped, banking away, practically out of control.

Then they were up and moving again, even as gunfire roared from the back of the mansion.

Flanagan had seen movement just beforehand, but the pirates were smart, staying back in the dimly-lit ballroom instead of getting right up to the window. Still, even as glass shattered and bullets *snap*ped entirely too close by overhead, he spotted a muzzle flash and fired back at it. There was too much noise to hear if he'd hit the shooter, but the muzzle flash disappeared.

Bianco slung the EVOLYS onto his back and drew his Glock. "I'm out."

"Stay behind me, then." Flanagan got to his feet, dumping the rest of his magazine through the windows before he dashed forward, reloading as he went, while Santelli, Kirk, and Curtis took up the fire.

Bounding successively in short dashes, covering each other by fire, the Blackhearts raced toward the end of the mansion. Wade was already at the corner, and he popped it quickly with Burgess, the two of them doing a "high-low," with Burgess on a low knee and Wade leaning out over him. Then they hooked around and disappeared.

The rest of the Blackhearts closed in as they neared the end of the mansion. Curtis was running half off-balance, the muzzle of his EVOLYS pointed at the sky as he struggled to get his last belt loaded on the move. Santelli ran with him, his body between Curtis and the mansion, weapon up and slamming rounds through every opening he could see, just to keep the pirates—and possibly any of Fontaine's security that hadn't joined them like Raford—from sticking their heads up.

The fire from inside the mansion *had* died down. Some of that was probably because of the Blackhearts' suppressive fire. Some was also probably because they had moved fast enough that they were outpacing the enemy's OODA loop.

Some of it was also probably because a lot of the shooters in there were dead.

Now speed was security. As Flanagan came around the corner, he saw that Wade and the others were now in a dead sprint down the line of rocks that pointed almost directly at the docks and the *Dream Empire*, still tied up at the end of the pier.

Unfortunately, the yacht wasn't the only boat there.

The *Lyubov Orlova* floated at anchor just aft of the yacht. She actually looked small next to the massive opulence of the *Dream Empire*, and she was, over a hundred feet shorter. But two speedboats had just arrived at the pier across from the yacht, and a dozen gray-clad shooters were moving quickly across the pier toward the gangplank leading up onto the aft helipad, where Flanagan could just see the last of the pirates' MD-500s still sitting, rotors turning.

That wouldn't have been such a problem, except that there was another pirate in the bow of the formerly derelict cruise ship, and he had a belt-fed. And it wasn't a very long shot from the bow to the side of the mansion.

That machinegunner had a clear line of sight on the ground they had to cross, too.

With a flickering blossom of flame, he opened up, glowing tracers zipping toward the Blackhearts and their prisoner. Two of the contractors went down immediately, the man with no shirt collapsing with half his neck and his head shot away. The rest went flat, diving for cover behind the rocks.

This was a bad spot. Flanagan got behind a rock, twisting around and checking the windows above them, just in time to see movement. He snapped his rifle up, trying not to flinch as bullets smacked off the stone above his head, streaks of red sailing off into the night with evil whines, and opened fire just before the silhouette in the window, barely visible against a dim glow from deeper inside the mansion, started shooting. Flanagan's own bullets smashed through the glass and punched into the man's plate, shoulder, and head. He spun out of sight and disappeared.

Just as he twisted back around to see if he could get a shot at the pirates down on the pier, who were probably moving on them while they were suppressed from the bow of the *Lyubov Orlova*, Fontaine made his move.

Brannigan's grip must have loosened slightly when he'd dived for the ground. Fontaine suddenly twisted out from under him, ran to the edge of the cliff just beyond Curtis and Santelli while tracers flew around his ears, and jumped off.

Brannigan cursed, twisting around to go after him, but another burst of machinegun fire forced him down into cover again.

Flanagan wormed his way forward on his belly, craning his neck to see through his NVGs under his helmet. They weren't exactly designed to be used in the prone. They had to get some fire on those pirates before they got overrun.

Another long burst raked their position, smacking dust off the rocks and chips off the wall of the mansion, forcing those still alive to get even lower, and then Curtis opened fire behind them. More hostiles were coming up from the rear of the mansion.

They were pinned.

***

Hank and Puller turned back toward the stern. "We've got to take that helicopter out, but if their mothership's *right there*, then things are about to get a lot hairier."

Puller snorted. "I don't see how. Seems to me that hitting a helicopter with a machinegun in the door from a hatchway with no actual cover from only a couple yards away isn't exactly anything less than 'hairy.'"

Hank had to shrug and concede that the doc had a point. Still, they had to move. "If we move fast enough, maybe we can make it work."

"I admire your optimism." Puller lifted his muzzle toward the overhead and put a hand on Hank's shoulder. "On you."

Appreciate the vote of confidence. He felt the sudden wild urge to laugh. It *was* his hairbrained idea, after all. It was only fitting that Doc let him go first.

They exploded out through the hatch almost as one, just as the machinegun opened up from the bow of the cruise ship just off the end of the pier.

The noise and the light show as a stream of red tracers spewed through the night toward the shore and the mansion apparently was just enough of a distraction. The helo's door gunner wasn't looking at them as the pilot began to lift off, the skids just barely coming off the pad as both Blackhearts opened fire.

The door gunner was the first to die. The two of them raked their fire across the fuselage, more concerned with getting as much lead on target as fast as possible than with accuracy. At that range, however, it would have been hard to miss.

The MD-500 slammed back down onto the pad as the pilot slumped, red painting the holed acrylic canopy to his side.

The rotors kept turning, but he hadn't gotten far enough off the pad to actually crash.

Puller turned to the port side, reloading as he practically duck walked toward the rail. Hank quickly followed as the machinegunner raked the mansion from the bow of that pirate ship out there. They were exposed as hell on the helipad, but right at the moment that gunner seemed to be focused on the island itself.

Maybe the pirates wanted the yacht as undamaged as possible.

He realized, belatedly, that the main reason Puller was heading for the side was that the gangplank was still down. The pirates would have easy access to the deck if they got to the pier.

When they got to the rail, hugging the thin outer hull that provided some concealment, if not cover, he peered over and saw that it was worse than he thought.

A dozen gray-clad shooters were on the pier, moving forward at a run, while the machinegunner raked the rocks off to the side of the mansion. He had no way of knowing for sure who was out there, but something told him that it was probably his dad and the rest of his teammates.

"I've got the gunner." Puller was already aimed in.

"Take him." Hank was a little frustrated that he had to say it, but there *were* only two of them.

Puller took a single shot, and the machinegun fell silent. Then Hank took a deep breath, popped up from behind the gunwale, and opened fire.

The pirates were about halfway down the pier. They hadn't bothered with much dispersion, since they were just trying to get across the open danger area under cover of the machinegun fire. His first ten shots dropped three of them before they realized they were in trouble.

One of them, a tall man with a graying beard, pivoted, dropped to a knee, and tried to return fire. His rounds went high, though; he didn't have a good enough shot. Hank forced himself not to flinch at the muzzle flash, put his red dot right on the man's face, and stroked the trigger.

The gray-bearded pirate's head snapped back like he'd been punched, and he seemed to float there, still erect, for a moment, before he fell over onto his back.

Then a torrent of fire roared out from the rocks and cut down the rest.

***

The door wasn't opening. As hard as El Salvaje wrenched on the pry bar, it would not give. His earlier hopes were rapidly being dashed, but he didn't know what else to do.

"Hey, what's that?"

He pivoted, letting go of the prybar and letting it fall to the perforated steel decking. The other pirate was up on his rifle, looking at something below them, in the water.

El Salvaje couldn't believe his eyes. Looking more than a little like a drowned rat, Joshua Fontaine dragged himself up onto the pier, right where El Salvaje and his pirates had climbed out of the water only a few minutes before. He looked around carefully, then, half-crouched, he ran toward the speedboat where the bodies of his staff were still cooling.

The other pirate didn't hesitate. His rifle barked, the thunder of its report deafening in the close confines of the rock and the steel stairwell. Fontaine stumbled and dropped to one knee, clutching his stomach. The pirate shot him again, and he pitched over and fell into the water, just in front of the speedboat's bow.

El Salvaje saw everything he had banked on die with the billionaire. Another sort of man might have despaired.

It wasn't his way, though. He'd just have to pick up where he'd left off. He stepped back, shot the pirate in the back of the head, and then, as if nothing had happened, he started down the steps toward the dock. The speedboat would at least get him to Los Cristianos.

***

With the fire lifted and the sounds of fighting from inside the mansion dying down, the Blackhearts moved quickly toward the cliff. Maybe they could find Fontaine and intercept him before

273

he got too far. Brannigan led the way, his jaw set, fury burning in his chest. He'd be damned if he let that snake get away.

As he neared the lip of the cliff, the throaty roar of a nautical engine echoed off the cliffs, and a big, sleek, gray speedboat seemed to leap out of the cliff itself, swerving slightly to clear the mouth of the sound before racing out into the night.

A handful of shots followed it, but the coxswain was swerving violently and moving fast. He was also low, and it was almost impossible to get a clear shot at him.

"Cease fire." Brannigan didn't want Fontaine dead, anyway. Not yet. He turned to Raford. "There's a dock down there." It wasn't a question, but the demand was clear enough.

"Only a handful of us were ever allowed down there, but yeah." Raford shrugged. "It's kinda James Bond, but he's a billionaire. They're weird, anyway. We didn't really question it."

"You know the way down to it?"

"Yeah. Come on." He hefted his rifle, obviously well aware that he still had it on the Blackhearts' sufferance. "I don't know if he will have left any indicators as to where he's going, but it's worth a look."

Brannigan nodded and waved at him to proceed. "We'll be right behind you." The threat—no, the *promise*—didn't need explanation.

They moved carefully, retracing their steps back the way they'd come. A few sporadic shots still echoed through the mansion, but it seemed almost as if the carnage down on the pier had taken some of the starch out of the pirates. Raford carefully made entry on the dining area, though not before calling out, "Friendly!" That might or might not have been a good idea, depending on who was inside, but the bodies scattered on the floor and the ground outside suggested that Curtis had laid enough fire down that the pirates who'd attempted to pursue them had either all been killed, or else had fallen back to try another way.

"Can I use the radio?" Raford had circled around the edge of the room, staying out of the kill zone in the center, and paused at the doorway.

274

"Not yet." It was still a delicate situation, but without knowing for sure which way the rest of Fontaine's people were going to jump, not to mention how many of them there were, or how many pirates, he didn't want to broadcast anything that might give the bad guys any information.

Raford nodded, his mouth tight, and then quickly cleared his way through the doorway. There were more bodies on the floor, both contractors and pirates.

He suddenly pivoted toward the foyer, his weapon coming up, only to be interrupted by a shout of, "Friendly!"

Raford snapped his muzzle toward the ceiling. The other contractor approached quickly, though his eyes widened when he saw the Blackhearts behind Raford. "It's cool," the long-haired contractor assured him. "Trust me."

The red-bearded man looked uncertain, but he nodded. "Cool." He didn't sound all that certain, either.

"What's going on in here?" Raford asked. Brannigan's eyes narrowed, and he felt his impatience rising, but if Fontaine had been on that boat, he was gone. Getting down to the docks wasn't going to get them on the man's trail any faster.

"Those fuckers just lost their heads and went chasing after this bunch." The red-bearded man nodded toward Brannigan. "We must have smoked four of them right then, and the rest either ran right into machinegun fire or holed up in the ballroom. Jake's still smoking them out. Looks like most of the rest of the place is clear, though." His eyes moved to Brannigan again, and the question was obvious.

Raford gripped the man's shoulder. "Look, it's a long story, but we've got to get down to the docks."

The man frowned. "The 007 docks?" He looked at Brannigan again, almost sheepishly this time. "We're not allowed down there, remember?"

"Unless it's an emergency, and this is kind of an emergency, don't you think?" Raford studied the man's doubtful expression for a moment, then lowered his voice. "Look, as soon as he said these guys were pirates, I knew he was dirty. Turns out, he was dirtier than we thought. *And* if what we just saw is what I think it was, he just left us to face the pirates on our own."

The red-bearded man nodded then. "Yeah, something was off about that radio call. I think we were all too busy to think much about it, though. Okay, lead the way."

Raford nodded and started down the stairs. Brannigan and the others followed, though they still kept their muzzles up to cover the foyer as they passed. They weren't *that* trusting.

It didn't take long to flow back to the room where they'd captured Fontaine. The basement was quiet as a tomb, at least until a sudden storm of gunfire thundered above, though it sounded like a bunch of muted *thump*s through the door. Then everything went quiet.

Red Beard listened to his earpiece a moment. "Ballroom's clear."

Raford nodded and led the way down the steps to the door. He got it unlocked easily enough, but it stuck when he tried to open it. He finally had to kick it open, and it caught on a prybar lying on the deck outside.

The door opened onto a perforated steel landing, with another two flights of stairs leading down to an underground marina. Two speedboats were still tied up to the concrete piers on either side of the cave, which was still lit by lights hanging from conduits bolted to the stone ceiling.

The cave was an abattoir.

The first body, dressed in gray fatigues and combat gear, lay on its face on the deck in front of them, still dripping blood and liquefied brain matter through the holes in the perforated steel deck. More lay on the piers below, though most of them were apparently civilians. They also looked like they'd been tossed onto the pier, rather than having died there.

They started down, weapons up, just in case. Nothing else in the cave moved, except for the faint sway of the boats on the water.

"John. Look." Flanagan had moved out along the wall, nearest to the bodies, and was pointing into the water.

276

It took a moment to haul the final corpse out of the water, but Brannigan knew who it was before they even brought the dead face out of the water. He'd recognized Fontaine's red shirt and light-colored khakis.

He looked up toward the exit. "Well, that's it for him. I wonder who that was on the boat?"

EPILOGUE

It didn't take long to clear the *Lyubov Orlova*. It looked like the bulk of the pirates had been committed to the assault on the mansion, and were now lying dead on the pier, the yard, the beach, or inside the house itself. The handful of men still aboard the old cruise ship surrendered quickly, without a fight. One of them confirmed that the gray-bearded man Hank had shot had been Cain, the top pirate.

The remaining pirate ships had faded, turning aside and sailing away as soon as the fire from the *Lyubov Orlova* had ceased. They'd still have to be dealt with, but that wasn't Brannigan's concern at the moment.

The MH-X Stealth Hawk settled on the aft helipad of the *Dream Empire*, and Hauser stepped out, jogging forward to meet Brannigan at the forward hatch. The big, blond operator shook the Colonel's hand. "Damn good to see you in one piece, sir. The brief we got made it sound like things got kinda hairy."

"They did." Brannigan ushered the big man, one of Clayton Abernathy's eerily secret black ops group, into the aft lounge. The bodies of the pirates had been policed up and disposed of, though not before extensive identifying photos had been taken. Most of Fontaine's surviving security had cooperated eagerly, though a few Raford had identified as suspect were currently being held with the remaining pirates. "We've been making the

279

most of the accommodations for the last forty-eight hours, though."

"So I see." Hauser looked around the yacht with an appreciative nod. Then he got down to business, jerking a thumb over his shoulder. "We're not here to take your prisoners off your hands, I'm afraid. That's going to be the *New York*, that will be on station in about ten hours. I wanted to get the data dump as soon as possible, though." He rubbed his square jaw. "We've already got assets looking for the remaining pirate ships. Getting to the bottom of Fontaine's operation is going to take a little longer."

Brannigan nodded. "I figured. Any ideas so far?"

"He was a hedge fund manager turned 'entrepreneur' who got greedy." Hauser shrugged. "He wouldn't be the first rich asshole to decide to turn to terrorism and crime to line his pockets. We'll have to see if there was anything more to it."

"Well, hopefully it's all over." Even as he said it, though Brannigan wondered.

Was this kind of thing ever really over? What skeletons had Fontaine had in his closet that might come out and stalk the light of day?

Hauser was thinking the same thing, though not just about Fontaine. "It's a concerning thing, what's happened. Most modern-day pirates have been ragtag tribal militias and gangs. 'Cain,' it turns out, was formerly Captain Adrian Mills. Dude was in DEVGRU for a while, before he was quietly forced to retire." At Brannigan's raised eyebrow, Hauser shook his head. "No, not the same situation as yours. Mills deserved it, and more. It's probably no surprise he turned pirate. What *is* a bit of a surprise is how he got almost two hundred men to go along with him. The guy didn't have much of a rep as a charismatic stud. He was always an asshole."

"Well," Brannigan said, pouring a pair of glasses of Fontaine's expensive whiskey and handing one to Hauser, "if you need a hand rounding up the rest, let us know. We kind of need to recoup after this fiasco. I don't think we can count on Fontaine's organization to pay us, now."

Hauser smiled slightly as he lifted his glass. "I'll pass it on, but I also won't mention the fact that I suspect that you and your boys might be able to find plenty of remuneration around here."

Brannigan returned the smile and raised his own glass. "Your discretion is admirable, Master Sergeant Hauser."

LOOK FOR MORE HARD-HITTING ACTION SOON, IN:

BRANNIGAN'S BLACKHEARTS

CONCRETE JUNGLE

AUTHOR'S NOTE

Thank you for reading *Marque and Reprisal*. I'd wanted to do a somewhat straightforward pirate hunting story for a while, though this one turned out a little less straightforward than I'd initially planned. I hope you enjoyed it, twists and turns and all.

To keep up-to-date, I hope that you'll sign up for my newsletter—you get a free American Praetorians novella, *Drawing the Line*, when you do.

If you've enjoyed this novel, I hope that you'll go leave a review on Amazon or Goodreads. Reviews matter a lot to independent authors, so I appreciate the effort.

If you'd like to connect, I have a Facebook page at https://www.facebook.com/PeteNealenAuthor. You can also contact me, or just read my musings and occasional samples on the blog, at https://www.americanpraetorians.com. I look forward to hearing from you.

Also By Peter Nealen

The Brannigan's Blackhearts Universe
Kill Yuan
The Colonel Has A Plan (Online Short)
Fury in the Gulf
Burmese Crossfire
Enemy Unidentified
Frozen Conflict
High Desert Vengeance
Doctors of Death
Kill or Capture
Enemy of My Enemy
War to the Knife
Blood Debt
Marque and Reprisal

The Maelstrom Rising Series
Escalation
Holding Action
Crimson Star
Strategic Assets
Fortress Doctrine
Thunder Run
Area Denial
Power Vacuum
Option Zulu
SPOTREPS – A Maelstrom Rising Anthology

The Lost Series
Ice and Monsters
Shadows and Crows
Darkness and Stone
Swords Against the Night

The Unity Wars Series

Printed in the USA
CPSIA information can be obtained
at www.ICGtesting.com
LVHW042314130624
783200LV00031B/571

9 798218 035617